Praise for *I Thought You Were Dead*

"Chosen by independent booksellers as a recent No. 1 Book Sense Pick, *I Thought You Were Dead,* a novel about the bonds between dogs and humans, is heartfelt and nostalgic in tone . . . Stella's wisdom sets the luckless Paul on a brighter life path. It's her nobility . . . that gives the story its power."　—*USA Today*

"[*I Thought You Were Dead*] has a low-key, indie-movie vibe, with Stella sounding like *Juno*'s older, world-weary aunt."
　　　　　　　　　　　—*The Washington Post Book World*

"With an irresistible voice, a completely relatable hero, and a dog named Stella who will steal your heart away, Pete Nelson has crafted a cunning and completely winning novel in *I Thought You Were Dead.* Read it, and you will fall in love."
　　　　　—Susan Cheever, author of *American Bloomsbury*

"In the guise of a novel, Pete Nelson has spun a beautiful ballad out of the humblest elements: an old dog, a drinking problem, a Minnesota family and a woman torn between two lovers. Not at all coincidentally, he's also written a truly outstanding talking-dog story . . . With exquisite tone control, he has given us a story that's sweet and loving but never sentimental."
　　　　　　　　　　　　　—*Milwaukee Journal Sentinel*

"Stella the dog is always charming. And there's a dignity and gravity to Paul's affection for her . . . Their friendship [is] one of the best ever put down on paper."　　—*St. Louis Post-Dispatch*

"Hilarious and heartbreaking, Pete Nelson's *I Thought You Were Dead* will stay with you long after you've read the last page—a brilliantly funny, highly original, and heartfelt novel about a man who needs all the help (i.e., love) he can get and who finds it in delightfully unexpected places."

—Mary Helen Stefaniak,
author of *The Cailiffs of Baghdad, Georgia*

"'I thought you were dead,' Stella says to Paul when he returns home from a bar, on page one of Pete Nelson's new novel. Delivered by an aging, arthritic Labrador/Shepherd mix, the line displays the dry wit and dog logic that makes Stella and, by extension, much of this novel a delight . . . Yes, Stella talks. And the conversations are so charming and matter-of-fact that it hardly seems worth asking from whence this special power comes."

—*Bark* magazine

"Pete Nelson has crafted a sweet, charming story about a man, his dog and the people in his life . . . A walk with Gustavson and Stella is a journey not soon forgotten."

—*The Charleston Post and Courier*

"If you think your dog is not only the best listener in your life, but you can actually hear its sage advice in your head, you should read Pete Nelson's *I Thought You Were Dead* . . . Nelson describes the friendship between man and dog with a lot of heart and understanding."

—*The Oregonian*

"Airy and almost miraculous . . . It's very wise about the way devotion—between animals and people, between people and people—can keep us going."

—*The Palm Beach Post*

"Nelson delivers readable prose and a flawed, likable character who is easy to root for. The author does a good job portraying the complexities of adult relationships without artifice."
—*The Cedar Rapids Gazette*

"A sweet little novel . . . about relationships . . . Stella has a wry voice that might, just might, also be the voice of Paul's inner better angel. And if dogs could talk, they probably would talk like Stella—kindly, sensibly, usually about food . . . Alternately hilarious and heartbreaking."
—*Minneapolis Star Tribune*

"Ultimately, *I Thought You Were Dead* is about the catastrophes that make a person realize his life is a mess, then do everything he can to put his life back together—perhaps, in the process, creating something better than he dared to hope for."
—*BookPage*

"In this age of extended adolescence, here's a coming-of-age novel about a middle-aged man who's had no luck at much of anything, especially love. The fact that Pete Nelson can tell such a story without making the narrator's charming talking dog seem unusual is proof of his power as a writer. This book will make you laugh, cry, and want a dog you can really talk to."
—Wyn Cooper, poet and author of *Postcards from the Interior*

I Thought You Were Dead

Also by Pete Nelson

A More Unbending Battle
Left for Dead
That Others May Live
The Christmas List

I Thought You Were Dead

A Love Story

A NOVEL BY

PETE NELSON

Algonquin Books of Chapel Hill   2011

Published by

ALGONQUIN BOOKS OF CHAPEL HILL

Post Office Box 2225

Chapel Hill, North Carolina 27515-2225

a division of

Workman Publishing

225 Varick Street

New York, New York 10014

First paperback edition, Alqonquin Books of Chapel Hill, March 2011.

Originally published by Algonquin Books of Chapel Hill in 2010.

Printed in the United States of America.

Published simultaneously in Canada by

Thomas Allen & Son Limited.

This is a work of fiction. While, as in all fiction, the literary
perceptions and insights are based on experience, all names,
characters, places, and incidents either are products of
the author's imagination or are used fictitiously.

Library of Congress Cataloging-in-Publication Data

Nelson, Peter, [date]

I thought you were dead : a love story : a novel /

by Pete Nelson. — 1st ed.

p. cm.

ISBN 978-1-56512-597-1 (HC)

1. Human-animal relationships — Fiction.

2. Dogs — Fiction.   I. Title.

PS3614.E449I33 2010

813'.6 — dc22   2009047626

ISBN 978-1-61620-048-0 (PB)

10 9 8 7 6 5 4 3 2 1

First Paperback Edition

For Jen and Jack

I Thought You Were Dead

Part 1

Winter/Spring

Individual heart cells beat at their own rate when separated from one another, a phenomenon easily observed beneath a microscope. It has long been known that when they are pushed together, they will synchronize their pulses. Recent studies have shown, however, that heart cells begin to synchronize slightly *before* they touch. It is not known how they signal across this distance. Some scientists speculate that this method of communication may be able to cross great distances and may explain how social animals bond, or how pets seem to sense when their masters are coming home, or even how people fall in love, one heart calling to another.

—Paul Gustavson, *Nature for Morons*

1

Two of Them Going Nowhere

In the winter of 1998, at the close of the twentieth century, in a small college town on the Connecticut River, on the sidewalk outside a house close enough to the railroad tracks that the pictures on the walls were in constant need of straightening, not that anybody ever straightened them, Paul Gustavson, having had a bit too much to drink, took the glove off his right hand, wedged it into his left armpit, and fumbled in his pants pocket for his house keys.

The snow was coming down hard, which meant the plows would be rumbling all night, clearing the roads. It was early March. Paul would have to shovel in the morning, a favor he did for his landlady, who lived upstairs and hadn't raised the rent in years in part because of the kindnesses he'd done her. His go-getter neighbor would already have finished snow-blowing his own drive, salting it, sanding it, probably drying it with a hair dryer before Paul got out of bed. Paul didn't mind shoveling, even though he'd shoveled enough snow as a kid, growing up in Minneapolis, to last a lifetime. He had to be at the airport by noon to catch his flight back to the Twin Cities, a flight that might not have been necessary had he been more on the ball. Some days were better than others.

"I'm home," Paul said, letting himself in and closing the door to keep out the cold.

"I thought you were dead," the dog said. Her name was Stella, and she was a mixed breed, half German shepherd and half yellow Labrador, but favoring the latter in appearance. Fortunately, she'd also gotten her personality from the Labrador side of the family, taking from the Germans only a certain congenital neatness and a strong sense of protectiveness, though since she was the omega dog in her litter, it only meant she frequently felt put-upon.

"Once again, I'm not dead."

"Joy unbounded," she said dryly. Stella had no sense of permanence and therefore assumed Paul was dead whenever he was out of sight, hearing, or smell. "How was your night?"

"I went to the Bay State and heard the blues," Paul said. His head swam as he bent over to scratch her behind the ear, jingling her collar.

"Do you realize you're only slightly less routinized than a cat?"

"No need to insult. Do you want to go for a walk or what?"

"A walk? Yes. I think a walk would be nice. Is it cold out? I don't want to go if the weather's bad."

"There's no such thing as bad weather," he told her. "Just bad clothes."

She could still walk to the door, though sometimes Paul had to lift up her hind end to help her get off her dog bed. Usually he took the dog with him wherever he went, but tonight he'd left her home because of the weather. They lived in an apartment on the ground floor of a double-decker between the railroad tracks and the cemetery in Northampton, a small college town in western Massachusetts.

Stella paused on the front porch, gazing apprehensively at the snow, then took a cautious step forward.

"Hold it," Paul said, picking her up and carrying her down the three concrete steps to the sidewalk. He'd built a ramp for her to walk up, made from an old door with carpet squares nailed to it, but walking down the ramp was difficult for her. He set her down gently. She walked ahead of him, sniffing at the Sliwoskis' bushes, and at the house next door to that, and in all the places where she'd stopped and sniffed every night for the seven years they'd lived there. She stumbled occasionally.

That made two of them.

Paul inhaled deeply through his nostrils. He felt snowflakes on his face. The neighbors across the street still had their Christmas lights up. The neighbors next to them were watching television. At the corner house, he looked up. The student who lived there, Journal Girl, he called her, was again at her computer, her profile lit blue in the second-floor window. Sometimes she was brushing her hair. She was lovely.

He examined the pavement at his feet beneath the corner streetlamp. The snow was falling in flakes fat enough to cast shadows that, as the flakes fell, converged in the circle of light cast by the sodium bulb overhead. He stood in the exact middle of the convergence and imagined he was absorbing some kind of boreal energy, then stopped himself before anybody saw.

"Did I tell you you're going to be spending a week at Chester's house?" he told the dog.

"No problem," Stella said. "I like Chester."

"What's not to like?"

"Why am I going to Chester's house?"

"I have to fly home. My dad had a stroke."

"What's a stroke?"

"That's when part of your brain dies," Paul said. "Either you get a blood clot that blocks an artery so your brain doesn't get enough blood, or else an artery bursts and you get too much blood. I looked it up."

"And too much blood is bad, but not enough is bad too?"

"I guess," Paul said.

"A conundrum."

"A conundrum," Paul agreed. "An irony."

"So part of his brain died?" she asked.

"Something like that," Paul said. They walked.

"What part? How many parts are there?"

"Lots. They don't know how bad it is. I was talking to a guy at the bar who said if they get to you in time, they can limit the damage."

"A guy at the bar said that?"

"Yup."

"Always a good source for reliable medical information," she said. "I'm sorry for you."

"He was shoveling the walk."

"Your dad or the guy at the bar?"

"My dad. So it's my fault. We should have bought him a snow-blower. I was supposed to do some research and find out the best one to get, but I hadn't gotten around to it. We were worried about him shoveling. There's a family history of strokes and heart attacks."

Paul scraped a handful of snow off the hood of a car and tried to make a snowball, but the snow wasn't wet enough.

"I'm confused," Stella said, pausing to sniff at the base of a fence post. "If there's a family history, then how is it your fault?"

"He was exerting himself," Paul said. "If we'd bought him the snowblower I was supposed to research, he could have taken it easy."

"Shoulda, woulda, coulda."

"Even though he probably wouldn't have used it. He liked the exercise."

"There you go, then. You can't live your life second-guessing yourself."

"Dogs," Paul said, turning left on Parsons.

"Where to?" Stella asked.

"I need to walk a little bit," Paul said. He was headed toward the cemetery.

"The sign says NO DOGS," Stella reminded him.

"Let's live dangerously," he said, turning his collar up to keep the snow from falling down his neck. He took a glove off and checked his back pocket to make sure he had plastic Baggies to pick up after his dog. He did. They walked in the street, keeping to the tire tracks. The sound of his feet crunching in the snow reminded him of his teenage years, before he was old enough to drive, the miles and miles he'd walked, in blizzards even, looking for friends, for adventure, for something to do, anything to get out of the house. It pained him now to recall how much he'd once craved being free from his parents. He'd be free of them soon enough, the stones in the cemetery reminded him. Walking among them, it was hard to pretend that wasn't true.

"Beautiful night," Stella said, trying to make things better. "I love how quiet it is when it snows."

"Me too."

"Though it makes it hard to smell things."

"Why is that?"

"Water doesn't evaporate in the cold the way it does in the heat," Stella explained patiently. They'd already had this conversation.

"Know why they put this fence around the cemetery?" Paul asked, reading the names on the grave markers. One of the town's celebrities, Sylvester Graham, was buried here. An orator and health-food advocate, he was widely misidentified as the Father of the Graham Cracker, though he'd only invented the flour the cracker was made from. The other regional celebrity was Emily Dickinson, who'd lived across the river in Amherst. He wondered if they'd ever met, as contemporaries or as ghosts.

"Why's that, Paul?" Stella asked, though she'd heard it a dozen times.

"Because people are just dying to get in."

"That's a good one," Stella said. "Wasn't the road outside the cemetery where Emily Dickinson got pulled over for recluse driving?"

"I've told you that one before?"

"Once or twice," Stella said. In fact, he told it every time he told the cemetery-fence joke, and in the same order. He had other jokes he felt obliged to tell in specific circumstances; whenever he saw a kitchen colander, for example, he would advise the cook, "Be careful not to sing through that — you'll strain your voice." The dog tolerated it. Better than some people, Paul always said.

When they got home, he carried her up the front steps and set her down on the porch. Inside, she took a drink of water in the kitchen, sniffed her food bowl for recent additions, and then went to her bed by the radiator. L.L. Bean, red plaid, down filled, only the finest, she told the other dogs in the neighborhood, though Chester, her boyfriend, swore it was poly fill, but then, he was a golden — in other words, no rocket scientist. She let out a grunt as she lowered her weight to the floor, then appeared satisfied. Paul threw his coat over a chair and sat on the couch.

He took the TV remote control in hand and began at the top, channel 98, surfing down slowly, pausing just long enough at each channel to pass judgment. No, he did not want to invest in real estate, or car polishes, or stain removers, or hair or skin care products endorsed by aging actors and actresses. He could remember back when cable TV was first introduced in the seventies. "People will pay a monthly fee to watch the shows, so there will be no need for commercials — it will be *commercial-free television*," they'd said.

Paul turned the TV off. And Karen said he had no self-control. She never did like to watch television. He'd known that about her from the start and married her anyway. He had only himself to blame. It was a mistake he wouldn't make again, assuming he'd ever have the opportunity to repeat it.

He was tired and wanted to go to bed. Flying made him anxious, which meant he was going to have a rough night sleeping. He realized only as he locked the back door that he'd forgotten to check messages on his answering machine. There were two.

The first was from Tamsen, the woman he'd been seeing for the past three months, not exactly a true romance, more a strange but mutually satisfying exchange of courtesies, a benevolent closeness that allowed for physical contact, which it made him slightly tumescent merely to recall. Yet to qualify as a true romance, the relationship would have to hold promise for both the near and the distant future, and as far as Paul could tell, the long-term prognosis was poor. *"Hi, Paul — it's me. Just calling because I had a terrible day. It's not looking good at WebVan. Everybody around here is freshening their résumés and stealing office supplies, and here's a bad sign — Derek had his favorite pinball machine taken out for 'repairs,' or so he said, but I'll bet you anything he's hiding it somewhere so they don't repossess it when the whole thing goes belly-up. So anyway, I just wanted to talk to you because I miss you and I need to hear the sound of your voice. It's eleven now but you can call me and wake me up if you want. Have a good flight tomorrow if I don't hear from you, and call me when you get to your parents' house. I know it's going to be hard for you but you can do it. I know you can do it. Okay? Your dad's going to be okay. So call me."*

She had a sexy voice, slightly smoky and tinged with a Northeast Corridor Boston-Rhode Island-New York accent that made her seem tougher than she really was. It was far too late to return her call.

The second message was from his mother, who always began her messages, "Hi, Paul — it's your mom," as if he wasn't going to recognize her voice.

"Hi, Paul — it's your mom," she said. *"It's about eleven o'clock here, and I'm at Mercy Hospital. Your father is still resting comfortably and your sister is here and I'm going back just as soon as I get some coffee. Pastor Rolander was here visiting but he's left too. I think Bits will meet you at the airport, and she has your flight number and all that, so don't worry. I'm looking forward to seeing my little boy. Love you lots. Bye."*

It was nice to think there was at least one person left on earth who thought of him as a little boy.

Paul filled a glass with ice and poured himself a scotch, adding an extra splash for good measure, because it had been an extradifficult night, and tomorrow was likely to be worse. He took the drink to bed with him, where he read another paragraph of *Anna Karenina.* He'd been reading the book about one paragraph a night for the past three years. He heard toenails clicking against the floor. Stella had risen from her dog bed all on her own and had come to join him.

"You want up?" he asked her.

"Sure."

"Promise not to whimper in the middle of the night to be let down?" he asked. "I need my sleep. Chester's owners are going to come get you and take you to their house while I'm gone."

"No whimpering, I promise," she said.

He lifted the dog up onto the bed, where she made a nest for herself at his feet. He tried to read. Levin was convinced that Kitty thought he was an asshole. Paul was inclined to agree with her. He put the book down. He wondered if his father knew the difference anymore between being asleep and being awake, or if he had no words in his head at all and felt trapped, bound and gagged. Maybe the opposite was true and he was engaged in some kind of unbroken prayer and felt entirely at peace. Strokes could occur in any part of the brain, couldn't they? Each stroke was probably unique, immeasurable or unpredictable to some extent. His mother said that before it happened, Paul's father had complained of a headache and his speech had seemed a little slurred, though she hadn't made anything of it at the time. "I saw him shoveling, and then when I didn't see him anymore, I thought he'd gone down the block," Paul's mother had told him on the phone. "Then when I went to look for him, I saw him lying on the sidewalk and I thought at first that he'd slipped on the ice."

When he didn't get up, she'd dialed 911, fearing he'd had a heart attack. The operator told her not to move him because jostling could cause a second heart attack. Paul's mother had covered her husband with blankets where he lay and stayed by his side. They took him in an ambulance to the hospital, where doctors diagnosed a stroke. There they gave him a drug to dissolve the clot, but it would only work, they said, if it was administered in time, before too much damage had been done to the tissues in the brain that were being deprived of blood and therefore oxygen. Maybe the old man simply thought he was dreaming and couldn't wake up. Maybe it was a good dream. Maybe it wasn't.

"What?" Stella asked. "You sighed."

"Just thinking," Paul said. "If you could be a vegetable, what vegetable would you be?"

"Is a tomato a fruit or a vegetable?"

"There's been some debate. Why would you be a tomato?"

"To get next to all those hamburgers," the dog said.

"But if you were a tomato, you wouldn't want to eat hamburger."

"Of course I would. Why would I change, just because I'm a tomato?"

"You'd want tomato food. This has got to be the stupidest conversation we've ever had," Paul said.

"Actually, this is fairly typical," the dog said.

"You think my dad is going to be okay?" Paul asked.

"Sure. He's a tough old bird, right?"

"He used to go to the park and play pickup hockey with the high school rink rats until he was, like, sixty-five years old."

"The only guy alive who thinks Gordie Howe was a quitter."

"That's right," Paul said. "The only guy alive who thinks Gordie Howe was a quitter."

"Your dad's not a quitter."

"That's got to be in his favor."

"On the other hand," Stella said, "everybody gets old and dies. You know that, don't you?"

"Of course I know that."

"It's supposed to work that way. If it didn't, the whole planet would fill up with decrepit, useless old wrecks everybody else would have to take care of. And that wouldn't be good, would it?"

"No, that wouldn't be good."

"If you ask me, you humans have already artificially extended your life spans to the point where you're seriously screwing up the environment for the rest of us. You're supposed to die at forty or forty-five, tops. You're not supposed to gum up the works by hanging around for an extra thirty or forty years."

"*That's* a bit insensitive."

"Nothing personal."

"Look who's talking," Paul said. "How old are you? Fifteen? What's that in dog years?"

"Fifteen and a half," she said proudly. "And it's all relative. In tortoise years, that's nothing. In butterfly years, it's forever. I want your dad to be okay, but if he's not okay, that's no less desirable, in the grand scheme of things. That's all I'm saying. If he goes, it means more food for you."

"It's not a question of food," Paul said.

"Paul," Stella said, "*everything* is a question of food. Everything except where you lie down. And even that has to be somewhere near food. If you had a choice between sleeping somewhere that was soft and warm but a thousand miles from food, and sleeping in a place that was totally uncomfortable but right next to the kitchen, you'd sleep where there was food."

"I'm just a bowl of Iams to you, aren't I? That's all I am."

"You're more than a bowl of food, Paul. You're a dish of water too. You even pick up my shit." Sometimes she'd crap in the middle of the sidewalk downtown and turn and say, "Be a dear and get that, would you, Paul?"

"All I'm saying," she continued, "is that there's a line. And above the line, life is good, so keep on living, because you're healthy and alert and everything is okay. But below the line, life isn't good. Below the line, you're in pain, or you're hurting others, or you don't enjoy seeing your loved ones anymore, or you're embarrassed all the time because you're incontinent and you're pissing on yourself. Below that line, pulling the plug is better than not pulling the plug. Just play it by ear when you get there."

"I'll take it under advisement," he said.

She nestled in, resting her head on his leg.

"If he dies," she asked a moment later, "will that make you the alpha dog in your family?"

He'd once explained to her how wolves organized themselves as social animals, referencing research he'd done for the book he was working on, tentatively titled *Nature for Morons*.

"No," Paul told her. "That would be my brother, Carl."

"Oh," Stella said. "So you're not even going to try?"

"Don't worry about it — I lost that battle a long time ago," he said. "That's one thing you and I have in common. You don't remember, but you were the shiest pup in the litter when I got you. Your siblings used to knock you all over the place."

"In that case," she said, "you might want to bring some sort of offering . . ." But he was asleep before she got the words out.

She sniffed the air, then cocked her head to listen a moment. She heard the furnace in the basement kick on. A truck, some-where far off. The pilot light in the gas stove hissing. A mouse scratching, somewhere behind the mopboard in the kitchen, and of course, her master's breathing, his heart beating, his teeth grinding slightly, something he did when he was stressed. Other than that, all seemed to be in order.

How difficult it was now to remember her siblings. She could remember running wild through the weeds, usually last in the order, but it never bothered her to be last, as long as she had someone to run with. She remembered a farm and, vaguely, a fat man playing the banjo in the twilight, singing:

> What you gonna do when the liquor runs out, sweet thing?
> What you gonna do when the liquor runs out, sweet thing?
> What you gonna do when the liquor runs out?
> Stand around the corner with your mouth in a pout,
> Sweet thing, sweet thing, sweet thing.

"Good night, Paul," she said. He was snoring, but that never bothered her either.

Come Home, Waffle Belly

His sister's given name was Elizabeth, but everyone called her Bits. She was two years older than Paul, fair haired but not blond by Minnesota standards. She was waiting at the gate, alone, and gave him a big hug. She'd left the kids at home with her husband, Eugene. "They wanted to come meet you," she said, "but I was afraid with the snow they might cancel your flight."

Bits was his favorite sibling, despite the fact that when they were young, she'd occasionally tortured Paul, the baby in the family, as older siblings do. He had to admire the inventiveness with which she had tormented him. For example, she used to pin him to the ground, with his older brother Carl's help, and sit on him and pull his shirt up and press a tennis racket against his belly and then rake the extruded skin with a hairbrush, so that when she took the tennis racket away, he had what she called a waffle belly. She was even tempered, the fixer, the go-between middle child and the anxious one, fretting over details on a bad day but levelheaded on a good one. Her house was only a mile and a half from their parents' house, so she'd always been the one to drop by and check in on Harrold and Beverly to see if they needed anything.

"How is he?" he asked his sister.

"He's stable. He's not good, but he's not getting any worse. You'll see. How was your flight?"

He made a so-so gesture with his hand. "I don't think I've ever had a good conversation on an airplane."

"I'm sorry," she said. "Did they feed you?"

"Nothing," he said.

"I think the coffee shop at the hospital is still open. The food'll make you ill, but if you get sick, you're already in a hospital."

He'd also had four vodkas on the plane and needed to pee. Airport bathrooms annoyed him, guys bellying up to the urinals with their bags over their shoulders, knocking into you with their luggage and making you tinkle on your shoes. He contemplated draining one of the nip bottles he'd stashed in his suitcase but decided to wait until later. People were waiting for him.

As they drove, she filled Paul in as best she could. Their father had had about as bad an ischemic stroke as you could have, she said. The only fortunate aspect was that he hadn't had a hemorrhagic stroke, since burst blood vessels were harder to treat than clots. The damage was primarily to the right hemisphere of Harrold's brain and to the motor cortex. He would need to relearn how to do virtually everything, she said. He could move his right hand and lightly grip with it but was otherwise paralyzed. He had some spasticity in his left foot and leg, indicating live nerve action, and he seemed to be aware of his circumstances, but he had had two severe seizures in the first twenty-four hours. He was being closely monitored. She warned her brother that he might be shocked when he saw their father, with so many tubes and wires and machines hooked up.

Bits maneuvered her minivan past familiar landmarks, a Rexall drugstore, a sporting goods store, the Sears Building. When he got to the hospital, Paul found a men's room near the gift shop, drained another nip, popped a Life Saver, ran his fingers through his hair in the mirror, and then went to face the music.

"I hate this place," he said as they walked down the hall, following a blue stripe painted on the floor. Paul had been to Mercy

Hospital three times before, the first time for stitches when a kid in sixth grade hit him in the eye with a snowball, and the second time after he'd broken his arm playing high school football. The last time was when he'd visited his namesake, Grandpa Paul, who'd lain in his bed after cancer surgery, shriveling up like a mushroom on a windowsill.

"I was in labor for thirty-seven hours the last time I was here," his sister said. "Oh, the memories."

"They should bill you by the hour," Paul said. "They'd move people out faster."

"I did feel guilty for malingering," Bits said, "but I was having such a good time."

Paul stopped her in the hallway.

"I have to ask," he said. "Are you mad at me?"

"For what?"

"I was supposed to be pricing snowblowers," Paul said. "If he hadn't been shoveling, this might not have happened."

"I was mad at you for maybe five seconds," she told him. "You're not why a blood clot stuck in his head. And if it wasn't shoveling, it would just have been something else. He could have had a stroke lying in bed. I said the same thing to Mom. She was blaming herself because she thought if she'd been watching out the window, she would have seen him when he fell. You can't watch somebody all the time. If you could, my kids wouldn't have so many stitches in their heads."

The door to his father's hospital room, just down the hall from intensive care, was slightly ajar, so he opened it slowly. Paul's mother, Beverly, was off on an errand, a nurse said. Bits went to look for her. Before she left, she gave Paul's arm a squeeze and said, "Don't worry — he won't bite you."

The vodka numbed him, but not enough. His first impression was that his father, with his dentures out and his glasses off, and his snow-white hair, and the tubes in his nose and in his veins,

looked a lot like Grandpa Paul, the difference being that Grandpa
Paul had been semiconscious and cheerful right up to the last
moment. Paul's father's eyes were closed, his breathing percep-
tible only at close range. A pink plastic apparatus resembling a
handlebar mustache connected to clear plastic tubes brought
oxygen to his nostrils. IV drips fed drugs and serums and nutri-
ents into both arms. A half-full catheter bag hung at the foot of
the bed, collecting urine. Other sensors taped to various parts of
his father's body brought data to a multitiered monitor, report-
ing things like temperature, heart rate, blood pressure, and Paul
wasn't sure what else. An array of unused equipment had been
pushed against the far wall. Somehow the first impression was
that this was more of a science project than a human drama, or
a scene from some doctor show on television, not quite real. He
wondered what his father might be thinking. He was wearing a
hospital johnny, white cotton with blue diamonds on it. On the
bed stand next to him was a bouquet of flowers, an empty glass,
a Diet Coke can, a half-consumed sleeve of Ritz crackers, a Bible,
and his mother's reading glasses. The television mounted in the
corner of the room was off, but Paul wanted to turn it on, in dire
need of a distraction. How ineluctably strange, Paul thought, to
be able to move, see, talk, hear, and comprehend, while his father
couldn't. Harrold had been the source of whatever strength Paul
possessed. If the old man had taught him anything, it was how
to persevere.

"Where are you now?" he wanted to ask.

His father was only seventy-two but looked ninety in the fluorescent light, waxy and pale. In a sense he'd come full circle, for
the odd thing was that Paul's earliest memory of his father, one
of the earliest memories he had, was of Harrold lying in a hospital bed, a different hospital, in a different era, without a tenth of
the technology surrounding him today. Paul had been just shy
of three years old and had no memory of the accident itself, but

he remembered seeing his father with bandages around his head and tubes up his nose, after he'd driven off an icy road and into a bridge with the whole family in the car. They were coming home from a pre-Christmas reunion organized by some of Harrold's navy buddies, men he'd served with in the Pacific. Paul could remember holding Grandpa Paul's hand, walking down a long hospital corridor that smelled of disinfectant, hearing voices in the air, doctors' names coming over the public-address system. He remembered being told that if he was good he could buy anything he wanted in the gift shop, only to discover sadly that there was nothing there he wanted. He remembered being told to keep very quiet, until he came to believe any noise he made might accidentally kill somebody, so he kept *very* quiet.

They'd stopped first to see his mother, who'd been less seriously injured. Beverly had managed a weak smile and squeezed his hand. Then they'd gone to see Harrold, who looked at Paul but couldn't speak. Carl had broken his shoulder and had a bandage on his head for a while, and Bits had bumped her head and suffered cuts from flying glass. She still had a scar above her right eyebrow, which over the years had become a line that made her look permanently bemused. People who didn't know her sometimes thought she was being sarcastic or ironic when she wasn't. Paul had emerged from the accident more or less unscathed, a few cuts, a chest bruise where he hit the headrest, and a collapsed lung that was easily reinflated. The kids had stayed with Grandpa Paul and Grandma Lula while their parents recovered.

Paul remembered something else. He remembered meeting a man in his father's hospital room, a big, barrel-chested guy with a blond crew cut, in a military uniform, probably one of his father's navy pals. He remembered the uniform and in particular the military decorations the man had on his chest and sleeve. That was all. His father never talked about the time he spent in the service or, for that matter, about the accident. Death had no meaning for Paul at the time, so he hadn't been worried, just impatient, waiting for his family life to resume its normalcy.

"You did it once, tough guy," Paul whispered. "You can do it again."

He was thinking of mortality and related issues (meaning, fulfillment, accomplishment and failure, final judgment, eternity, et cetera) when his sister rejoined him.

"Mom's down the hall. She said she'd be right back. We were going to order Chinese. They told us it was okay to eat in the lounge," she said. "I haven't even had a chance to ask you about you. How are you doing? Do you ever see Karen?"

Paul wondered if Harrold could hear them. If he could, he gave no indication.

"It's hard not to in a small town," Paul said. Nobody in the family had known what to say about the divorce, owing, in part, to the fact that against all odds, no one in his family had ever been divorced, but that was okay because he didn't want to talk about it either. "She's still with the arts council, so she's downtown a lot, but so far we've managed to avoid each other."

"Would you say you're on good terms with her?" Bits asked.

"I wouldn't go that far," he said. "We've moved on."

They were interrupted when Paul's mother came in and gave him a long hug, and he hugged back, grateful for the kind of family that can't divorce you and go off and find somebody else to live with.

"It's so good to see you," she said. "I'm sorry you had to fly home under these circumstances, but I'm glad you're here. I'm sure your father is glad too." She moved to the bed and leaned over her husband. "See who's here, Harrold? It's Paul."

Paul was hoping, for reasons selfish and otherwise, to observe a sudden spike or two on his father's heart monitor, but the beat was steady and unchanged. Beverly returned to Paul.

"My goodness," she said. "Your hair has gotten so much darker."

"Mom," Paul said. "You've been saying that ever since I went away to college. My hair turned dark when I was five. It hasn't changed since then."

"I know," she said. "I just can't get over it."

Paul kept his mother company while Bits went to pick up dinner. A nurse asked them to wait in the lounge while she calibrated and adjusted the technology surrounding and attached to Paul's father.

"How are you holding up?" Paul asked Beverly.

"Well, you know," she said, "when you get to be our age, you have to be aware that this sort of thing can happen. Two of our friends from church have had strokes."

Beverly was five foot two and shrinking. One day, he'd told her, she'd be the size of a raccoon, and then they could fly with her in a crate and take her to all the places she wanted to see. Her hair was gray but full. Today, she seemed thinner. She sat on the couch, moving aside a pile of out-of-date magazines. Paul sat next to her. She spoke of what the doctors had told her so far. She seemed oddly calm, self-assured in a way he'd never seen before. Paul always figured he'd inherited his insecurity from her and his intransigence from his father. She'd made notes on a small pad and referred to them to fill Paul in. The doctors had warned her that they couldn't predict how impaired Harrold would be, or for how long. It was once thought patients couldn't recover much beyond the progress made in the first six months, but newer therapies and medications had extended the recovery period by as much as four years.

He was being given aspirin and Heparin to thin his blood, Beverly told Paul, to prevent new clots from forming in his legs and to protect against pulmonary embolisms. He was also being given Prozac for his emotional state, since stroke damage in the right hemisphere often caused depression. Harrold could not produce speech, and it was too early to tell to what extent he could understand it. He was clearly confused and likely to have difficulty concentrating.

The best news was that he wasn't going to get worse and was unlikely to have another stroke, Beverly said. Paul was impressed by how much his mother had taken in. He wondered if the doctors had told her everything, or rather if she'd heard everything they'd said. It was human nature to selectively edit the picture to make it as rosy as possible. He remembered what Bits had said about Beverly's blaming herself for not watching over Harrold more closely.

"It sounds like the sort of thing that could have happened at any minute," Paul said. "Nobody knew. He was in good shape before any of this."

"The doctors said he's in very good physical shape for a man his age," Beverly said. "He may be moved to a stroke unit in a day or two."

"I just want you to be in good shape too," Paul said. "You still have to take care of yourself."

"Oh, don't worry about me," Beverly said. "You know, there's a very nice little chapel downstairs, across from the coffee shop, where you can go pray if you need to. I've been asking God to check in and keep an eye on your father."

While researching animal behaviors, Paul had come across a study by scientists who'd concluded, supported by all the most recent data and statistics, that contrary to popular belief, prayer and optimism and/or a sense of humor had no measurable effect on the prognosis or survival rates of critical hospital patients, but that didn't mean it wasn't a good idea for the families waiting in hospital lounges.

"Good to know," he said.

"Your brother has been so helpful," Beverly told him. "He insisted on having a neurologist be your father's primary physician. I think our regular doctor's feelings were a little hurt. They were talking about moving Harrold to a nursing home instead of rehabilitation because of his age, but Carl put his foot down. I don't think I would have known what to say."

"Has he been by today?" Paul asked. It wasn't hard to imagine his brother throwing his lawyerly weight around a bit. Make all the lawyer jokes you wanted, but it was nice to have one in the family when you needed one.

"He should be here any minute," Beverly said. "He's coming after his meeting. Didn't Bits tell you?"

"I don't think so," Paul said. "She might have."

Carl was an attorney for IBM, pulling down big money and supplementing it with his various investments. It was a path he frequently urged Paul to follow, even though Paul didn't have much financial savvy, as Carl liked to remind him. Carl had a strange way of complimenting him first before insulting him, saying, "Gosh, Paul, you know — you always had all the creative talent in the family, which means you must have brains, so why is it you don't know diddly-squat about money?" Paul had mixed feelings about seeing Carl. He loved his brother, but Carl drove him nuts.

"He's been really so helpful," his mother said. "It's good to have you home. I wish you lived closer so we could see you more often."

"So do I," he said, though the East Coast suited him fine.

There were three other people in the lounge with them, an old woman watching CNN on the television in the corner and a young mother with a toddler up long past his bedtime. When Bits arrived with the food, Beverly asked the others if they were hungry. The old woman smiled politely and shook her head. The young mother said thanks but that they'd be leaving as soon as she could have a word with the doctor. Bits set the food on a round table in the corner, lifting five white cardboard cartons with wire handles from a brown paper bag and spreading an array of individually wrapped plasticware on the table. She'd bought paper plates as well. She said she'd run into Carl in the parking garage and that he was getting everybody pop from the soda machine and would be along shortly.

A moment later, Paul heard Carl's footsteps approaching, distinct from those of the hospital workers in their soft-soled shoes. He was genuinely glad to see his big brother. Carl embodied the word *classy,* with his wide-wale black corduroy pants and black cashmere crewneck sweater over a blue pinstripe no-iron oxford shirt, his brown Cole Haan loafers with tassels on them, his red hair (their parents had considered naming him Eric), the only kid in the family who had red hair, cut in a Robert Redford shag, with a meticulously trimmed red beard to match.

"I stopped by the room," Carl said, setting the sodas on the table and hugging his mother. "Dad's asleep." He turned to Paul. "You made it okay? Airline give you a medical discount?"

"They did," Paul said.

"Anything new?" Carl asked Beverly.

Beverly filled him in. Little had changed since Carl's last visit. Harrold had had a slight fever, but his temperature had returned to normal after antibiotics were added to his IV drip. Carl announced that he was starving, and Paul remembered he was hungry too. They opened the cartons and distributed the contents, speaking in hushed hospital tones.

"Everything's going to be okay," Carl told Beverly. Paul marveled at his brother's confidence, but Carl had always been confident, whether there was any basis for it or not. "How goes the struggle?" he asked Paul, wielding his chopsticks expertly while Paul used a fork. "Still working into the wee small ones? What's the new project? One of those Idiot books, right?"

"Morons," Paul corrected him. "The Idiot books are a bit more technical than ours."

"Those Idiot books are a great gimmick. What's this one about?"

"Nature."

"*Nature for Morons?*" Carl said. "God, are you perfect for that."

The reference was to Paul's Boy Scout adventures. Carl, who'd joined Mount Olivet Troop 110 four years earlier than Paul, had progressed all the way to Eagle Scout, whereas Paul had been kicked out for smoking before he made First Class. It wasn't tobacco that Paul and his patrol mates had been smoking. It wasn't marijuana either. It was everything else in the forest — sarsaparilla leaves, skunk cabbage, spleenwort, lamb's-quarter, and various other flora indigenous to the coniferous biome of northern Minnesota — each experimental doobie rolled in Zig-Zag papers with a club moss filter. Nothing they smoked got them high, but it seemed an investigation worth pursuing. Carl was the one who caught them. Paul had argued that by the letter of the law, troop rules forbade smoking only tobacco or pot, but Carl knew a scout's higher duty was to the truth, even if it meant ratting out your own brother. Paul later considered getting booted from the Boy Scouts a blessing in disguise, soon discovering it was a lot more fun to hang out at the beach with the in crowd (or even the out crowd) than to go to scout camp, but he was pretty upset about it at the time.

He let the insult pass. It was not the time or the place, but he felt his guard go up.

"Was that your idea?" Carl asked.

"It was the editor's, actually," Paul said. "I think he's trying to atone."

"Atone for what?"

"He was with the Greenpeace group that went up to Labrador to spray-paint the baby seals," Paul said.

"Well, he should feel bad," their mother said. "That's terrible."

"They weren't vandalizing them, Mom," Paul said. "They were trying to stop the seal hunters who were clubbing the seals for their fur. They decided they'd spray-paint them fluorescent orange to make the fur useless."

"Well, that's better," Beverly said.

"Not really," Paul said. "All baby seals have to protect themselves from polar bears is their camouflage coloration. The bears ate them all. Probably still talk about it. 'Night of the Smorgasbord.'"

As they ate, they discussed the practical matters before them. Carl had had a long conversation with the person who would be coordinating Harrold's rehabilitation. As soon as possible, he wanted to get Harrold to the point where he could dress and feed himself, the risk of depression being greatest in patients who gave up hope of ever living independently again. When Harrold came home, he'd be unable to climb the stairs, at first and probably for quite some time, but a bed could be set up in the sunroom. Carl had arranged for a physical therapist to work with Harrold, once he came home, for nine hours a week, and for a speech and language therapist to work with him an additional nine hours a week. He and Bits and Erica and Eugene would drop by as often as they could to help with Harrold and to take some of the burden off their mother. If that proved untenable, they'd probably need to consider nursing homes, but all in good time. Insurance would cover most of the expenses. Paul said he wanted to pay an equal share of whatever it cost, but the fact was that Carl's annual income was easily ten times Paul's, so that an equal share and a fair share were two different numbers, and both of them knew it.

Carl had also made plans to buy their parents a computer

after the woman he'd spoken to advised him that there were rehabilitation programs available where patients with only the partial use of one hand could click a mouse to solve simple puzzles to sharpen their minds and could even communicate with others by clicking to answer yes-or-no questions on their computer screens. If greater motor control returned, patients could eventually click on icons or letters to spell out words. Any stimulation of the speech centers of Harrold's brain would be therapeutic, promoting neurogenesis and simply helping Harrold relearn how to pay attention.

"Maybe you and Dad could instant-message each other," Carl suggested to Paul. He turned to Beverly. "It's time you guys got online anyway."

Paul agreed that he could do that. Beverly seemed hesitant. Carl asked her why.

"I just don't think I want to be on the Internet," she said.

"Because?" Carl asked.

"Well," she said, "I don't know much about it, but I don't want those hacker people using my credit cards. I know they can get into things and steal your information."

She agreed only after Carl assured her that there was nothing to worry about and that if it made her more comfortable, he'd be happy to put the AOL account in his name and use his own credit card to pay for it.

Paul ate. He thought of all the family meals they'd eaten together, sitting at the kitchen table, Harrold reading the paper but lowering it occasionally to participate, Carl cleaning his plate clockwise and chewing loudly, albeit with his mouth closed, Bits kicking Paul in the shin under the table, Beverly rising every few minutes to fetch refills and seconds from the stove (and always finishing her own meal last), saying, "Don't be afraid of the potatoes," or "Help yourself— don't be afraid of the asparagus," until her children mocked her, pretending to be frightened by the potatoes or terrified by the asparagus, and then everyone would laugh. He remembered the fights too. In the hospital lounge, someone was conspicuously absent. It was all wrong.

Beverly said Pastor Rolander had called to say there was going to be a special prayer offered in church tomorrow for Harrold's recovery. Carl said they'd decided they were still going to go ahead with the birthday party for his son, Howard, which they'd planned long before Harrold's stroke, after church at Carl's house, just family and cousins. Bits agreed that the children would be too disappointed if they canceled.

"Life goes on, right?" Carl said. "I was going to stop in to see Dad before church, and then maybe after the party we can bring the kids back here to see Grandpa. Unless you think that would be too much."

"He'd love that," Beverly agreed.

When it came time for everyone to grab a fortune cookie from the carton in the middle of the table, Paul declined. He'd decided, somewhere in the course of the day, pondering his father's current situation, that he needed to start thinking about his own health and how to improve it. Turning down desserts occasionally might be a good first step. He'd never cared that much for fortune cookies anyway. Half the time, they were stale or soggy. His brother looked up.

"Aren't you going to eat your cookie?"

"I don't think so," Paul said.

"You at least have to read your fortune." Maybe it was Carl's imperious tone, but suddenly Paul remembered all the old wars. They kept their voices down, but the tension escalated.

"No, thanks," Paul said.

"Why not? It's fun."

"Why should I?" Paul said. "I'd be very surprised if what it says in the cookie bears the slightest relationship to my actual future, considering it was written fifty years ago by a man in China who never met me and who's probably dead by now."

"That's not the point," Carl said. "It's fate."

"What is?"

"What cookie you get."

"There's only one left," Paul said. "What choice do I have?"

"Then that's the one that was meant for you."

"If I don't want one," Paul said, "that's fate too."

"No," Carl said, "that's free will. Fate is why you have to open your cookie."

"I don't *have* to open my cookie if I don't *want* to. I don't *have* to do anything."

"Then I'll open it for you," Carl said, reaching for the plate. Paul managed to grab the last cookie before Carl could.

"It's my cookie, right?" he said. He picked it up, crossed the lounge, and asked the young mother if her little boy would like a treat. She thanked Paul, took the cellophane bag from him, tore it open, and handed the cookie to her three-year-old, who turned it over and over before taking a bite, the fortune falling to the floor with the other half of the cookie. The young mother picked up the crumbs from the floor, glanced at the fortune briefly, and then threw it in the wastebasket, her child too young to appreciate it.

"There," Paul said, returning to the table. "Apparently fate wanted him to have it."

Bits rolled her eyes, having witnessed similar scenes countless times. Carl scowled and said nothing, but Paul knew that deep down, Carl wanted to go dig the little strip of paper out of the wastebasket and read it. Paul foiled him by helping Bits clean up and dumping their leftovers into the wastebasket on top of the fortune.

When Bits offered to give him a ride to their parents' house, he told her he'd ride with Beverly.

"You go on ahead. I think I'll stay here one more night," Beverly said. "The chair in your father's room folds out. It's really quite comfortable. If you'd just check when you get home to make sure I didn't leave anything plugged in . . ."

"I already checked, Mom," Bits said. "We'll be fine. I have my key."

"I'll be home to change clothes before church," Beverly said, gathering up her coat and purse. "I think everybody needs to get some sleep."

They walked her to Harrold's room. Paul was surprised to note, as he leaned in to kiss his father good night on the forehead, that Harrold had tears running down both his cheeks.

"The nurse said that's just a neurological response," Bits told him. "Supposedly it has nothing to do with how he's feeling."

"Supposedly," Paul said. As Beverly used a tissue to dry her husband's eyes, Paul realized it was the first time he'd ever seen his father cry.

3

Brrzzlfft!

A s his sister drove, Paul stared out the window. The city had changed since he'd moved away, but mostly at the extremities, where its distant suburbs continued to expand into the surrounding farmland, and at the center, the downtown area where commerce and culture collided. Between the center and the outskirts, it all looked much the same. They passed his old high school, which Bits said was now a school for the performing arts, attracting kids from all over the city. Paul saw the alleyway where he used to get high before homeroom. He recalled the day he thought the pot he'd smoked was oregano or Minnesota ditch weed, a rip-off, then realized, as the bell rang, that he'd been reading and rereading the first sentence of his *Scholastic Weekly* for over an hour.

The house was a three-bedroom stucco Federal-style home in South Minneapolis. His parents had put on a new roof the summer before, with plans to sell, but they hadn't found any condos to their liking yet. There'd been talk of their finding some retirement community down south, in Arizona or Texas, but it never got beyond talk. He couldn't imagine them living anywhere but Minnesota.

Bits showed him where Beverly hid the spare key, under a flowerpot on the front porch, then used her own key to let them in. Paul dropped his bags at the bottom of the stairs. Bits told him he might want to build a fire in the woodstove and asked him if there was anything he needed. It was going to be strange. As best he could recall, he'd never spent a night in the house alone.

"Just the phone," he told her.

Bits asked him who he was calling. "You've got a girlfriend?"

"Yes, she's a girl, and yes, she's a friend."

Bits furrowed her brow. They were in the kitchen.

"What's that supposed to mean?" she said, leaning against the counter. "Are you seeing this person or not?"

"Sort of."

"What do you mean, 'sort of'?"

"What are you?" Paul asked. "A private detective?"

"Don't get all whiny, Paulie," she said. "I'm just asking because I didn't think you were ready to jump back into the dating pool."

He noticed his mother had removed his wedding pictures from the photo gallery she kept on her refrigerator door, including the five-by-eight of him and Karen cutting their wedding cake, him in his tux, her in her gown and veil. He wondered what Beverly had done with the photographs. She had boxes of thirty-year-old Christmas cards in the attic. She'd never get rid of something as historically significant as a wedding picture.

"I'm not ready," he told his sister. "That's the whole point. I'm in the pool but only up to my ankles. It's sort of a mutual I-don't-want-a-relationship relationship. We just really like each other, but we're trying not to get ahead of ourselves."

"Is it exclusive?" his sister asked.

"For me it is," he answered. "She has a preexisting relationship."

"She does?"

"Yeah, but it's not going anywhere. She's free to see me if she wants to, and she told him about me. There's nothing sneaky going on. Nobody's playing anybody. We're very open about everything — there's no rule that says you're not allowed to date more than one person at a time."

"Well," his sister said, "just make sure she's good to you. I don't want you getting involved with the wrong person."

"That's exactly why we're hanging out. If I met the right person right now, I wouldn't know what to do. We're not getting involved. That's what makes her right."

As much as he'd always loved women (beginning in second grade, when he'd been unable to take his eyes off Miss Lasseter's pendulous boobs for the entire school year), he'd recently come to the conclusion that he didn't know very much about them. He honestly couldn't say if he thought about love too little or too much. He recognized that there was a mystery and a magic to it and had spent the past twenty years trying to solve the mystery, even though he knew he ran the risk of destroying the magic. By the end of his relationships, he'd usually spent more time analyzing and thinking about love than he'd spent actually enjoying or participating in it. Sometimes it seemed as if it was the guys who gave it the least amount of thought who had the best luck, the one-dimensional monobrows with minimal vocabularies whom women seemed drawn to. For Paul, the longer his relationships went on, the more confusing they became, and the whole point of his relationship with Tamsen was never to let it get that far. Keep it simple. She wasn't really wrong for him except insofar as she wasn't really available either. Had she been fully and immediately available, asking for or expecting more than he could offer, he'd probably run the other way, though winning her affections was nevertheless his goal. It didn't make sense, but it was fun as long as he didn't overthink it. He knew he wasn't going to have much luck explaining that to his sister. After the divorce, he and Bits had talked on the phone at length about what went wrong and how he and Karen had been a bad match from the start, and how Bits had had misgivings as early as the wedding.

Paul made her promise that if she ever had misgivings again, she would speak up immediately.

"What's her name?"

"Tamsen."

"Tamsen? I like it. What sort of name is Tamsen?"

"It's an old family name," he said. "French, I think."

"She has a last name?"

"Prouty."

"And she's old enough to name all four Beatles?"

"Pete Best, Stu Sutcliffe, Billy Preston, Brian Epstein, George Martin, and Alan Freed too. She's only five years younger than me."

"You're sure you're ready to date someone from within your actual peer group?" his sister said. "That sounds like a pretty big step."

"You're the one who told me I needed someone who could kick my ass," he said.

"She kicks your ass?"

"No," he said, "but she could."

"How did you meet?"

"We had lunch together," he told his sister. "Strictly business. At first."

Tamsen had called to ask if he'd be willing to link his book's Web site to an e-commerce site she was working for. His name was on the cover of a book called *Windows 95 for Morons,* but he'd only finished the project, he explained, after taking over for the original author, who died before he could turn in the first draft. She told him not to worry about it. Her employer, a company called WebVan.com, just needed actual content to attract browsers to their Web site, meaning articles, news items, humor pieces, short stories, even poetry. That first phone call, they talked for over an hour. When she said she was going to be in Worcester for a business conference and suggested they meet for lunch, his heart raced.

"Is she divorced?"

"Yeah, but I wouldn't want to see someone who wasn't."

"Kids?"

He shook his head.

"They tried but they couldn't get pregnant."

"So what's this other relationship she has?" Bits asked. "It's not serious?"

"He's a radiologist," Paul said. "Stephen. He and his wife are separated and getting divorced, but they have two boys, ten and twelve. I guess it makes things fairly complicated. Her best friend, Caitlin, told me she likes me much better."

"'She,' Tamsen, or 'she,' Caitlin?"

"Caitlin likes me better than she likes Stephen," Paul clarified. He'd met Caitlin at a dinner party and had "passed the best-friend test with flying colors," according to Tamsen. He usually felt as if he came off more awkward than charming, but it had been a fun party. Caitlin had confided to Paul, in the kitchen, that Stephen was predictable and a bit boring, almost a slightly taller version of Tamsen's ex-husband. Caitlin said she thought Tamsen needed someone who brought out her creative side.

"But as I said, she's free to see whoever she wants. And so am I. Not that I want to. We have a deal to be completely open and honest with each other and nonjudgmental. We can say anything to each other."

"That's the stupidest thing I've ever heard," his sister said.

"You could be right," Paul said. "If it doesn't work out, we still have jealousy and deception to fall back on."

"It's your call," his sister said.

"Which is why I need a phone," Paul said. He hoped he wasn't too late. "I promised I'd call when I got home from the hospital."

"Can I listen in?" Bits asked. She'd eavesdropped once in high school, when Paul had nervously phoned a girl, and never let him forget what he'd said: "I like what's you about you . . ."

"No," he said.

His sister offered to pick him up in the morning before church, but he said he'd ride over with Beverly. He hadn't brought a suit to wear, but he had a nice shirt and could borrow a tie from his father's collection, probably one of the same ties he'd borrowed back in high school, and throw a sweater over it.

When Bits had gone, he opened the refrigerator, though he knew better than to think he'd find a beer or a bottle of wine or whiskey anywhere in the house. Upstairs, he threw his suitcase on the bed in the guest room and opened it. He had five nips left. The liquor stores would be closed tomorrow, so he saved four to tide him over and opened one as a nightcap, then went into his father's office to use the phone.

The idea of talking to Tamsen still excited him. That first time on the telephone, they'd been professional and stuck to business initially, but in no time they were sharing personal details, their favorite bands, places, and foods. Their tastes were similar, and he'd wanted to know more. He'd driven to Worcester two days later to meet her for lunch with nothing in mind other than to play it by ear. He found the restaurant without much trouble, a sushi place where they'd ordered plum wine. She was far prettier than he'd dared to hope, approaching petite with straight shoulder-length hair the color of Mexican rosewood. She had hazel eyes that caught the light, expressive eyebrows, good cheekbones, smooth skin, perfect teeth, and lips that he could only think of as kissable. Her hands were small and soft but her grip was firm. Her body was (it was only natural to compare) better than Karen's, who had something of a boyish build. Again, they'd eased into each other, talked about business, the weather, sports, New England, politics. She played poker. She liked to go to the beach by herself and listen to CDs of female jazz vocalists who only needed one name, Ella and Billie and Bessie and Blossom and Judy. She had a fish tank. She'd taken cooking classes but often had yogurt and carrots for dinner. They'd talked until it became clear to both of them that they wanted to move beyond chitchat.

He'd asked her about her family. Her brother, Mike, lived in California. Her mother, Judith, lived in Kingston, Rhode Island, a teacher in the South County school system (that they were both teachers' kids was one of many similarities). Tamsen's father, John, had been an engineer for General Electric who traveled a great deal on business. Her fondest memories of him were of sitting side by side on the couch watching reruns of the TV show *Hogan's Heroes* when he came home from work. He'd just turned fifty when he was diagnosed with cancer. Tamsen had been engaged to a man named Donald, but they moved the wedding day up when they heard, even though she'd begun to have doubts about the relationship — in fact, she'd told Paul, she knew deep down that it wasn't going to work, but she'd been in denial and felt she couldn't call it off because of her father's illness. She wanted him to think she was going to be happy.

When it was Paul's turn, he limned his own failed marriage for her in brief, taking care not to sound bitter or blaming, aware that poor-mouthing one's ex was bad form. When Tamsen asked him if he was dating anybody, he told her honestly that he'd forgotten how. He'd asked women out twice and had been shot down both times, his overtures too tentative and timorous. Tamsen had advised him that if he wanted someone to know he was interested in her, he had to tell her in no uncertain terms, at which point he put his arms around Tamsen and kissed her. It was the most impulsive thing he'd ever done, resulting in the most exciting kiss he'd ever experienced, like in the movies, surprising him as much as it surprised her, given that he had zero confidence as a lover, husband, or partner. The plum wine had emboldened him, but his first thought was to apologize. The way she smiled and kissed him back told him that no apologies were necessary and that he'd correctly interpreted the signs and signals she'd been sending. They'd kissed three more times, the last when they were standing in the parking lot, and she said she had to go, but not before revealing that her psychic had told her she was going to meet someone whose name started with *P.* He didn't believe in psychics, but he knew better than to say so. She'd kissed him good-bye in a way that didn't say good-bye at all. "Brrzzlfft," he'd said. He'd meant to say an actual word.

After the day he'd had, he liked thinking about her. The idea of her gave him peace. In his father's office, he dialed her number from memory.

The message on her answering machine said, *"Hi, this is Tamsen. Please leave a message, and if this is Paul, I went out, but feel free to call and wake me up, or else call me in the morning."*

He hung up, but not before he heard her machine beep, which meant she would know someone had called and hung up and would probably guess it was him, and that was awkward. Now he had to call back and actually say something.

He stopped to parse the meaning of her message. The fact that she'd left a personal message for him was good, because it meant she was thinking of him and wasn't worried about who else (Stephen) might call and hear it. The fact that she said she'd gone out but didn't say where she'd gone probably meant she was with someone (Stephen?) and that was bad. But she'd said "feel free to call and wake me," and that was good because it meant she wasn't sleeping over at his house, and he wasn't sleeping over at hers. But she'd added "or else call me in the morning," and that was bad, because it could mean she was at his house, or he was at hers and she was screening her calls, and either way she would not be reachable until the following day. Unless it was good and meant only that she really wanted him to call and didn't care when.

He had to think. It was true that they'd agreed to be open to each other and that nothing would be off limits, but that said, when they were together, he tried to avoid the subject of Stephen, and she did too. He knew that if he was going to prevail in the rivalry, he had to be the one who was the least jerky — the one she could complain to about the other, and not the one she complained to the other about.

He stared at the phone, the same vintage black Bakelite rotary-dial telephone he'd stared at for a significant portion of his adolescence, under nearly identical circumstances, trying to work up the courage to call a girl, trying to think of what to say. Same room too, his father's office having formerly been the bedroom Paul shared with his brother. It now contained a twin bed instead of a bunk bed, a set of filing cabinets, and the massive rolltop oak desk his father had inherited from Paul's grandfather. The walls were decorated with photographs — one of his father with his college buddies, another of Harrold with his navy buddies (Paul examined the photograph and tried but failed to identify the navy buddy he'd met in the hospital, the barrel-chested guy with the crew cut) — as well as various awards and recognitions of achievement Harrold had garnered over the years, including a Minneapolis School System Teacher of the Year award. Being the son of a teacher had placed Paul in a difficult position in high school, his kinship tantamount to an traitorous alliance with the Enemy. To show his friends that he could be trusted as a "regular guy," he smoked pot and drank and got in trouble at every opportunity. Harrold Gustavson was considered one of the more acceptable teachers in the school, not popular in the palsy-walsy way some teachers were, but highly respected, even by the juvenile delinquents and the stoners and the jocks, for being fair and honest and for simply being a good teacher, intense, everyone said — an hour in his class was like a week in anyone else's. Paul had avoided his father's class for the same reason he avoided talking about school at home. It was a question of establishing an identity for himself, apart from his family, which required some sense of autonomy and privacy. Other kids could do stuff at school that their parents never knew about; Paul never had the luxury. From eighth grade on, he left his house to hang out at his friends' houses every chance he got, to get away from what he considered oppressive and ubiquitous parental supervision. Away from prying eyes, he could use swear words in his conversations, smoke cigarettes, drink beer, goof around with chicks, let his hair down and relax — he could be himself. At one time, that meant being whatever was the opposite of who his father was. Now, surrounded by so many representations of his father's accomplishments, with nothing of note to show for his own sorry life, default contrariety didn't seem like such a good idea.

Staring at the telephone was no more productive now than it had been when he was a pimply-faced teenager, and led him to the same conclusion: "Just call — you'll think of something." He dialed again. Twice, his finger slipped from the hole in the rotary dial and he had to start over.

"Hi, this is Tamsen. Please leave a message, and if this is Paul, I went out, but feel free to call and wake me up, or else call me in the morning. Beeeeep . . ."

"Hi, it's me," he said. "I'm home and it's about ten o'clock your time. Just calling to say good night. I was thinking I might ramble on and see if I could fill your entire tape but that would be wrong. We went straight to the hospital from the airport and had dinner there. My mom is actually staying there tonight, so I've got the house to myself. It's a little spooky. I'll tell you all about my dad when I talk to you, but the basic word is, he's stable and resting and not likely to get any worse, so there's no emergency, exactly, except that they still don't know how bad it is. There's positive indications and negative ones and they're still doing tests. I'll keep you posted. We're all sort of spent. I had a little spat with my brother, which I will also tell you about later.

"Anyway, I really was going to ramble on and on to see if I could make you laugh at how I just kept going on and on and on and on, but actually I won't do that. I wish you were here. I'm in my father's office, which used to be my bedroom, mine and Carl's, and I'm looking at all these awards and honors he won, and it's making me think I really need to get some honors and awards. Maybe when I get home, I'll see if I have an Old English font and print myself up some awards to hang in my studio."

This was good. He spoke slowly. He could imagine the smile on her face. She'd said she loved the way he made her laugh. This was worth points.

"I know I promised not to ramble on and on and fill up your whole tape, and I won't, I swear, but right now I wish you were home. If I was there, I'd get *Casablanca* from Blockbuster and put it in the VCR because you said you've never seen it, and then I'd rub your feet while we watched it. Tell the truth, it's a little weird to be sitting on this bed, having fantasies about you. I don't know if I told you this, but all the prepubescent fantasies I had as a kid generally involved situations where girls were forced to sleep with me, where we'd be trapped in cave-ins or shipwrecked on a deserted island or stranded by a plane crash at the North Pole and I'd rescue these various damsels in distress and none of them ever voluntarily offered their affections. They only kissed me because I saved their lives and because I was literally the last man on earth. Doesn't say much for my self-esteem, does it? Anyway, we can talk further about this, but I'd really hate to ramble on and fill up your entire tape."

He paused, counting slowly to five.

"Gosh. It's really cold here. Is it cold there? It's cold here. How much snow did you get? I'm really sorry to just ramble on and on like this. Seriously. Anyway, I shouldn't ramble on and on and on, but I wanted to tell you I miss you and I wish I could talk to you. To tell the truth, part of me hopes my dad gets better so that someday he can meet you, because it would make me sad to think he never did . . ."

He caught himself. He'd broken an unwritten rule, a tacit clause in their agreement to live fully in the present moment and not talk too much about the future. He needed to put the cat back in the toothpaste, as his mother, prone to malapropisms, might have said.

"Okay, now I definitely think I shouldn't have said that. Don't get me wrong, I would love for you to meet my family, obviously, someday — not right now, necessarily — and I'd obviously love to meet your mom and all that, but we're probably not at that point yet in our relationship where we can start talking about meeting each other's families . . . not that there's any reason . . ."

"Beeeeeeeeeeep."

"Sonofabitch!" he said, slamming the phone back in its cradle.

It had been a long day. He hoped he would be back on his game tomorrow.

4

King Carl

*T*hat's what you fought about?" Stella said. "Paul — a *fortune cookie?*"

"There was a little more to it than that," Paul said.

"Not even that he ate your cookie," Stella continued. "I can understand getting mad at somebody if they ate your cookie. You're telling me he was trying to get *you* to eat your *own* cookie — do I have that right? I'm just trying to understand this."

"He's controlling," Paul said. "He thinks he knows what's best for everybody. I suppose he means well, but it's so irritating."

When Paul got back to Northampton, he'd taken the trash out, watered his plants, and then dumped the contents of his suitcase into the laundry basket. He'd played the messages on his answering machine, the last of which was from Tamsen, saying she wanted to drive up to see him that night. He'd called her back, got her machine, told her he was heading to the Bay State for a beer later and to find him there, and then drove to collect Stella, who'd been staying with her friend Chester, the retriever with the heart of gold and the brain of stone.

Her first question, once he'd lifted her into the car, was how his father was feeling. He told her what he knew. He'd visited the hospital every day during his stay, sometimes with his mother, sometimes with his sister or alone, reading out loud to his father from the newspaper and adopting a disparaging tone when mentioning those goddamn Democrats, which he assumed his father would find therapeutic. On Paul's final visit, his father had been conscious and awake, his eyes open and able to follow people around the room, but he was otherwise unresponsive. Paul had sat by his father's bedside and held Harrold's hand (he hadn't done that since he was four) and felt it twitch slightly.

"I think he was glad we were there," Paul had explained to Stella, "but it was hard to tell. It's very strange when you can't look at someone's face and guess what they're thinking. You don't realize how much that matters until it's absent."

"How's your mom dealing with it?"

"She's upbeat, actually," Paul said. "Everybody's rolling up their sleeves and saying, 'Let's get to work.'"

"Why do you need to roll up your sleeves?"

"It's just an expression."

Stella silently considered Paul's report, then said she thought something was still bothering him. That's when he told her he'd had a fight with his brother, adding the story about the fortune cookie because he thought it was funny.

"I don't think it would have killed you to eat the cookie," Stella said dryly. "Just to keep the peace. That's all I'm saying."

"It's the principle," Paul said. "That's what you would have done?"

"And the fortune too," she said. "That would have solved both your problems. Besides, if you eat something you don't want to eat, you can always swallow grass and throw it all up later."

"Easy for you to say," Paul said, but she was right, again. Blessed was the peacemaker. "In humans, they call that bulimia. Plus there wasn't any grass. There was snow on the ground. What do dogs do in the winter when they need to throw up?"

"Change the subject if you want to," Stella said. "I just think you have a really strange relationship with your brother. It sounds so petty. And I mean that in the pejorative sense. Don't you love your brother?"

"Of course I love my brother," Paul said. "I just wish he lived in New Zealand."

"Is that a nice place?" Stella asked.

"It's a very nice place," Paul said. "Good location too."

As Paul drove, he thought of all the times, growing up, when he'd wished far worse for his brother. The time Carl had walked away from the chessboard, refusing to either finish the game or officially resign, with Paul two moves from checkmate and about to beat his brother for the first time in his life at anything. Then there was the time Carl stole the shoelaces out of Paul's sneakers when his own broke, or finished the milk when Paul still had cereal left, or licked the centers out of the Oreos and then put them back in the bag, or the times he'd made Paul burn his marshmallows making s'mores by outfencing him over the campfire with his roasting stick (for years, Paul pretended he liked burnt marshmallows). Yet despite the basic sibling rivalry stuff of early childhood, for the first ten years of his life, Paul had wanted to do everything Carl did, wear the same clothes, get his hair cut the same way. When Paul entered junior high and the war between them intensified, Paul couldn't help thinking, "This is how you repay me for a lifetime of adoration?"

He looked at Stella, who was staring at him, her head cocked.

"It's hard to explain," he told Stella. "Do you remember when you were just a puppy and you lived on a farm with your brothers and sisters, and you were" — he had told Stella once that she was the runt of her litter, and that had hurt her feelings — "the *nicest* dog in your family, but your older brothers were bigger than you, so if there was a bowl of food on the floor or a table scrap, they ate it first and never let you have any?"

"Vaguely," Stella said.

"Well, it's sort of like that," Paul said. "With people, you get in these relationships and you never grow out of them."

"With dogs, you don't have to grow out of them," Stella said.

"There's a social order. That's what you want. I understand if you don't know what your place is. That could be confusing."

"It never bothered you when your brothers got to eat first?"

"They were bigger," Stella said. "It was more important to me to be the nice one. And maybe it's not my place to say, but I always thought you were the nice one too. That's why we get along."

He reached across and scratched her beneath the ear. She leaned into it.

"There's nothing wrong with being omega," he said. "It's the people who are humbler than thou who bug me. Besides — that wasn't what the real fight was about. That was just when I got my hackles up."

She looked puzzled.

"These," Paul said, reaching across again and grabbing Stella's fur behind her collar.

"That's my neck," she said.

"Hackles are the feathers on a chicken's neck."

"Do I look like a chicken to you?"

"Horripilation, then," Paul said. "The way your fur rises when you're trying to look tough to avoid a fight. To scare the other dog off."

"It doesn't sound to me like you were trying to scare your brother off," Stella said. "It sounds to me like you were trying to make your brother mad. If you didn't want to make him mad, you would just have eaten the cookie. It wouldn't have killed you."

"All right already," Paul said. "Next time, I'll eat the cookie."

"So what was the real fight about?" Stella asked.

"Money," Paul said. "About which I couldn't care less, by the way. He had us all over for Sunday brunch after church because it was my nephew's birthday and they didn't want to reschedule the party. He has this huge house in a very wealthy neighborhood in Edina. It's very intimidating."

"But of course, you couldn't care less," Stella said.

"It's just different," Paul said. "His neighborhood is full of lawyers and bankers and doctors. They make more money than I do."

"So why don't you become a lawyer or a banker or a doctor?" she asked.

"That horse left the barn a long time ago. It's like you were saying," he told her, "about roles. I like what I do, but I never know what I'm doing next. It's feast or famine." His literary agent, Mauricio Levine, was good at encouraging Paul to keep a cheerful outlook. "Just remember what Churchill said: 'The secret to success is learning how to go from failure to failure without loss of enthusiasm.'" Maury had brought Paul his first big break, a chance to finish *Windows 95 for Morons* when the original author died suddenly of what Maury called "an unrelated illness." Paul still wondered how it could have been related. They needed to come up with an option book. Paul suggested *Love for Morons*, but unfortunately the publisher already had a husband-and-wife team working on it who'd been married and divorced four times, to each other, which Paul had to agree was hard to top. The editor finally suggested *Nature for Morons*. "These things are golden, but finish it quick so you get paid, because I think the publisher is going out of business," Maury advised. "That's publishing," he added.

"With Carl, there's no famine. It's all feast," Paul continued. "I'm not saying he hasn't earned it. He works really hard. Probably too hard."

Paul's brother had always pushed himself, "always biting the candle off at both ends," as their mother had once said. He never slept, always training for something, a marathon, a 10k, a half Ironman. His clean good looks, kind eyes, and gentle manners had won him plenty of East Coast girlfriends in college, though when he finally hooked up for good, it was with Erica Stephenson, a fellow Minnesotan in the same law school class at Yale. As a Yale undergraduate, Carl had striven mightily to be accepted in the right circles, invited to the right parties, granted access to the Old Boy network. Yet when his fiancée said she wanted to practice law in Minnesota, to be near her parents, Carl gave up any thought of signing on with some high-powered Boston or New York or Washington, D.C., law firm. Paul wondered if Carl regretted his decision. No one would ever know it if he did.

"You work really hard too," Stella said. "I think you should be paid as much as a lawyer or a doctor."

"I couldn't agree more," Paul said. "I'll bring it up at the next meeting. Be glad you never had to get a job."

"I live with you, don't I?" she said. "That's work."

"Lucky for me, you're a working breed," Paul said.

"Half," she corrected him. "My other half is sporting. So what was the fight about? What about money?"

After the birthday party, Carl had told Paul he wanted to have a word with him in his office. Carl's home office featured an exquisite L-shaped rosewood desk console, with the biggest computer monitor Paul had ever seen. The walls were decorated with all the various awards Carl had won over the years, beginning in kindergarten. Carl's athletic trophies sat atop the bookshelf, along with photographs of Carl, exhausted, crossing finish lines with his arms up in the air and his red armpit hair showing. Paul was surprised to see that his brother had bought ten copies of *Windows 95 for Morons,* with one propped upright on display atop a Stickley bookcase.

"He said he and my dad had been working on a living will as a way of avoiding estate taxes," Paul told Stella. "My dad wants to give his money to his children while he's still alive, not to the government. If you die, the government takes a huge chunk of your money so your family can't have it."

"I'd like to bite the ass of whoever thought of that," Stella said.

"You're not alone," Paul said. "Anyway, after he retired, my dad started playing the stock market and changing his investment strategies. Rolling stuff over, whatever that means."

"Even I know what *roll over* means."

"Different kind of *roll over*," Paul told her. "Carl said it looked like my dad was going to gift each of his kids with a little over three hundred thousand dollars."

"Is that a lot?" Stella asked.

"It is to me," Paul said.

"You want all the money you can get, right?"

"Sure," Paul said, "though they've done studies that prove people with a lot of money aren't any happier than people who only have a little." She gave him a tilted quizzical look. "It's human nature. You just always think you want more. And then you get more and that makes you want more still. It's better to be content with what you have."

"Well, duh," Stella said.

"That's your nature," Paul said. "For humans, it's harder than it sounds. I had a bit of a falling-out with my dad a few years ago on this very subject. I called home to ask for a loan because Karen and I had gotten into some financial trouble. I was making the do-what-you-love-and-the-money-will-follow argument, and my dad said, 'Sometimes you need to think of somebody other than yourself. Sometimes you do what you have to do for the people you love, particularly when doing what you love isn't working.' He saw me as a failure. Needless to say, I never quite got around to asking for the loan."

"Needless to say."

"I don't claim to be Mr. Financial Genius," Paul said. Stella gave him a look that he ignored. "That doesn't mean my brother has the right to exclude me from the decision-making process."

Paul explained that Harrold had, in the process of drafting a living will, granted Carl durable power of attorney. Carl told Paul, in his office, that he thought it would be a good idea, given the present uncertainty, to postpone the disbursement of the living will in case something bad happened to Harrold, some worst-case scenario where they needed the money to pay for extended care. Paul had countered that the point of a living will was exactly to prepare for worst-case scenarios, and that if their father had another stroke and didn't survive it, the money would go to pay the estate taxes, which was exactly what Harrold didn't want.

"He made it sound like I was being greedy. Or cold."

"But you're neither of those things," Stella said.

"Thank you," Paul said. "That's why it hurt. Then he dropped the real bomb. He told me he was going to fire Arnie Olmstead, my father's broker. Arnie'd worked with my dad all his life. He goes to our church. They used to carve balsa-wood totem poles together when we were all in Indian Guides."

"What's Indian Guides?"

"It was this YMCA program where white guys dress up and pretend they're Indians," Paul said. "Fathers and sons. The point is, Carl was using his power of attorney to take over my father's investments."

Carl said he would have told Paul sooner but Paul had never shown any interest in such things before. That was true. Carl lectured him about how the market had changed with the Internet, how more information was available now than ever before and more people were playing the market who didn't know what they were doing, which meant more volume, higher highs, lower lows, a faster, more volatile roller coaster, and more passengers who weren't wearing their seat belts. Paul read the paper every day but usually skimmed the business section. He knew the market had been wacky, records set every month, with catastrophic corrections and new Black Fridays ever looming. Carl's argument was that Arnie Olmstead was behind the times and unable to react were something drastic to occur. "We have a responsibility," Carl had said. Carl's plan was to manage their father's investments online, where you could make quick trades without having to pay huge brokers' fees. "Everybody's doing it," he said. He intended to keep everybody informed. "Just let me watch over things for the time being. If you have any doubts as to my ability, you're free to examine my records anytime you want to."

"So you wanted to be included, even though you don't have any money and you don't care about money and you don't know anything about the stock market," Stella said. "I'm not trying to be critical. I'm just trying to keep things in perspective."

"I appreciate it," Paul told Stella. "I just don't trust him. I learned not to. I trusted him before and he screwed me. I swore it wouldn't happen again."

"What did he do that makes you not trust him?" Stella asked.

"Where do I start?" Paul said. "Like the time I was at a party and Debbie Benson wanted to go skinny-dipping. That's where you take off all your clothes and go swimming. Usually at night after you've been drinking. It's supposed to be sexy."

"It's not?"

"Not in Minnesota," Paul said. "Not where there are mosquitoes the size of chickens. Plus the water was freezing cold, which has a nice effect on girls' bodies but not so much for guys, if you know what I mean."

Stella looked puzzled again.

"Anyway, I was way past curfew when I got home because I'd been driving around the lakes for an hour so as not to reek of alcohol. I came in and my father was waiting up for me, and he said he wanted to know if I was taking pot. My mom was usually the one who waited up, so I knew it was serious. I said you don't *take* pot, you *smoke* pot. He said, 'Pot is a drug, is it not? And you take drugs.'"

"Alcohol is a drug too, isn't it?" Stella asked.

"I guess it is, but you don't say, 'I take alcohol.'"

"But you do say, 'I took a drink.'"

"I freely admit it was a stupid argument," Paul said. "But I'm denying up and down to his face, saying I don't smoke pot and never have, and he pulls out a big old Baggie full of weed and asks me if it's mine. Which it obviously was, but I'd hidden it under a loose floorboard in the attic that you had to move six huge boxes just to get to, so no way anybody could accidentally find my stash. The only other person in the house who knew about my secret hiding place was guess who? Carl. He narced on me. In my own house. You don't do that to your brother. You just don't."

They were home now. Paul helped Stella out of the car, lifted her up the steps, and set her down on the porch while he unlocked the front door. Inside, he turned up the thermostat, got a beer from the refrigerator, and sat on the couch. Stella took her place on the dog bed by the radiator. Paul picked up the remote control, then decided against watching television.

"I have to say," Stella said, "I still feel like something else is bothering you. You have that guilty-conscience look."

"A hangdog look?" he asked.

She'd never cared much for the expression.

"I think maybe I did a bad thing," he told her.

"What did you do this time?"

He'd asked Carl, once their meeting in his office was over, if he could use his computer to check his e-mail and to see if he could get Tamsen online. She wasn't online, so he sent her a quick note to tell her that all was well and that he would call her when he got home. He even considered using his brother's phone to call her.

He needed to talk to somebody. He was trying hard to give his brother the benefit of the doubt; yet evil thoughts came to him unbidden. Did he need to protect himself, even if it was only a remote possibility that Carl was going to screw him somehow? Flipping through the Rolodex on Carl's desk, he found Arnie Olmstead's telephone number and decided he could at least give Arnie a call to get a second opinion. He needed a pen or a pencil to write the number down.

Carl's desk drawers were immaculate. The top middle every-thing drawer, which should have been stuffed to overflowing with miscellaneous crap, was instead neatly organized with plastic sectional dividers, every paper clip in its proper place. He found the pen he was looking for, but he couldn't resist further investigation. In a deep side drawer, he found what had to be every operations manual and appliance warranty Carl had ever received, stored in alphabetical order. In a drawer below that, of interest, in a protective clear Plexiglas case, was a baseball auto-graphed by Harmon Killebrew, the former Minnesota Twins player who'd been a childhood hero of Paul's and apparently Carl's hero as well.

After writing down Olmstead's number, he was about to log off and rejoin his family downstairs when he saw an icon on Carl's computer desktop marked "PINs."

Paul couldn't believe his brother would be so stupid as to write down his PINs and keep them all in one place. A quick click, though, showed that Carl had multiple PINs. Paul had only one personal identification number, 7285, which was his name if you dialed it on a telephone, and he used that PIN for all his various accounts. Carl's PINs, his ATM password, his AOL password, others that Paul didn't recognize, were listed alpha-betically, including, after Citibank but before Discover, a PIN la-beled "Dad's Online Portfolio." It was a relatively simple matter to hit the Print button and make a copy of the list. The bottom line, he'd reasoned, was that if he decided later that it was the wrong thing to do, he could always tear up the copy and undo the transgression, but if it was the right thing to do, he'd never get another chance.

"He said I was free to examine his records anytime I wanted to," Paul explained to Stella.

"That may be what he said, but I doubt that's what he meant," Stella replied. "If you're asking my opinion."

"I didn't exactly think it through," Paul said.

"Well. You had a lot of other things on your mind," Stella said. "With your dad in the hospital. You know that in a way, you're lucky."

"How am I lucky?"

"Not everybody knows who their father was," she said. He looked at her.

"German shepherd," Paul said. "Pretty sure."

"So you've said," she replied. "I would have liked to know more."

"I think you put your finger on it," Paul told her. "I'm not saying I'm not lucky, but I think the hardest part was that I always had this fantasy that one day my dad and I would go fishing or something, and then we'd sit around the fire and drink fifty-year-old Macallan and have some big heart-to-heart. I know who he is, but I don't feel like I know him. Or actually, it's more like he doesn't know me. And now I won't get another chance."

"I thought your father doesn't drink."

"It's just a fantasy," Paul said.

"Are you glad you went home?"

"I suppose so. I couldn't say for certain if he even knew I was there," Paul said. "I think I went so I'd get credit for going. Like how you go to funerals because you're afraid if you don't, the dead guy's ghost is going to point his bony finger at you and say, 'Why weren't you at my funeral?'"

"Well, that's just silly," Stella said. "Of course he knew you were there. He'd know it even with his eyes closed."

"What makes you say that?"

"Well," Stella said, "I know you're there when my eyes are closed."

"How?"

"I don't know," Stella said. "I just do. Pheromones. But I'll bet you if I know, he'd know too. He's your father."

He picked up her paw and squeezed it three times.

"Do you know what that is?" he asked her.

"That's my paw," she said. "Are you going to tell me another word for part of a chicken?"

"I mean the three squeezes," Paul said. "It's a secret signal my mother taught me when we were at the hospital. Three squeezes means 'I love you.' I guess they've been doing it with each other all their lives, waiting in lines in airports or sitting next to each other at weddings. They'd hold hands and give each other three squeezes. He did it in the hospital, right there while I was saying good-bye. The doctors said it could be a sign that he's getting better."

Paul tried to remember the moment he'd held his father's hand and felt it twitch. Had it twitched once? Twice? Three times perhaps? He couldn't say.

Part 2

Spring/Summer

Pain is the primary negative reinforcement nature uses
to teach the lessons all species need to learn to survive.
In a study done at UCLA and at Macquarie University
in Australia using brain-scanning technology to observe
activation in the brain's anterior cingulate cortex or pain
center, human subjects confronting loneliness or heartache
resulting from being excluded from a social group or
network experienced pain as real as if their skin were being
burned. In other words, the need to belong to a group or
to be connected to someone else is fundamental to our
survival, so that it is the very pain of heartache that keeps
us coming back for more, to make the pain go away.

At the same time, the endorphins released when we're
in love, affecting the pleasure centers in the brain, are
known to lower our IQs and inhibit long-term objective
memory. Thus we are hardwired to fuck up again and again.
Species known to aggregate in social groupings, canids or
ungulates, for example, show similar releases of pleasure-
giving hormones—endorphins, dopamine, oxytocin, and
the like—when aggregated, and similar activities in the
anterior cingulate cortex during periods of isolation or

separation. Members of the canid species, including dogs and wolves, are second in this regard only to humans. Social animals also tend to exhibit greater temerity and are built more for endurance than nonaggregate species. Dogs and wolves, for example, are believed to have the most efficient cardiovascular systems of all mammals. Wolves regularly hunt down prey faster and stronger than they are simply by outlasting them over great distances, often running up steep hills through heavy snows without tiring. Canadian researchers studying sled dogs attached heart monitors to a team of malamutes and discovered that sled dogs running at top speed could sustain heart rates exceeding 300 beats per minute for hours, a rate once believed possible only in shrews. This does not come as news to dog owners, who already know that no animal has a heart quite like a dog's. Social animals therefore have high tolerances for both pleasure and pain and can abide fluctuations between the two for long periods of time.

—Paul Gustavson, *Nature for Morons*

5

Exile in Beersville

P emmican!" Stella said. "My favorite. Thank you."

He'd given her the present he'd brought her. The pickin's for dogs at the Minnesota-themed gift shop at the airport were beyond slim. Every time he flew home, he brought Stella back a bag of Chippewa pemmican, meat cut in strips and dried Native American–style. He'd brought her Slim Jims once but they hadn't agreed with her. He'd remembered at the last minute to pick up a gift for Tamsen too, rushing through the airport gift shop with five minutes to spare before his flight boarded. Everything on the shelves screamed "I meant to get you a real gift but actually I forgot until I got to the airport." He had to choose between a ceramic loon, a bottle of maple syrup (but bringing maple syrup home to New England was like carrying coal to Newcastle), a Kirby Puckett bobble-head doll, or a snow globe with Paul Bunyan and Babe the Blue Ox inside. He'd settled on the snow globe as having the highest kitsch value.

He showed Stella the snow globe, turning it upside down, then righting it.

"That's lovely," she said. "How does it do that?"

"There's water inside," he told her.

"Why doesn't the snow melt?"

"It's plastic or something," he said.

"Can I have my pemmican now?"

"Let's bring it to the Bay State," he told her. "I'm meeting Tamsen there. You can eat it in the doorway. Just don't let people see or everybody is going to want some."

The Bay State Hotel bar was listed in the American Registry of Seedy Dumps, which gave it five stars for having everything a true derelict might want — dollar beers and two-dollar whiskeys, skanky urinals and wet bathroom floors breeding all kinds of molds and fungi, dim lights and dirty mirrors behind the bar so you didn't notice how old or bald or fat or drunk you were getting. The jukebox featured George Jones drinking songs, Marvin Gaye, Al Green, Otis Redding, Miles Davis's "All Blues," Frank Sinatra's *Songs for Swingin' Lovers*. The walls were wood paneling, decorated with clown portraits and beer mirrors and Toby mugs on a plate rail just below the ceiling, and a couple of dozen ceramic busts of sailors and leprechauns realistically rendered in porcelain at about a third of actual scale. The dour bartender, Silent Neil, hadn't spoken or even turned around to look at the television since Bill Buckner let the ball dribble through his legs in the sixth game of the 1986 World Series. Stella took her customary post just inside the Bay State's front door. She was allowed inside but preferred the doorway, explaining, "I'll roll on a dead carp, I'll even eat cat turds, but that place grosses me out."

During his separation and divorce from Karen, and in the détente that followed, the Bay State had become his sanctuary, literally, a place she'd promised not to frequent so that he could feel secure, knowing he wasn't going to run into her there. He'd reciprocated by giving her the bar at the Hotel Northampton as a safe haven, though she didn't seem nearly as bothered by the whole situation as he was. Of course, that meant if she went on a date, she'd go to the bar at the Hotel Northampton, which had floor-to-ceiling windows facing the street, not that Paul ever parked across the street and spied on her with his binoculars . . . or anything.

"The traveler returns," Doyle called out as Paul walked in.

Paul regarded his friends. Doyle was a drummer in a blues band. Brickman was a sandy-haired, Kennedyesque stockbroker. Bender was a photographer. McCoy was a jazz piano player who got asked on a regular basis, "You're really talented — why don't you move to New York?" Yvonne ran the computer lab at UMass. D. J. and Mickey taught psychology, he at UMass, she at Amherst College. The code of conduct at the Bay State was that nobody judged anybody — live and let live, and accept people for who they are. Paul found it easy to live by such rules. It felt good to be home.

He raised his beer to O-Rings, who didn't do anything for a living, as far as anybody knew. Nevertheless he somehow always had money for pinball and owned four of the machine's top five all-time record scores. O-Rings lived with Marie, a sweet woman, and they'd just had a baby, but somehow it hadn't cut into O-Rings's pinball schedule or reduced the number of pints of Guinness he downed every night. He'd been called O-Rings ever since the space shuttle *Challenger* blew up, for reasons that were no longer clear.

"So how's your dad?" Doyle said. "Do they know how bad a stroke it was?"

"He can't walk and he can only move his right hand."

"I get like that," D. J. said.

"On a good day," Mickey added.

"So what's the prognosis?" McCoy asked. "Can he talk?"

"Nope," Paul said. "I think I'll be able to get online with him and he'll be able to answer yes-or-no questions by clicking the mouse, but that's about it. We haven't got it all set up yet."

"Bummer," Doyle said.

"How old is your dad?" McCoy asked.

"Seventy-two, " Paul said.

"When's his birthday?" Yvonne asked.

"I don't know. It's in July."

"You don't know when your own father's birthday is?" she chastised him. "What kind of shitty son doesn't know when his own father's birthday is? I'll bet he knows when yours is."

"Well, he was there when I was born," Paul said. "If I was there when he was born, I'd probably remember too."

"Let's drink to Paul's dad!" Doyle proposed. Everybody raised their glasses and said, "To Paul's dad!" Paul joined them.

He found a stool open at the bar next to his friend Bender, the photographer, and asked him how he was.

"I suck," Bender said. "I shot a wedding four years ago but I never got around to printing the pictures. Now I just heard they're getting divorced, but I can't find the negatives."

"They still want the pictures?"

"Go figure," Bender said. "I just want to get paid."

"I have a question for you," Paul said. "You're a fitness guy — what's better exercise, running or bicycling?"

"Better for what?"

"For getting in shape. Losing weight."

"Well," Bender said, "running burns more calories, but cycling is easier on your body. Especially your knees. Why?"

"I took a vow," Paul said. "Seeing my dad inspired me. Maybe *scared* me is a better word." He considered telling Bender about the fortune cookie and his fight with Carl but changed his mind.

"If you're only going to do one, you should run," Bender advised. "Running is a four-season sport. If you want to cycle, you probably have to join a gym in the winter. Or get a good stationary bike. I don't have room for one in my apartment."

"You ride a bike at the gym? You like it?"

"It depends on who's ass I'm staring at on the bike in front of me," Bender said. "You have to take what you get — passing's not an option. You get behind a fat guy and it sucks, but if it's a tight little Smithie, you can get a Lycralock that's transcendental. Running is also cheaper."

Paul resolved to purchase, the next day or as soon as possible, a pair of running shoes and get started on a new regimen. A glance in the mirror mounted on the wall behind the bar only strengthened his resolve.

He had his eyes closed, listening to the jukebox, when someone approached him from behind, put her hands over his eyes, and kissed him on the top of his head.

"Knock it off," he said. "My girlfriend's going to be here any minute."

He opened his eyes and saw Tamsen. She turned him to face her and kissed him again, briefly, breaking it off with a subtly arched eyebrow that said there was more where that came from.

"I missed you," he said.

"I missed you too," she said. It was about a two-hour drive from Providence to Northampton, through what Paul considered to be the least scenic part of Massachusetts, relatively flat and with few roadside attractions.

"You look like you need a shot of tequila," he told her.

"Just a cup of coffee," she said, taking off her coat, an expensive black leather jacket with a down-filled lining that kept her both warm and chic. She left her silk scarf wrapped around her neck. She was always colder than he was, a fact he attributed to her smaller mass-to-surface-area ratio. "Is the coffee here any good?"

"That's a good question," Paul said. "I don't think anybody's ever had it. I'd be surprised if it was."

Neil brought her a cup with cream and sweeteners.

"How was driving?" Paul asked.

"Terrible," she said. "You're sure Stella is going to be okay in the doorway?"

"She prefers it there," Paul said. "She thinks it's too skanky in here."

"I have something for her — do you mind if I give it to her here?"

"Go ahead," Paul said. "She's not picky."

Tamsen took from her purse a half pound of shaved roast beef she'd purchased at the supermarket before leaving. She fed it to the dog slowly, petting her between bites and talking to her. Stella shot Paul a look that said, "You can have the rest of the pemmican."

Paul regarded his girlfriend, his paramour, his significant other — whatever the proper term was. Her black boots gave her an extra two inches of height, though she did not seem self-conscious about her height. For that matter she did not seem to display any noticeable body-image neurosis that he'd been able to detect. She stayed fit by working out three or four times a week in the company gym. Paul thought how nice a pair of tight jeans looked on her.

She next took from her purse a new red bandanna, folded it on the diagonal, and tied it around Stella's neck. The dog seemed to momentarily preen, lifting her head as if to see her own reflection in the glass door.

When Tamsen returned to his table, Paul noticed the bounce in her step, a spiritedness he found inspiring even when he failed to match it: it pulled him forward.

"You don't mind, do you?" she asked him, seating herself next to him. "I thought she'd like a little color."

"I like it," he said. "I think she does too."

"I was going to get her a string of pearls, but it might be too Barbara Bush," Tamsen said. She sipped her coffee.

"I have something for you too, when we get home," he told her.

"What is it?"

"It's a surprise."

"Is it cash?"

"No, it's not cash."

"Cash always makes for a thoughtful gift. Just so you know."

"It's not cash."

"Okay. I can't wait to see it."

When she looked around a room, she was more likely to move her eyes than to turn her head, though when she disapproved of what she saw, she tended to tilt her head forward slightly and gaze from beneath a subtly furrowed brow. She wore contact lenses during the day but needed reading glasses when she took her contacts out at night.

She dressed well for work, a bit expensively, she admitted, though her new salary made nicer things affordable, and she changed into old jeans and T-shirts at night, sweatpants and cotton tops, loose-fitting shorts and baggy pullovers, her wardrobe of a color spectrum that favored Bacon over Monet, few pinks or powder blues and plenty of browns, rusts, and blacks. She was frequently misplacing her keys or reading glasses, as her father had before her. One of Paul's favorite things about her was her sneeze, which could knock the plaster off a wall, an explosive, fricative roar with a high-pitched shriek in the middle of it that turned heads in restaurants. She always stifled it politely behind a Kleenex or napkin, but those times when she was caught short without either, she let go and blushed afterward.

"Now I'm starting to feel sane," she said after sipping her coffee. "You must have had a pretty insane week yourself. Are you all right?"

"I'm starting jogging tomorrow," he said. "I just decided. I'm going to start slow and work up to maybe three miles a day. I'm also on a diet."

"Good for you," she said.

"I'm cutting back on ice cream too, for starters," he told her. "No chocolate cake after midnight. No between-meal pizzas, and no more chocolate malts with breakfast. Just a few sensible rules."

"Excellent idea," she said. "So tell me everything about your trip."

He told her about his father and how hard it was to see him fallen and stricken, and the odd feeling, despite the fact that he'd moved away from Minnesota and established his independence long ago, that somehow the ground he stood on was less solid than before, or that he was less sure of himself.

"How's your brother?" she asked.

"Filling the power vacuum," Paul said. He told her about the problems with his brother and about his fear that stepping aside to let Carl run the show was going to cost him somehow.

"He's taken the whole thing over," Paul said. "He even fired Dad's broker so he can manage Dad's investments himself, on-line. I know he knows what he's doing, but I'm not sure I trust him."

"Look, Paul, you have to be really careful not to let money make things ugly or weird between you. I see it at my job all the time. I know you and Carl already had a strained relationship; I'd hate to see this push it over the edge. In the end, it's not worth it. You know that, don't you?"

"Anyway, we'll see," Paul said. "Actually I have a confession to make." He told her how he'd found and copied his brother's PINs, "just in case," and explained his reasoning at the time. He acknowledged, though, that since then, he'd had the feeling he'd done the wrong thing. He asked her what she thought.

She looked at him.

"What?" he wanted to know.

He had a terrible sinking feeling, realizing he'd just fallen in her eyes.

"You want me to wave my hand and absolve you of this?" she said.

"So you definitely think it was wrong?"

She laughed, more a laugh of disbelief than hilarity.

"Gee, give me a second to sort through my right and wrong folders. Stealing . . . stealing . . . oh, here it is, in the *wrong* folder." She regarded him for a moment. "You're really not sure if this is right or wrong?"

"Well, no," he said. "It's not a question of right or wrong. It's wrong. It's just a question of how wrong."

"What difference does it make?" she said. "Wrong is wrong. It's not a sliding scale, as Sister Michaeletta used to tell us. It's not like stealing a candy bar isn't as bad as stealing a fur coat. Stealing is stealing."

He felt crushed. For the first time, he'd disappointed her. He felt as if all the progress they'd made toward becoming closer was being negated.

"Look, Paul," she said, "I'm not your moral compass. I'll talk to you about whatever you want to talk about, because that's the deal, but alarms go off when I feel like you want me to solve your problems. I'm just trying to take care of myself right now. I hope that doesn't sound cold. I don't think you're a terrible person or anything. I just don't want you to pass the responsibility for your decisions off on me. Do you see what that does?"

"I do," he said.

"I'm sorry, but Donald used to do that and I'm a little sensitive," she said, softening her tone. "Like he wanted me to be his mother or something. He used to ask me to wake him up in the morning, so I'd make sure the alarm was set, but then he'd sleep through it and be mad at me, and I'd say, 'Wake your own fucking self up — you're not in high school anymore.' And I knew if I wasn't there for him to blame, he never would have overslept. The alarm clock would have been enough. It was like I was his moral overdraft protection or something."

"He sounds like an asshole."

"He *was* an asshole," she said, again softening her tone. "And it's not fair to blame you for that. I'm your equal, Paul. And I'm your friend. You can talk to me about anything, but if you want to confess and be absolved, I can't do that."

"No," he said. "You're right."

"I'm trying to be nonjudgmental here," she said. "I mean, it's *your* life . . ."

"Can you understand what I was thinking?"

"Of course I can understand it," she said. "If you think he's going to do something, why not just ask him to show you the books? Why isn't that the first option? He even told you you could. Tell him you want him to teach you about investing."

Paul made a face.

"I'm sure I was just being paranoid," he told her. "There's just this history . . ."

"Look — what do you want me to say? It's your business. He's your brother. Men are such idiots when they start getting competitive. I give up."

He took the list of PINs from his pocket, ripped it into a dozen pieces, and threw the scraps into the wastebasket. When he'd finished, she leaned over and kissed him. She was wrong about lacking the ability to bestow absolution.

"You said you got your dad a computer?" she asked.

Glad to shift topics, he told her about the shiny new IBM he'd helped his mother set up, with all the newest chips and the most

RAM and the biggest hard drive and an extralarge monitor. He explained how they were going to get his father online. She asked what the prognosis was.

"They gave him a drug that's supposed to dissolve clots, but you have to administer it within an hour or so of the stroke, and since they didn't really know how long he'd been lying there when my mother found him, they're not sure how much good it did him. Some guys, if you give it to them quickly, are practically walking and talking within hours. He's obviously not."

"He'll get better," Tamsen said. "He was in good shape before it happened, right?"

"That's why I'm starting jogging," Paul said. "I totally mean it. Enjoy my beer belly while you can, because in six months, this sucker is gone."

"Well, I'm proud of you for starting," she said.

"I'm serious. Besides, it isn't even really a beer belly."

"It's not?"

"When I was in college, I wanted to look more mature, so I had a silicone belly implant."

"It worked."

"I'm thinking of having it removed."

"Are you gonna stop tweezing the top of your head too?" she asked.

"Think I should?"

"Up to you," she said. "Don't change on my account."

He looked around. Doyle, Brickman, Bender, D. J., Mickey, Yvonne, O-Rings, and McCoy had the far end of the bar pinned down. The blues band, which had been on break, was taking the stage again.

"You still interested in losing weight?" Tamsen asked him.

"Yeah. Why?"

She leaned over and kissed him again.

"Take me home, then," she said. "I want to give you a thousand-calorie burn."

"We talking sit-ups and push-ups?"

She whispered in his ear, "I'm thinking of an entirely more pleasurable form of exertion."

He smiled. He was terrified.

6

Enterprises of Great Pitch and Moment

He kissed her in the parking lot. She pressed him up against her car and kissed him back. He felt a stirring in his loins, only to realize it was her hand. Until he was primed and stiff and ready to ravish her, he wouldn't be able to relax, which made it all the more difficult.

"Hold that thought," she said with a smile, releasing him and getting into the car.

"I'll do my best," he thought. "Maybe this time will be different."

He lifted Stella into the backseat. As Tamsen drove, Paul tried to think of anything but sex, because he knew overthinking it was precisely his problem. He and Karen had been crazy for each other when they first met. Their love life began to abate the day they'd gotten engaged, lost somewhere in the friction of planning the wedding. The sex between them died long before the love did, but sex was the canary in the coal mine, an early warning he hadn't heeded. He knew that sexual intimacy was a partnership, but he nevertheless blamed himself entirely when he started to lose his erections. He'd never been so sexually driven, in any of his relationships, that he could carry forth regardless of what his partner was thinking or feeling. It was Karen's very eagerness that aroused him, her passion and her abandon, more than how she looked or what she wore.

A marked diminution of passion was, as he understood most marriages, not uncommon. There was always something else to do, or she was too tired, or they had to wake up early, or she brought work home that she needed to finish. Maybe tomorrow . . . maybe this weekend . . . maybe next week . . . The first few times he failed, Karen gave him the "It's okay, it happens, just hold me" speech. The longer they went without sex, the more important it became to succeed the next time they tried. The more important it was, the more self-conscious he was and the more pressure he felt. The more pressure he felt, the more he failed. The more he failed, the less she initiated anything or pressed the issue, knowing it would only make him feel bad. It was a downward spiral. They tried therapy, but it only made both of them even more self-conscious. Eventually they became more like brother and sister than husband and wife, a compromise they could live with, but not indefinitely. He told himself that he wasn't truly impotent — that he was just a failure with Karen, a victim of "situational impotence," and that under different circumstances, with the right woman, he'd be his old self, a stag in rut, a mighty lion. Wouldn't he?

"You're thinking too much," he warned himself.

It also occurred to him, on the drive home, that he wasn't just competing against himself — there was Stephen, the radiologist, with whom Tamsen was already sleeping.

"Be Zen. Take the time she gives you and be glad," he thought.

By the time they reached his house, he realized he'd failed once again to hold the thought. Perhaps he'd get it back. She had a bag full of clothes with her, as well as a large black bag full of books and papers, which Paul set down on the kitchen floor. Stella sniffed at her bags.

"No more roast beef," Tamsen told the dog, taking off her coat, "but maybe tomorrow we can go to the store."

Stella shot Paul a look as if to say, "You can go. I'm living with her now."

"Don't worry — next time I stay for more than one night, I'm making you your favorite meal," Tamsen said over her shoulder. "What was your favorite comfort food when you were a kid?"

"Beef Stroganoff. What's yours?"

"Campbell's onion soup with toasted garlic bagels," she said. "It renders me fairly toxic but I love it."

"What's all this?" he asked, regarding her luggage.

"Reading," Tamsen said, kissing him. "Marketing decided we needed an on-site astrologist, so I have to go through these clippings. Actually we're linking to a site called Zodia.com that's supposed to do your chart in twenty seconds — all you do is type in your time and place of birth. Want me to do yours?"

"Pass," he said.

He went to his bedroom, and when he returned, he handed her a box he'd wrapped and tied with ribbon, though he'd had some trouble getting the bow tails to curl. The expression on her face was one of puzzlement as she removed the Paul Bunyan snow globe from the tissue paper. His first thought was that he'd bombed out.

"I wanted to get you something specific to Minnesota," he said. "I almost got you a painting on a redwood plaque of an Indian maiden who looked like Janet Jackson, but I figured you already had one."

She kissed him.

"I love it. Why Paul Bunyan?"

"He's from Minnesota," he said.

"My father brought one of these home from one of his trips

once," she said, tipping the snow globe upside down. "They always remind me of him."

"What did your brother get?"

"Gas station road maps. He collected them. They used to be free. I need a bath," she said. "Care to join me?"

"Sure," he said.

While Tamsen got the tub ready, he stood in the middle of the living room, channel-surfing like a zombie.

"She loves you, you know," Stella told him. "That's what she told me."

"She said that?"

"Yeah."

"Just now?"

"Uh-huh," Stella said. "While you were in the bedroom. Oh, dear. I hope she wasn't telling me in confidence."

"What were her exact words?"

"She said, 'He's a bit of a bozo, but I can see what you see in him.' What's a bozo?"

"I am," he said. "What else did she say?"

"That's it. She said, 'He's a bit of a bozo, but I can see what you see in him,' and then she sighed and bit her lip. FYI, I think she might be in heat."

"All right, then," Paul said. "You mind sleeping out here tonight?"

"Not at all," the dog said. "You seem nervous."

"Little bit," he said.

"Why? I just told you she loves you."

"It's hard to explain," Paul said.

"Tub's ready," Tamsen called out.

He went to her. She'd turned out the lights in the bathroom and lit candles.

"Where'd you get bubble bath?" he asked.

"I brought it with me. We got a giant box of free samples in the office from Bed Bath and Beyond. Oh, please — I *don't* want to talk about the office anymore! If I mention work one more time, you have my permission to shush me." She kissed him. He put his arms around her. She undid his belt and tugged at his shirt. She pulled his shirt off him and undid his shoes. She pulled down his pants and then removed his shorts.

"Get in," she commanded. She undressed, got in the tub with him, and started washing him. He would have closed his eyes, but if he did, he would have missed the way the candlelight played off her perfect skin. That a woman so attractive would find him appealing seemed extraordinary. He thought of the last few months that he and Karen had actually slept together, how he'd slide his foot across the mattress and touch her under the covers, foot to foot, and she'd jerk away as if he had leprosy. The feeling transcended loneliness. He felt like poison. As Tamsen washed him, he thought of how long he'd ached to be touched like this. He tried to concentrate on the feeling, though he knew he couldn't will his penis to become erect through sheer force of concentration.

She washed him, touched him, kissed him, trying to reach him. He closed his eyes, trying to simply enjoy it, trying to focus, the way the therapist he'd seen with Karen had tried to teach him. When he opened them again, he saw himself sitting on the toilet, watching himself in the tub.

"Nothing yet, huh?" Paul on the Toilet said.

"I'm not talking to you," Paul in the Bathtub said. "Leave me alone. Don't you see this is — "

"Exactly the problem," said Paul on the Toilet, finishing the sentence. "Of course I see it — I'm the analytical one. Try relaxing. Try breathing deeply through your nose and holding it in.

Count to six. Now let it out. You need to be relaxed to get an erection."

"Go away," Paul in the Tub said, irritated. "You're ruining this."

"*I'm* ruining this?" Paul on the Toilet said. "*You're* the one who called for me, pal, so don't pin this on me. Take some responsibility. I'm just trying to help."

"You're not helping."

"Paul?" Tamsen said.

"Yeah, yeah," Paul told her. "I'm really tired. I guess I must have just closed my eyes for a second."

"You're not getting off that easy," she said, kissing him again. For a second, he thought she'd meant to say "easily," a comment on his lack of responsiveness. Paul on the Toilet watched as Tamsen did everything she could to get Paul in the Tub aroused. She climbed on top of him, lifted a taut nipple to his mouth, pulled at him, bade him touch her and moaned with pleasure as he did, and held him close as she shuddered, and Paul on the Toilet admired her passion, her style, her imagination, and her determination, and he liked watching the soap bubbles run from her smooth skin as water and suds splashed about the room, but it was Paul in the Tub who needed to be present in the moment, and he was not.

"I'm sorry," he said when Tamsen at last desisted and simply held him, resting her head against his chest.

"Shh," she said. "You don't have to say anything. It's all part of the mystery. Sometimes I can have an orgasm like — " She snapped her fingers. "And sometimes it's like — " She pretended she'd forgotten how to snap her fingers, flailing them palsied in the air. "It doesn't matter."

"I heard about a woman who had orgasms every time she sneezed, and when the doctor asked her if she was taking anything for it, she said — "

"Just pepper," Tamsen said softly, holding him. "You told me that one. No jokes. You don't have to entertain me to get me to like you. I just want you to feel comfortable with me. It's going to happen, and I'm going to be here when it does."

"I think I drank too much," he said. "I've had a lot on my mind."

"You have."

"I was hoping to do better," he said.

"Paul, stop — I don't care. I just like being with you. I think you're cool."

"You think I'm *cool*?"

"I think you're *way* cool."

"No one's said they thought I was cool since seventh grade."

"Who said it in seventh grade?"

"Mary Schwandt," Paul said. "She passed me a note. It said, 'Dear Paul, I think you're really cool. A bunch of us are going down to the park tonight to beat up Randy Bubniak, and I was wondering if you want to come with us. Love, Mary.' "

"Who was Randy Bubniak?"

"Just this kid I'd known since kindergarten. I guess he was somewhat on the effeminate side. I told him he probably didn't want to go down to the park for a while because some kids were going to be waiting for him."

"See? That's exactly what I mean. Nine out of ten seventh-grade boys wouldn't have said anything. That's one of the many things I love about you. Sometimes I think you don't see it, and that kills me. You only see the negatives."

"What are the other things you love about me?" His hidden question was, "What do you mean when you say that, and is it the same thing you mean when you say it to Stephen? Do you love him too?" This wasn't the time or place to bring up Stephen.

"Why?" she said. "Do you have to have a reason to love somebody? It's what you feel — it's not a conclusion you reach through logical deduction."

"I don't have to have a reason, but I try to understand it when it happens," he said. He remembered how frightening the idea of romantic love had been to him when he'd first encountered it, when he understood it only as some overwhelming and mysterious force that comes over you, beyond your control, out of the blue. He'd worried, lying in bed in seventh grade, that he might fall in love with somebody he didn't want to fall in love with — what would he do then? He wanted to have some say in who he did or didn't fall in love with. Tamsen was right. He did need a reason. He'd always needed a reason.

"Let's get in bed," she said. "I feel like I want to sleep with you for three days."

"I could go for that," Paul said.

"Paul," she said when they were in bed. "Just don't brood. We've been brought together by something larger than sex. There's no clock running on it. Okay? I just want to know you. I want you to know me."

"Okay," he said. He would try not to brood. "Tell me something nobody else knows, then. Tell me a secret. Something you want. Something nobody else knows about."

She paused. "You have to promise not to repeat this to anybody. I've been taking singing lessons."

"You have?" he said. "Who from?"

"From a woman named Sheila Clark. She's got a trio in Providence. Stephen and I saw her one night, and when she was on break I told her I'd always wanted to sing, and she said she was starting a class and I should sign up, so I did. Sort of on an impulse."

"Does Stephen know?" Paul asked.

She shook her head. "He was in the bathroom," she said. "It's so embarrassing. Sheila's been trying to help me figure out why it's so hard for me. I can speak in front of a thousand people at a tech convention, but the idea of opening my mouth and singing in front of people terrifies me. I think it's because in my fantasies, I'm just like the singers I listen to on CD, but when I hear myself in reality — Sheila tapes us — I want to cringe."

He was thrilled to know something about her that Stephen didn't know.

"Sing something for me," he said. She demurred. "Please."

After a pause, she sang, softly, barely above a whisper, " 'Am I blue?' Not with you . . . ' " She stopped. "I can't."

"You have a beautiful voice," he said. "I'll bet if you sang full out, you'd be great."

"Ugh," she said. "That's not going to happen. Your turn."

"Okay," he said. "I write poetry. Just once in a while. I can quit anytime I want."

"Can you tell me a poem?"

"There was a young man from Japan, / Whose poetry just wouldn't scan. / When asked, 'Why's it so?' / He replied, 'I don't know, / Unless it's that I always try to fit as many words into the last line as I possibly can.' "

"Seriously."

"Seriously, I don't have anything serious memorized," he said. "I could e-mail you something if you want."

"I want."

He held her close and closed his eyes and listened to her breathing until sleep came over him. When he woke up two hours later, he was fully aroused, like a teenager looking at his first *Playboy*. He considered waking Tamsen up but knew the feeling would probably fade before he could do anything about it.

He went into the bathroom, struggling at first. A warm shiver swept over him from head to toe as he peed. He shuddered.

"We'll get her next time," he told his penis.

"We'll get who?" Stella said from the fuzzy bath mat where she'd been lying.

"I wasn't talking to you. Go back to sleep."

"Yes, master," she said sleepily. "Are you all right? You seem bummed."

"Minor setback," he said.

7

The Secret Life of Jimmy Carter

The next day, after Tamsen left (giving him a sweet kiss to assure him all was well between them), he went to Kmart and bought a pair of sweatpants, a sweatshirt, and a pair of running shoes. He was stretching on the kitchen floor in his bathrobe when Stella walked in and saw him.

"What in the world are you doing?" she asked him. "Did you hurt yourself?"

"Not yet," he said. "I'm stretching. I'm going to start jogging."

"You?" Stella said, suppressing a chuckle.

"What's so funny?"

"I think that's great," she said. "I'm sure you'll have a terrific time. Why now?"

"I'm going to change my life," he told her. "I made a vow after I saw my father."

"So you're going jogging?"

"Dieting too. I'm serious. I realized I've let myself slide since the divorce."

"Just since the divorce."

"You're no one to sit there telling me I'm out of shape. When's the last time you got any exercise?"

"While you were gone. Chester and I ran several miles through the snow, chasing away a couple of ferocious deer. Twelve miles,

I believe it was. Maybe you should check with your doctor. When's the last time you had a physical?"

"They're just going to point to the body mass index chart on the wall and tell me I'm too short for my weight. How am I supposed to get taller at my age?"

"Does this have anything to do with your penis?" she asked.

"This has nothing to do with that," he said. "Though it couldn't hurt. I decided this when I was in Minnesota. Care to join me?"

"Sounds like fun, but I'll pass," Stella said. "I'd only slow you down."

"I doubt that very much," Paul said. He looked out the window. The snow in the streets had melted to slush. He could think of plenty of reasons to wait until conditions improved. Then he pictured his father again, trapped in his hospital bed.

He changed to go running. He'd decided things were going to be different hundreds of times before, but this time he really meant it. He laid the sweatshirt and his new sweatpants on the bed, as well as a baby-seal-orange stocking cap (for safety), but before he dressed, he regarded himself naked in the mirror, to get a good mental "before" picture.

He looked doughy. Unimposing. A pushover. He'd smoked until he was thirty — that hadn't helped anything. He was five foot eleven, with decent posture, standing up, but with a tendency to slouch when he was sitting down, particularly in movie theaters, where he was usually quite uncomfortable, mostly owing to his not having an ass. He wished he could say he'd worked it off, better yet that he'd laughed it off, or lost it in Vegas, but the sad fact was that he'd been born without one, part of his heritage. For centuries, his Viking ancestors had rowed boats across the wine-dark seas of the North Atlantic seated on hard wooden planks — no doubt it was a question of erosion more than of genetics or evolution.

In compensation for his hereditary asslessness, he had decent-looking legs, though a bit bowed. His feet were well shaped but his little toes turned in and tended to grow calluses and to blister if his socks were too thin. Structurally, his left leg was sound but his right knee was shot, the anterior cruciate ligament snapped and the lateral meniscus cartilage all but gone after a softball accident years earlier. His orthopedic surgeon told him afterward that he was no longer allowed to participate in any sports because of the further damage he might do and the risk of developing arthritis later in life. Paul looked at his legs. Arthritis wasn't as bad as a stroke, and that was what he was worried about.

He was going jogging.

Nothing was going to stop him.

"From this day forward," he silently resolved, "every other beer will be a light beer. And every two out of three if I'm also eating Klondike bars."

He had good shoulders, broad and square, and nice hands, or so he'd been told. His chest was smooth and hairless. The hair on his head was sandy brown and thinning, but only noticeably so if he stood directly beneath an overhead light, a reason to avoid motel bathrooms. He examined his face. He hated the way he looked in photographs but liked the way he looked in mirrors, except when the mirror was lying flat on a tabletop and he could only glimpse himself by bending over, and then gravity pulled at the loose skin on his face and neck and made him look jowly and ancient. A friend had warned him, "Once you turn forty and you're in bed with a younger woman, never be on top unless the room is pitch black, because she could open her eyes and suddenly think she's in bed with Jimmy Carter."

He had "quiet good looks," in Tamsen's words. He did not have bags under his eyes or wrinkles or frown lines, and his lips were not as thin as those of most Scandinavian men, not the down-turned narrow slits evident on his ancestors' faces in old family photographs, immigrants in their New Land finery, men and women who never smiled, because their lives were hard and their memories pained them, and because the shutter speeds were so slow back then that you had to assume a pose and freeze for at least five seconds. No Norwegian man had ever been able to hold a smile for more than three.

"Make an appointment with a dentist," he told himself.

"Find a dentist."

"Or get a job with dental coverage. And a physical. Yeah, right."

"Stop being so passive."

His new jogging shoes were lighter than air and soft underfoot. He felt as if he was walking on somebody's sofa. He'd loved sports as a kid, fantasizing, as boys did, that one day he might turn pro. Horsing around and wrestling and playing kickball and catch with Carl made him aggressive and competitive. Before he broke his arm in a preseason football game in ninth grade, he'd been a four-season jock: baseball in the summer, football in the fall, basketball in the winter, and track in the spring. After the accident, he'd sat out games and practices for over a month, during which time he discovered all kinds of things: girls, tobacco, alcohol, drugs, girls. After that, he never really gave a damn anymore about sports, satisfied to ride the pine and muse without ever coming close to matching Carl's athletic accomplishments or his own prior expectations.

"I was an athlete once. I can be one again."

Seeing his father lying in the hospital had given him a sense of mortality that he hadn't had before. He'd waited long enough. It was time to get healthy.

He tightened his laces, stood up, took a deep breath, and touched his toes, making a loud grunting sound. "Stretching is overrated," he said to himself. His belly bulged slightly over the drawstring of his sweatpants. He wore an oversize sweatshirt more because he needed something bulky to cover his gut. He took one last look in the mirror and thought, "It's a miracle that Tamsen is attracted to me. If the psychic hadn't told her I was the one for her, where would I be?"

The fact that she'd chosen him was impossibly flattering and good for his ego. She told him he didn't look anything like Jimmy Carter, but then, what else was she going to say?

"Maybe some day I'll run in a marathon with Carl. I'll get in great shape and kick his ass," he thought.

"First things first. Just start running."

"Maybe I will run with you. I've changed my mind," Stella said. "How far are we going?" Even as out of shape as he was, he knew Stella was too old to keep up with him, try as she might.

"Uh . . . I'm going to need you to stay here and guard the house while I'm gone," he told her.

"Fabulous," she muttered, turning and circling once before lying on her bed. "We wouldn't want anyone breaking in and stealing the boxer shorts you left under the bed, would we?"

HE STEPPED OUTSIDE. The air was cold and dry, the sky a cloudless blue, the sun bright. He briefly considered waiting to begin his new regimen until some day when it was warmer, but he recognized the lame excuse for what it was. There was no way to start but to simply start, one foot in front of the other. He began walking to the corner and told himself as soon as he reached the fire hydrant, he would pick up the pace.

At the hydrant, he ran, turning right on Parsons and right again on Bridge, past the post office, where the employees were ominously cheerful and pleasant. He ran past Historic Northampton, a very old house across the street from the post office that was no doubt filled with very old things. Nobody he knew had ever been there, and nobody he knew knew anybody who'd ever been there, or anybody who had any plans or intentions to go there, though the building was open to the public six days a week, preserving history by more or less keeping it to themselves. At first he was surprised at how easy it was to run after years of inactivity and sloth. Then he was surprised at how briefly that feeling lasted and how tired he soon became.

He headed downtown, Northampton a picturesque arcade of boutiques and businesses and a destination for travelers from Montreal to New York City, who came for the shops and the restaurants. He ran past Stanley Prochaska's jewelry store, one of the oldest shops in town, and past the bridal shop, perhaps the only one in the country that featured matching bridal gowns for "hers and hers" commitment ceremonies, Northampton being famous as a major haven for lesbians. He ran past the leather goods shop, and the sporting goods shop, past couples clutching paper bags, men shopping with their women. He briefly recalled shopping with his ex-wife, holding her bag and saying things like, "Do we really need a new blender?" or "Doesn't the old toaster oven still work?" He ran past Thornes Marketplace, once a traditional department store that now housed a variety of independent shops and was kind of the crown jewel of the Northampton shopping scene. He ran past the building where he rented an office for himself, where he kept his work mess separate from his home mess, writing and staring out the window, sometimes with binoculars, just keeping an eye on things.

Paul ran, unzipping his Windbreaker at the neck, though the temperature was only in the forties. His legs were starting to ache, and his lungs hurt, but he kept going, past a store called Faces, which sold cheap furniture and lamps and posters and things to go in dormitory rooms. He ran past Betsy's Threads, a high-end clothing shop where Betsy had to keep track of all the social circles in town and remember which dresses she had sold to which women to make sure nobody showed up at the same party wearing the same thing. He ran past Intimate You, a sexy lingerie shop where the owner, a woman named Charlotte, knew everyone in town and, more importantly, knew who was wearing what beneath their clothes. She also had a good idea of who was having affairs and with whom, information garnered when men bought lacy bras or thong panties for their girlfriends, after which the mistresses brought them back to exchange them for the more appropriate sizes or styles.

He ran past Jake's No Frills Dining, where he'd gone for bacon and eggs and toast and coffee (but no frills) every morning for the past fifteen years. While Paul sipped coffee, read the *Globe,* and did the crossword puzzle, Stella would lie quietly in the café doorway, bothering no one, at least until the day the city said they were going to fine dog owners twenty-five dollars for tying their pets up downtown (there was a fine for not tying them up too), regardless of whether the offending pooch was snoozing peacefully in the sun or gnawing the toes off babies in their strollers. Paul couldn't begin to count the number of people in a typical day who smiled when they saw Stella lying contentedly in the doorway, but of course, nobody's going to call the dog officer and say, "I'd like to report a dog — it's not doing anything, but it made me really happy just to look at it . . ."

He ran down Main Street, where he often saw petitioners getting signatures to put candidates on ballots, and girls' soccer teams collecting donations, and New Age people offering incense or poetry, and disturbed zanies muttering things like "You don't leave witnesses, you *never* leave witnesses . . ." to themselves. Main Street was generally alive, seven days a week and year-round, with trust-fund mendicants, panhandlers and mooches, crow babies and white Rasta kids in Jamaican black, yellow, green, and red knit caps, Goth waifs and death punks who asked for spare change to make "phone calls," and, one time, a kid squatting on the sidewalk with a sign that read, PARENTS SLAIN BY NINJAS — NEED MONEY FOR KUNG FU LESSONS! He ran past a used-book store, and another used-book store, and a new-book store, and a store that had once sold crystals but went out of business when the crystals apparently told the owners they didn't want to be sold. He ran past importers carrying third-world knickknacks, and he ran past one of the dozen ice cream parlors in town, dairy being the last vice the local Birkenstockers allowed themselves. If a power failure were ever to shut down the ice cream parlor freezers, the streets of Northampton would be awash with slow-rolling waves of malted vanilla and lowfat frozen yogurt.

He kept running. He passed the Sunflower Laundromat, where everyone posted notes and notices on the community bulletin board. He ran past the Healing Cooperative next to the Laundromat, a kind of New Age clinic for psychic fairs and body workers and homeopathic remedies and treatments, with a pamphlet rack by the door, offering flyers for all the various local shamans and magical practitioners and caregivers. There he had to stop, wishing briefly that he'd brought along enough money to check himself into the Healing Cooperative for a full-body "gentle loving" massage.

He sat on the steps, panting, and felt light headed. He didn't expect to get in shape right away, but evidently he had further to go than he thought. He'd just begun to catch his breath when first his right calf muscle began to cramp up, then his left. He stood and walked it off, and after about ten minutes, he felt better.

And a minute later, he also felt proud of himself. By his own estimation, he'd come about a mile and a half. Most of the fitness gurus said that when you're starting out, it's important to go easy on yourself.

When he got home, he unlaced his shoes. Stella asked him how his run had gone.

"Terrific," he said. He filled the tub with water as hot as he could stand it. His feet hurt. His knees throbbed. He put his robe on again, went to the refrigerator, grabbed a beer, opened it, and then went to recover in the tub. After a moment, Stella came into the bathroom and stared at him.

"Is that part of your training too?" she asked him, staring at the beer.

"No," he told her, taking a sip. "This is my reward for exercising."

"What does it feel like?" she asked.

"What does what feel like?"

"Drinking. I'm just curious."

"It feels good. It relaxes you."

"What do you need to relax from? You don't do anything."

"From stress."

"What's stress?"

"What's stress?" Paul said. "Hmm. Well. You know when you see another dog coming toward you on the sidewalk, and he looks big and mean with his fur up on the back of his neck, so you get the fur up on the back of your neck too?"

"Horripilation."

"That's stress."

"Oh." She watched him as he swallowed. "So is there a big dog somewhere nearby or something?"

"No," Paul said. "That was just an example for you. Human beings have a lot of other things that stress us out."

"Like what things? You're lying in a tub of hot, soapy water, doing nothing as far as I can tell."

"Like stuff that happens. During the day. So people who have stressful days come home and get themselves a drink to unwind."

"After the big dog has gone away."

"Right."

"Wouldn't it make more sense to drink before the big dog gets to you?"

"I suppose."

"I mean, after the big dog is gone, where's the stress?"

"You have a good point," Paul said. "That's the difference between you and me. For you, when the big dog goes away, your fur goes back down and you forget all about it. People keep our fur up long after the big dog goes away."

"Why?"

"Because we're more highly evolved."

Stella had to think a moment.

"You know, the more you tell me about evolution, the less I understand it. Evolution means improvement, right?"

"Right."

"So thinking a big dog is there, when in fact there's no big dog there, is an improvement?"

"Not in and of itself," Paul said. "But we have a better long-term memory than you do. That's an improvement, but it makes it harder for us to forget the big dogs we run into every day."

"And that's why people drink?"

"Some."

"Do your mom and dad drink?"

"Never," Paul said.

"How about your brother?"

"Not as much as he should," Paul said. "He's got a lot of stress. Studies show that alcohol can relieve stress."

"And you feel better when you don't have stress?"

"Much better. I feel more like myself."

"Who do you feel like when you don't feel like yourself?"

"You're still you, but you don't feel like it," Paul said, knowing that wouldn't explain anything, not even to a human being. "You feel more in touch with things."

"Then why do you always lose your car keys?"

"Not those kinds of things."

"Then what kinds of things?"

"Look," Paul said. "It's like this. You feel sort of . . . in control and out of control at the same time. You're in charge of how out of control you get. And being out of control feels good because then you don't have the responsibility of being in control all the time, so you can kick back and be yourself. Like, when you're a baby, or a little kid, you're just you, just being yourself and not examining everything you do or worrying about what everybody else is going to think. You just basically feel good all the time. Then you get older, and you have to pay your bills, and other people expect things from you, and you never get a chance to just relax and feel good about everything."

"Except when you're drunk?"

"Not just when you're drunk. But sometimes when you're drunk, you feel very fine."

"How often?"

"I don't know."

"Half the time?"

"I don't know. Why? Why do you ask?"

"I don't know," Stella said. "Because you don't seem very happy. Especially not when you're drunk. Then you seem really sad. Is feeling sad feeling more like yourself?"

Now Paul paused.

"Does stress make you sad?" Stella persisted.

"No. Stress makes you anxious. It makes you feel up. But in a bad way."

"Does winding down make you sad?"

"Sometimes, I guess. You feel sad when things don't work out."

"Like with Karen?"

"Exactly."

"Or like when you can't get a boner?"

"Yes. That makes me sad."

"But getting a boner makes you happy."

"It makes me very happy."

Paul took the bar of soap and washed his hair. He wanted to change the subject. Stella was just trying to understand.

"Well, I think you have it backwards, if you don't mind my saying."

"Meaning what?"

"I mean I think you're switching the order of things. I think first you get sad, and *then* you don't get a boner. Or first you get happy, and *then* you get a boner."

"What makes you say that?" he asked.

"Observation."

"Observation?"

"How long have we known each other?"

"In human years?" Paul answered. "Almost sixteen years."

"And in that time, you've had how many girlfriends and wives?"

"One wife, please," Paul said. "What's your point?"

"My point is, all those years, all the times that you were in bed with people, don't forget — there were three of us in the room, not two. Ninety-nine percent of the time, I was watching you. I don't go off duty just because somebody else is there, you know — I still have to keep an eye on you, even if you aren't paying much attention to me. And what I've seen with my own two eyes, as a noninvolved observer, is first you get sad or stressed and *then* you don't get a boner, or first you get happy, and *then* you do. And drinking makes you sad. That's my observation. For what it's worth, but hey, I'm just a dog — what do I know? I was just wondering."

"Hmm," Paul said. "I'll get you a beer if you really want to know."

"No, thanks," Stella said. "I'm already relaxed."

"So if drinking makes me sad," he asked her, "what makes me happy? By your observation."

"People."

"People?"

"Yeah."

"Specifically how?"

"Meeting new people," she said. "Doing nice things for them. Works every time. You should watch yourself sometime."

"Hmm," he said. "Interesting."

8

Rules of Engagement

*H*is mother said Harrold was doing better. The doctors believed the clot-busting drug they gave him in the hospital, a medication called tPA, for tissue plasminogen activator, had reached his brain in time to reestablish blood flow and limit what would have been catastrophic damage otherwise. He was still paralyzed and without speech, but he could eat and focus long enough to watch reruns of the *Rockford Files* and *Gunsmoke* and *Highway to Heaven,* which, she said, seemed to bring a tear to his eye every time, the genuine kind. They'd set his bed up downstairs, with a twenty-four-hour live-in nurse for the first week and a visiting day nurse after that, in addition to the speech and occupational therapists who visited three times a week to work his legs and arms or to electrically stimulate his throat. It was all quite amazing, Beverly said. "You should see how good they are."

Carl made sure that the bills were paid and the checkbook was balanced and that the household was running smoothly again, for which Beverly was grateful. Carl and Bits and their families visited often or just took Beverly shopping when the day nurse was on duty. Paul's job was simply to try to engage his father in communication, to stimulate the parts of the brain that affected speech and response. It could prove difficult to measure whether it was doing any good, the therapist warned him, but it was certain to be a slow recovery and these were the first steps.

"I'm just so amazed at what they can do these days," Beverly said. "I remember a friend of my dad's who had a stroke, and he just sat in a wheelchair for the last twenty years of his life. This is all just so good. It's all good."

Paul took her word for it. He kept his expectations in check and got online with his father one night after dinner. Beverly was there to help her husband and to show him how to operate the mouse.

PaulGus: Hi. How do you feel today? I know you can't answer that question yes or no. I suspect I'll be doing most of the talking, so

HarrGus: YES

PaulGus: Interrupting is good. Feel free to interrupt me any

HarrGus: NO

PaulGus: I'm confused. No, interrupting is not good?

HarrGus: YES

PaulGus: Okay then, why don't

HarrGus: NO

PaulGus: Wait, wait, wait. Why don't we just start over and practice a little bit until you get the hang of this. Can you click on the Yes box?

HarrGus: YES

PaulGus: Can you click on the No box?

HarrGus: YES

PaulGus: Then please do so.

HarrGus: NO

PaulGus: Uh . . . okay then.

PaulGus: Are you still there?

HarrGus: Hi, Paul. This is your mother typing. I think

your father is feeling tired. Let's try this again in a few
days.

PaulGus: I don't know what I'm doing.

HarrGus: That's okay. We're all new at this. His eyes are
closed. Call me the next time you want to do this and I'll
make sure he's rested.

Part of the idea was simply to let his father know that he
wasn't alone and that there was somebody willing to listen. Paul
pictured his father as a kind of floating consciousness, like some
low-budget horror movie from the fifties where the mad scientist's brain was a bell jar full of glowing smoke.

The next time he tried, his mother assured him that his father
understood how everything worked and was rested enough to
give it another go. She said that she'd be in the kitchen but that
she wanted Harrold to try to do it on his own.

PaulGus: Good morning. How are you feeling?

HarrGus: NO

PaulGus: I mean, are you feeling good?

HarrGus: NO

PaulGus: Of course not. So you're feeling not so good?

HarrGus: NO

PaulGus: Do you want to do this?

HarrGus: NO NO NO NO

PaulGus: Why don't we try again tomorrow then?

HarrGus: NO

He tried not to become discouraged. It seemed to him that
perhaps the format wasn't working. The speech therapist Harrold was working with told Paul she thought Harrold's reading
comprehension was actually good. Some stroke patients developed a kind of dyslexia where written words and letters seemed

scrambled and incomprehensible, but Harrold had passed the tests she'd given him for that. Something else was holding him back. The therapist told Paul not to worry. So many different mechanisms come into play during the adaptive rewiring of the brain following a stroke. She believed Harrold understood the things that were said to him, and the words on the screen, but simply had great difficulty formulating a response.

Paul tried again a few days later.

PaulGus: Good morning, Harrold.

PaulGus: Are you there?

PaulGus: You need to click the mouse to tell me if you're ready. Are you there?

HarrGus: YES

PaulGus: This is Paul. I'd like to see if we could have a little dialogue here. Are you feeling up to it?

PaulGus: It's beautiful here today. Blue skies. Is the weather there nice?

PaulGus: Would you like to try this some other time?

PaulGus: I'm clearly not doing this right.

PaulGus: Just so you know, I'm not enjoying this any more than you are.

PaulGus: I apologize for that. Once I click Send, I can't take it back. I shouldn't have sent that. It was supposed to be a joke. I'm frustrated because I don't know how to help you.

PaulGus: Maybe it's too soon to be trying this. I can keep going but I don't want to force you to do something you don't want to do. Why don't we just give it a rest for a while?

PaulGus: Okay then.

He shut the computer off.

In the fifties horror movie, there'd be a good scientist gesticulating thoughtfully with his pipe as he pondered the big questions,

and maybe a comely female research assistant in a white lab coat
who carried a purse, even on the surface of Mars, and of course
a team of army generals who wanted to drop an atom bomb on
the brain in the bell jar, when the tap of a small hammer would
suffice. Paul felt alone.

He hoped no one was expecting too much from him.

9

Darwin Schmarwin

This magazine article," Paul said, looking up from his research on *Nature for Morons*, "says that dogs don't know why they bark."

"Says who?" Stella asked, looking up from where she lay by the radiator.

"Says this dog-evolution expert from Hampshire College," Paul said. "He's like the world's leading expert on canid behavior and he says that dogs just bark."

"That could be the stupidest thing I've ever heard," Stella said. "When someone's at the door and I go to the door to bark, what does he think I'm saying?"

"Well, I know, but —"

"When my bowl is empty and I'm standing at my bowl, barking, does he think I'm standing there asking for a weather report?"

"Wait, wait, wait," Paul said. "Let me finish reading this."

Outside, a clap of thunder shook the sky. Stella did not like the sound of it, not at all. She'd heard of too many dogs who'd been struck by lightning, some of them lying in their own beds, indoors. It could travel down telephone lines and television cables and leap out at you and burn you. Some thunderclaps, she'd heard, were so strong that the sound alone could knock your house down. Some of what she'd heard was exaggerated, sure, but there was simply too much anecdotal evidence to discount it all. She couldn't help it. She didn't like thunder.

"It says here," Paul read, trying to distract her, "that they compared the DNA of wolves and dogs and that the difference was a single haplotype, meaning that you and wolves are virtually identical, genetically."

But Stella wasn't listening — lightning lit the room. She silently counted, "One-a-Snausage, two-a-Snausage, three-a-Snausage . . ." When the thunder came, it came as a steady rumble that rattled her to the core. She looked at Paul but knew that there was nothing he could do about it. She tried to slow her breathing.

"You wanna come up on the couch?" Paul offered. "Come on up."

She pushed her front end up and then paused, waiting for the feeling to come around in her hindquarters. Her front end was still strong enough that if she walked herself forward, the hind part usually followed. She placed a paw on the couch cushion and waited. Paul reached over and lifted her up onto the couch. She laid her head against his thigh. He tickled the skin on her belly. For a moment she forgot about the storm raging outside.

"This is really interesting," Paul said, reading on. "This guy says that working dogs, breeds that either herd or guard sheep, are the most highly evolved of all the dog breeds. 'Indeed, it is useful to understand the behavior of adult dogs in terms of wolf pup behavior.' It's called paedomorphism — "

"Huh?" she said.

" — 'Meaning the adult of one species retains the juvenile characteristics of another,'" he read. "'The adult dog barks, just as the wolf pup barks, but adult wolves don't bark. Wolf pups, like adult dogs, will stay put in one place and wait to be fed, whereas adult wolves will do neither. Pups, like dogs, have the ability to bond with other species, a behavior adult wolves quickly outgrow, relating upon maturation only to conspecifics, one reason they tend to make poor house pets even when they're supposedly tame.' So when a border collie herds sheep, it says here, it will perform behaviors instinctively, doing things that are hardwired into its brain, because they're the same behaviors that wolves use to stalk and kill deer or elk. It's like dogs have been given incomplete genetic wolf instructions, because if they had the whole set of instructions, they'd kill and eat the sheep."

"Well, look," Stella said, lifting her leg when Paul scratched a particularly sensitive spot. "I'm sure this professor is a smart guy and all that, and he probably means well, but don't you find what he's saying to be just a bit . . . lobocentric?"

"Meaning?"

"Meaning it's always *wolf* this and *wolf* that," she said. "Comparing us to wolves. I get tired of it. It's ludicrous."

"How is it ludicrous?" Paul asked. "Wolves live in more complex societies than dogs do. Wolves fend for themselves in the wild. They can hunt down and kill an elk. Could you do that?"

"Why would I want to?"

"But *could* you?"

"You're missing the point, Paul," Stella said. "I don't have to. The answer is literally under your nose and you can't even see it."

"Meaning what?"

"Just that the implication is that dogs couldn't cut it as wolves. Like we're too stupid to hunt down elk or deer or whatever, like we're failed wolves."

"More or less," Paul said.

"Maybe I don't understand it," Stella said, "but when you explained evolution to me, you said the fittest individuals breed more successfully than less fit individuals."

"Right."

"So whoever is fittest has the highest population."

"Correct."

"Well, then," Stella said, "how many wolves would you say there are alive in the world today? Ballpark figure."

"The article says a hundred fifty thousand."

"Good," she said. "It's a hundred fifty thousand. Now, how many dogs are there? In the whole world, how many? How many just in this country, how many dogs?"

"Well," Paul said, "I'm not sure."

"Sixty million, in this country alone," Stella said. "So if there are, globally, say a hundred million dogs, a low estimate, and a hundred fifty thousand wolves, then who wins? Who's the fittest? Who's the most highly evolved? According to Darwin's own definition?"

"Dogs."

"I rest my case," she said. "What's it doing outside right now? It's raining. And where are the wolves? Out there in the rain. And where am I? In here, on the couch, warm and dry. I have food in my dish. I don't have to spend any of my time wondering where the next meal is coming from. So am I a failed wolf, or is a wolf a failed dog?"

"Well . . ."

"There's really no comparison. They're big and mean and they eat deer. Not impressed."

Just then a brilliant flash of lightning lit the sky, the brightest so far. He covered Stella's ears with his hands, but the thunder followed immediately, a colossal, booming explosion that rocked the house to its very foundation, followed by several aftershocks, and it didn't matter that Paul's hands blocked some of the sound, because Stella felt the percussion in her very bones and perceived the sudden drop in air pressure following the thunder as a kind of suffocating vacuum. Her heart raced. She felt as if she couldn't breathe.

"God, I don't like this, Paul, please," she said, "I can't take much more of this, I really can't . . ."

Then another flash, and an even louder thunderclap.

"There, there," Paul said, stroking and soothing his dog as

best he could. "It's okay. It's all right. It's all over now. Just calm down . . ."

"Easy for you to say 'calm down,'" she said.

"Everything is okay," he said, scratching her behind the ears and on the soft part of her belly. It felt to him as if she'd lost another pound or two. "I think you have one or two wolf genes left, or you wouldn't be afraid of thunder. Remember what you were just saying? You live indoors. You don't have to be afraid of thunder."

"That's true, but thirty thousand years ago when we moved indoors with you, you were still living in caves. Caves can't catch fire. Houses burn down all the time."

10

Virtual Canoe Trip

He was sore after the first time he ran, but the second time was easier than the first, and the third time was easier than the second. His goal was to run fifteen miles a week. His unspoken goal was to beat his brother in a race . . . someday. To keep track of his mileage, he ran on the Smith College Tartan Track, which was easier on his legs than running in the street. He made the foolish mistake, one day, of trying to time himself in a hundred-yard dash, a race he'd run in 10.5 seconds in high school. Allowing for age, atrophy, and disuse, he told himself he'd be satisfied if he could run it in under 20 seconds now. He tried to convince himself that his watch had somehow malfunctioned when he clocked himself at an appalling 38 seconds — either that or a hundred yards was longer than it used to be.

HOWEVER MUCH HIS muscles ached, he thought of his father and reminded himself that he was lucky he could move at all. Beverly had sent Paul an old photograph of himself and his father, taken after the two of them had finished a game of catch, the shadows of daylight savings time long at twilight, their faces painted orange by the fading sun's holy light, the two of them wearing matching Twins caps they'd bought at Metropolitan Stadium. Paul was struck by how young his father was in the picture, his strong shoulders and broad chest. If Harrold had ever had a moment of self-doubt in his life, Paul was unaware of it. Looking at the picture, Paul tried to put himself in his father's shoes. He couldn't.

He decided, one day after a run, to try again with his father. He'd hoped for immediate results, instant gratification, but perhaps it would be more a marathon than a sprint. He'd seen Karen in a restaurant earlier, having lunch with her sister and her sister's kids, Molly and Kevin. The encounter had left him depressed. It was one thing to have an ex-wife; it was another to have ex-nieces and ex-nephews. Nobody'd warned him about that. He used to play Chutes and Ladders and Candy Land with them on the rug. Now they were strangers, or he was. He couldn't even say hello and left quickly before they saw him. It was more weird than tragic. If he couldn't alter his own sorry state, maybe he could alter somebody else's.

PaulGus: Good morning. Or I guess I should say good afternoon. Are you ready to try to have a little conversation?

PaulGus: Just use the mouse to click Yes or No when I ask you a question.

PaulGus: Are you ready?

He needed to be patient. He was wary of saying anything too challenging.

PaulGus: I was watching a game between the Twins and the Red Sox the other day on ESPN. Did you see it?

PaulGus: They did a story on Harmon Killebrew. Apparently he's flat broke. That's sad, don't you think?

PaulGus: Killebrew had over 8,000 career at bats and not one bunt. I always liked that about him. No matter what the situation, he had the green light to swing for the fences. Did you like that about him too?

PaulGus: Wonder if that has anything to do with why he's
broke. You remember Harmon Killebrew, right?

He was of the theory that men invented sports to give them
something to talk about other than their feelings. Women
played sports, sure, but had they ever invented one? No need.
He couldn't think of anything more likely to draw his father
out. He pictured Harrold lying in bed, staring blankly at the
computer screen. Was he confused? Scared? Angry? When
Paul put himself in Harrold's shoes and tried to imagine what
Harrold might be feeling, his best guess was that Harrold felt
utterly and absolutely useless. "Useless" was not something
Harrold was familiar with. Paul was aware that perhaps he was
projecting his own interpretation. "Useless" was exactly how
Paul had felt after his divorce. Worthless and of no value to
anyone.

He allowed that perhaps he'd been using the wrong approach.
The speech therapist had told Paul he should feel free to chal-
lenge his father and push him a little bit. He considered taking
a more aggressive position, but how? Hectoring was out, ditto
badgering, cajoling, or scolding. There was always whining, but
that was hard to do online.

PaulGus: Look—let me just be honest. Maybe you think that
you don't need this, but I need this. I really need to talk
to you. You could just sit there and not respond, but I need
you to meet me halfway. I'm sorry if you find this difficult
or confusing, but you really have to try. People need you to
come back. Not just me. Your family needs you. Your wife
needs you.

PaulGus: I know it's hard. You can make mistakes. I just need
you to try. Okay? Are you ready?

There was a long pause. Paul waited.

HarrGus: YES

PaulGus: Excellent! Thank you. That's good. I'm guessing you must be feeling a bit lost.

HarrGus: YES

PaulGus: I wouldn't presume to know how you feel, but I do know what it's like to feel lost. In my marriage, for instance. Take my ex-wife, please. That's a joke.

HarrGus: YES

He felt oddly confessional. Why not? What was there to lose? The fact was, he'd always wanted to talk to his father about his failed marriage, not that there was anything anybody could have done. When he'd told his parents divorce was looming, they hadn't asked any questions, avoiding a touchy subject, no doubt. Paul had wondered how much they would understand anyway. His parents never fought about anything, though that didn't mean they agreed all the time. His mother held her opinions close and was infinitely amenable. It was a similar capacity for selflessness that had attracted him to Karen, her readiness to put others first. In the marriage, that "selflessness" evolved into an implacable resentfulness, an anger traceable (he'd theorized) to her position in her family birth order, the youngest of eight kids. Karen said she felt secondary, unimportant, convinced that his career meant more to him than she did, as did his friends, television, drinking, baseball, doughnuts, fishing . . . "I don't rank you — you do that to yourself," he'd argued. How could someone not believe you loved them, when all you knew, in your own heart, maybe the only thing you were truly clear on, was that you loved them? More to the point, how could you argue somebody into loving you? It didn't work that way.

PaulGus: Sometimes I think women accuse men of being unable to talk about our feelings when we say things they don't want to hear. Suddenly we "just don't understand."

I used to think, "Hey, I understand perfectly—I just don't agree with you."

HarrGus: NO

PaulGus: I don't think I ever saw Karen disagree with her female friends about ANYTHING. Seriously. So if you disagree, you must not be listening because obviously, if I heard what she said, I'd agree with her. What sense does that make? None whatsoever.

HarrGus: NO

PaulGus: Or she'd be clearly angry and sulking and when I'd say, "Is something bothering you?" she'd say, "No." Or she'd shut down and not say anything, and I'd ask her if she was all right and she'd say she was, but I knew she wasn't. What am I supposed to do? Respect the walls she put up, or break through them? It's so confusing. You can't listen to or agree with a mixed message. You're just screwed.

HarrGus: YES

It wasn't exactly a conversation, more like venting to a captive audience. He'd worked as a bartender back in graduate school and had witnessed men pissing and moaning about women and marriage. It didn't seem like too much to ask, even though men of Paul's father's generation weren't expected to be expressive about their emotions. You didn't talk about hardships or problems, because talking wasn't going to change anything and just kept things alive that needed to go away.

PaulGus: I wish I could hear your thoughts. You're one of the smartest people I know. Too bad we can't sit around a campfire and pass a bottle of Jack Daniel's back and forth. I always thought it would be fun to go camping one more time.

HarrGus: YES

PaulGus: Do you remember when we went to Indian Guides?

HarrGus: NO

PaulGus: Your name was Big Bear and my name was Little
Bear. Am I remembering that right?

HarrGus: YES.

PaulGus: It was so politically incorrect. Just short of putting
on minstrel shows. I don't imagine Native American
fathers and sons ever gave themselves white Anglo-Saxon
Protestant names and pretended they were living in the
suburbs.

HarrGus: NO

Paul's intention was to make his father laugh. Yet he realized
he was using humor to veer away from the very intimacy he was
seeking, a bad habit Karen had pointed out to him on several occasions. "See?" he thought. "Was too listening."

PaulGus: I can't imagine how confusing it must be for you. Do
you understand you've had a stroke?

HarrGus: YES

PaulGus: I know this is hard for you. I really appreciate that
you're trying. Actually, I'm in a piss-poor mood right now.
The woman I've been seeing is going out with another guy
tonight and I'm home alone. Bummer, eh?

HarrGus: YES

PaulGus: Not that I have any right to complain. My problems
don't begin to compare with yours.

PaulGus: I hope this gets easier and easier for you. There are
still people who need you. I need you. I need to be able to
talk to you. I've wanted to tell you that all my life.

HarrGus: YES

PaulGus: I wish I could just call you.

HarrGus: YES

PaulGus: So how about them Twins? Won't be the same without Kirby Puckett, will they?

HarrGus: NO

PaulGus: All right, then. Ursa Minor, logging off.

11

Forward or Back?

On the first truly warm day of spring, a bright, clear Saturday morning, Paul went for his longest run so far, over three miles, out past the community garden on the edge of town on Burts Pit Road, which everybody called Bird Spit Road. He was hoping to dispel his bad mood. He'd invited Tamsen up for the weekend, only to learn she was flying to Nantucket with Stephen to celebrate his divorce's becoming final. Paul wanted to tell her how lousy that made him feel, though being unpleasant would only push her farther away — you don't get love by acting unlovable. She'd apologized and invited him to visit her the following weekend, and he'd said yes, but it was hard not to think of her and Stephen, feeding each other clam chowder by candlelight.

He sat on the steps of his front porch after his run to cool down.

"Be glad you're a virgin," he told Stella.

"I'm a virgin?" she said.

"You are."

"I never had sex?"

"I don't think so," Paul said. "When you were younger, you went into heat once and I tied you up outside a drugstore, and I turned my back for twenty seconds and I came out and there was a little black mutt, like a schipperke, who was . . . um . . ."

"Who was what?"

"Striving mightily," Paul said. "But I think he was too short."

"Too short for what?"

"Too short to reach."

"Too short to reach what?"

"His goals," Paul said.

"What were his goals?"

"He wanted to have puppies," Paul said.

"With me?"

"Yup."

"He didn't even know me."

"He didn't care."

"Well, that seems rather inappropriate."

"You've been hanging around humans too long," Paul said.

"Were you too short to have children with Karen?" Stella asked.

"I wouldn't quite put it that way," Paul said. "But that was sort of the idea. At first. At the end, we were both glad we didn't."

"Why?"

"It's complicated," Paul said. "It's not like we made a conscious decision."

"Is that why you stopped having sex?" Stella asked. "To avoid having kids?"

"Is that why?" Paul said. "I never thought of that, but maybe. There was so much else that was wrong. And Karen and I stopped talking about what was wrong. If you stop talking about it, you're dead in the water."

"Too bad," Stella said.

"Fifty years ago, people put up with a lot more than they do now," he told her. "If Karen and I had gotten in a time machine and gone back to 1934, we would have been happy. Maybe not happy, but we would have stayed together. People settled for a lot less back then."

"Such as?"

"Like sex," Paul said. "Back then, people met, they kissed once or twice, they got married, they had a ton of sex for a year or two, and then they tapered off because they were so tired from milking the cows and plowing the fields. Now people meet, they kiss, they have a ton of sex, and then they get married and the sex tapers off, just like it always did, same exact curve, but now they think, 'Wow, we're not having sex anymore — it must be because we got married.' And then they get divorced."

"But there's no such thing as a time machine, right?"

"No such thing," Paul said.

"If you had a time machine, where would you go? Forward or back?"

"That's an excellent question," Paul said. Would he go back to the day he met Karen? Six months ago, he might have thought so. Now, no. That was progress. "I don't know. Maybe I'd go back to the night I skinny-dipped with Debbie Benson, but this time I'd bring along some mosquito repellent."

"You know what I think you'd do if you had a time machine?" Stella said.

"What?"

"I think you'd just leave it in the box because it would be too much trouble to read the manual."

"You're probably right," Paul said, lifting her up onto the front porch and setting her down. "They say you're supposed to live in the moment."

"As opposed to what?" Stella asked.

"As opposed to living in the past or in the future," he said. She tilted her head. "Don't look at me with that tone of voice. I'm not saying it makes sense. I'm just saying that's what people do."

"Do you?"

He tried to be Zen and not think about Tamsen on Nantucket. He tried to tell himself it was a good thing — that the more time she spent with Stephen, the sooner she'd reach a conclusion about him, possibly in Paul's favor.

When he went to visit her in Providence, he'd hoped Tamsen would throw her arms around him upon his arrival and say, "It's so good to see you. Nantucket sucked," but instead she'd simply kissed him and said, "I missed you." She'd invited him, the day before, to come meet with her book club, where he read poems by some of the poets he liked, and a few of his own. Afterward he and Tamsen and a few of the others from the book club, including her friend Caitlin, went for drinks at a place called the Wickenden Street Café, where Sheila Clark's trio was playing. Paul had bought Tamsen a couple of CDs he thought she'd like, a droll singer named Diana Krall and another named Eva Cassidy, who'd died young and was then rediscovered. Tamsen said she'd never heard such a beautiful voice. During a break, Sheila Clark invited Tamsen up to sing a song, but Tamsen adamantly declined despite the encouragement and cajoling of her friends.

In the car, Paul asked her, "So have you come out of the closet now about your singing lessons?"

"The closet's exactly where I should be singing," she said. "After I told you, I figured I had to tell Stephen, and after I told him, the cat was pretty much out of the bag."

Paul didn't say anything.

"I probably shouldn't be saying this," Tamsen said, "but do you know what Stephen did?"

"What?"

"He took me to a Céline Dion concert."

"Oh, no," Paul said, feeling more optimistic. "I'm so sorry."

"It gets worse. For her encore, she brought up Michael Bolton for a special guest duet. They don't have that much cheese in all of Wisconsin."

"Well, he didn't know," Paul said.

"I know," Tamsen said. "He meant well."

"You should give him some CDs by people you like so he can learn to tell the difference," Paul suggested.

"That's the problem. I already had," she said. "It's all right. My heart will go on."

He was feeling more comfortable by the time they got back to her place. He told her he had a friend in Boston named Murph who'd offered him tickets for a Red Sox–Yankees game, two weeks hence. "The guy knows everybody," Paul said. "He used to be the mayor's chauffeur. Now he drives a tour bus. You'd like him. I'll bet they're box seats. We could have sausage grinders on Lansdowne Street before the game."

Tamsen didn't answer at first.

"What's wrong?" Paul said. "We don't have to go if you don't want to."

"I'd love to go to Fenway Park with you," she said. "Could we go some other time? I've got something that weekend."

"Sure," he said. "Why? What have you got?"

"I wasn't sure how I was going to tell you this," Tamsen said. "Maybe we should talk later."

"About what?" he asked. "You can't just say, 'I wasn't going to tell you this,' and then leave it at that. I'm just going to fill in the blanks with something worse than whatever the reality is."

"I suppose not," she said. "I love you. You know that, right?"

"Why am I getting this gigantic uh-oh feeling?" he asked her.

"Stephen wants to take me to Paris," she said. "His wife is taking the kids to California and he hasn't had a real vacation for a long time . . ."

Paul felt as if someone had punched him in the stomach, though he tried not to let on. He actually wasn't sure he could have filled in the blanks with anything worse.

"I thought you just went to Nantucket with him."

"That was only a weekend. I've never been to Paris."

He didn't know what to say.

"I knew I shouldn't have . . . ," she began. "I'm not going to keep secrets from you."

He tried going back to the part where she said she loved him, but it was hard to stay with that thought.

"When are you going?"

"The next day," she said. "I mean, I could go to the game with you, but that's the night I need to pack. Unless I packed before . . ."

"How long will you be gone?"

"Two weeks," she said. "I didn't even use my vacation days last year."

"I'm sure you'll have a great time. Maybe Céline Dion will be performing at the Moulin Rouge," Paul said.

"Paul . . ."

"This isn't easy for me, you know," he said. He was caving in, collapsing inside. How much was someone supposed to take? "I've tried really hard to pretend I don't care. For all I know, maybe you should be with him. He's probably better for you in all kinds of ways — "

"Stop saying that," she said. "I can decide what's best for me. This whole situation isn't easy for any of us."

"I mean, where've we ever been?" Paul said. "Worcester."

"That's right," Tamsen said. "And as I recall, we had a rather fine time in Worcester."

Paul wanted to change the subject but couldn't.

"Just tell me something," he asked her. "Do you love me?"

"Yes, Paul. I love you. I just told you that."

"Do you love Stephen?"

"Paul," she said. "I don't think we should be talking about this. You're both — "

"Different," he said. "I know."

She paused.

"Now that his divorce is final," she said, "he thinks maybe we should start thinking about taking it to the next level."

"Is that how he put it?" Paul asked. "It sounds like a video game."

She didn't respond.

"So how do you feel about that?" he asked her. "Taking it to the next level."

"I think we need to talk about it. That's what we're going to Paris to figure out. I'm trying really hard to be honest about this. With both of you. I think it'll be good for us to get away from all the distractions. I'm not telling you this to hurt you."

"Why can't you figure it out in Cranston?" Paul said. "Or Rehoboth? People figure stuff out in Rehoboth all the time. Rehoboth is a very good place to figure things out. I've been there. There's absolutely nothing distracting in Rehoboth."

Part of him didn't want her to "figure it out." As long as she didn't, nothing would change. The status quo was hardly ideal, but it was better than change, if change was for the worse.

"Don't worry about it," she told him, but she seemed aware of how feeble her reassurance was. "You're my Paul. You're always going to be my Paul."

She reached into her purse and dropped a small metallic blue and silver object on the coffee table, a cell phone.

"I had to get one for work," she explained. "I'll leave you the number if you need to call me, but I'm sure it won't work in Europe. It only works here in large cities if I'm outdoors — the reception is terrible, but I might be able to check my voice mail."

He'd resisted getting a cell phone, mostly because it was another expense he didn't need, but he also thought of all the cool places he'd been and the people he'd met, looking for a pay phone. Sometimes he liked being out of reach. A cell phone was probably in his future, though, he knew.

She wrote her number on a piece of paper. He took it from her and thanked her.

He wondered if there was a way to salvage the situation. Nothing occurred to him. When she said she was tired and wanted to go to bed, he thought for a moment and decided he'd rather get in his car and drive home. It was late, but failing again in bed that night would be too much. He wanted to scream, punch a hole in the wall, beg her not to go — *order* her not to go — but if she was going to be in Paris thinking about him, he wanted the image that lingered to be a positive one. He told her he wasn't pouting or trying to be dramatic. He just wanted to go home. He tried to smile.

"Have fun in Paris," he said, rising to go. He turned around again when he'd reached the door. "You really do deserve to be happy. I mean it. That's what I want for you."

He wanted Stephen to choke on a croissant.

Thus when Paul's friend Murph called to ask him if he was still interested in the Red Sox tickets, a Saturday afternoon game against the hated Yankees, starting at three to accommodate national television, Paul apologized and said he still wanted to go but couldn't get a date to use the other ticket. Tamsen had told him, on the phone, that she didn't like the way they'd left things and wanted to see him before she left. About what? Paul wondered. Did she need to break up with him before she went to Paris? She said she'd be driving up that night, though she'd have to leave early the next morning. Murph said he'd be Paul's date, as long as Paul didn't try to get him drunk and take advantage of him.

"When has anybody ever had to *try* to get you drunk?" Paul said.

"Point well made, my friend," Murph said.

Paul hoped a Yankees-Sox game would take his mind off

Tamsen's going to Paris with Stephen. Murph told Paul to meet him at the will-call window. Paul arrived early and bought Tamsen a Red Sox cap at the souvenir shop across the street from the ballpark for her to wear on her trip. Paul hoped it would remind Stephen, every time he saw it (even in the photographs they looked at later), of Tamsen's split loyalties — assuming she wasn't driving up to give him bad news. He kept the receipt, on the chance that he would need to return the hat. Murph was a corpulent man with white hair and a florid face. He looked something like Tip O'Neill would have looked if he'd let himself go. The seats were incredible, boxes seven rows from the field, just to the third-base side behind home plate. Paul thanked his friend and asked him how much he owed him.

"Tut-tut," Murph said with a thick Back Bay accent. "Your money's no good here. You want a beer?"

Paul nodded. Murph made his way to the concessions area, and when he returned, he was carrying a tray containing four beers and a gigantic box of Cracker Jacks. "I get the prize in the Cracker Jacks," he said, handing Paul the tray.

"Jesus, Murph," Paul said. "I thought not even the pope could buy four beers at a time in Fenway Park." The strict limit was two per customer.

Paul drank his beers, and when they were gone, Murph went and got four more, commenting that he suspected management watered down the beer so that the fans didn't get too hammered, especially during Yankees games. With the sun on his face, Paul closed his eyes and enjoyed the buzz in the air, the gentle, rolling purr of the crowd, the smell of fresh-cut grass, and the spicy aromas of bratwurst and Italian sausages emanating from the grills beyond the Fenway confines. He loved the famous Green Monster, the forty-foot wall in left field, not because of the unique dimensions it gave the park, or the odd caroms it created when balls bounced off it, or the way it forced opposing coaches to alter their strategies. He loved it because of how it kept the city out and made you feel as if you were watching the game inside a fortress. Murph kept the beers coming, particularly after Paul told him the woman he'd been seeing was going to Paris with her other boyfriend.

"But I must warn you," Murph said. "I have only one rule, and that is that one does not discuss girlfriends or wives at Fenway. If we must discuss such things, I know a pub in Jamaica Plain we can go to after the game where the barmaids make the girls at Hooters look like the Bulgarian Women's Choir."

The Red Sox lost the game in the eleventh inning when one of the Yankees' third-string utility players — it was always a goddamn third-string utility player — hit a home run in the top of the inning.

Paul begged off joining Murph at the pub, explaining that he had to get back. He'd switched from beer to Diet Cokes at the seventh-inning stretch, aware that he would be driving home on the MassPike, where state troopers patrolled for impaired drivers, particularly after sporting events. Traffic was slow out of downtown Boston but picked up by the time he reached Newton. Yet he found himself unable to drive much faster than fifty, even after traffic cleared, because he could not shake the feeling that he was driving to his doom, in which case there was no hurry.

Why else would Tamsen be driving up to see him before her trip, if not to break up with him or part ways, however she defined it? Yes, it was possible that she simply wanted to see him. If that was true, it could wait, but if she had something else to say to him, something important they had to talk about, well . . . that could *really* wait.

He pulled off the interstate at a rest stop in Framingham to think. He sat in his car, thinking. He looked at his watch. Thinking wasn't working. It was approaching eight o'clock, the sun sinking low in the western sky. He didn't want her to come visit, but what could he say to stop her? Whatever it was, he would have to think of it in the next fifteen minutes or so if he wanted to catch her before she left her house, given the time she'd said he could expect her.

He finally went inside the rest stop, shouldered his way through the lines of travelers waiting to order their food at the McDonald's, and found a pay phone on the wall between the men's and women's bathrooms. He didn't know what he was going to say, but he told himself honesty was the best policy. As her phone rang, he watched a truck driver playing a video game called *Road Rage*. Getting it out of his system, one hoped.

When he heard her answering machine, he hung up, fished the piece of paper she'd given him from his back pocket, and dialed the number to her cell phone. The ring sounded like any other phone he'd ever dialed. He noted, as it rang, that every single person working behind the counter at the McDonald's was morbidly obese.

Perhaps because he was thus distracted (he later excused himself), when her voice mail announced itself, he impulsively decided to go with the next best policy, which was dishonesty. He had to say something, or she'd worry. A white lie, he told himself, knowing even as he spoke that he was veering from white into somewhere between battleship and charcoal gray. He told her he'd stopped at a rest area on the way home, but when he got back to his car, it wouldn't start, so now he had to deal with that. He told her he'd be fine, not to worry, but he couldn't say exactly when he'd get back to Northampton. He said he hoped she hadn't left Rhode Island yet and told her to have a great time in Paris.

He hung up, banged himself on the head with the receiver, then hung up again. The damage was done.

The best-case scenario was that she'd get the message, buy his story, skip the visit, go to Paris, and have such a terrible time that when she got back, she'd forget to ask about his car trouble. As he stood in line at McDonald's, waiting to order something for dinner, he worked through the remaining scenarios. One was that she wouldn't get the message in time and would drive to his house and wait there for him, which meant he couldn't go home. She would probably check her home machine or her voice mail, get his message, and turn around, but he still couldn't go home, on the chance that she might go to his house and wait for him anyway. He didn't dare call to check his answering machine because Tamsen might have let herself in and might pick up the phone. Worse still, she would get his message, get in her car, drive to Boston, and then head west on the Pike to stop at every rest area to find him and rescue him. He wouldn't put it past her.

After he'd eaten, he went to his car, took an adjustable wrench from his tool box, and loosened the cable on his battery, so that when he tried, the car really wouldn't start. Then he went to sleep in the backseat. If she found him, it would look as if he'd been telling the truth.

He'd had better nights.

When he got home the following morning, he played back a message on his answering machine from Tamsen. She said that she hoped everything was all right and that she'd call him when she got back. At least she hadn't driven all the way to find him missing. The damage was minimal, but it was damage all the same.

He pictured Tamsen and Stephen in Paris, laughing gaily, wearing berets and striped shirts and smoking Gitanes and agreeing that Paul was a loser and she was better off without him. He pictured them clinking their wineglasses together, toasting their future.

À votre santé.

Merde.

12

Scared

H e went to the Bay State the next night, but it did nothing to lift his spirits. D. J., Mickey, and McCoy were at the end of the bar. Brickman was in the corner, talking to a sweet-looking doe-eyed blond at least a dozen years his junior. McCoy moved down three stools and bought Paul a Guinness.

"Who's Bricks talking to?" Paul asked. A charming guy when he wanted to be, Bricks had flirted with countless younger women before, but somehow this girl seemed too young, too innocent. Bricks drove a Porsche. He would offer the girl a ride home, and she would see the car and say yes, and why not? She was an adult, presumably. Tonight, for some reason, Paul found it annoying.

"Don't know," McCoy said. "You hear my news? I'm moving to Paris. Maybe at the end of the summer."

Paul was shocked. Nobody ever moved from Northampton.

"Why is everybody going to Paris?" Paul said. "You know, that thing about the French liking American jazz players in France is just a myth. They hate jazz in France. They hate Jerry Lewis too. They hate everything."

Brickman and the doe-eyed blond rose from the table and left. The girl was laughing, tipsy, perhaps already thinking of the story she would have to tell her friends back at the dormitory tomorrow.

"If he touches her," Paul joked, "swear ta God I'll put him in the hospital."

"He could get a room next to Bender," McCoy said.

"What's Bender doing in the hospital?"

"Heart attack."

"What?"

"Why does everybody say that?" McCoy said. "Am I mumbling? He. Had. A. Heart. Attack."

"Bender can't have a heart attack," Paul said. "Bender spends five hours a day in the gym. If he can have a heart attack, I should be dead. How?"

They'd found him on the bike path out by the mall after he'd cycled to Bread and Circus to buy organic produce.

"Poor Bender," Paul said. "What hospital is he in?"

"I don't know," McCoy said. He called out, "Does anybody know what hospital Bender is in?"

D. J. and Mickey shrugged.

It was raining as he walked to his car. He took stock. Bender had had a heart attack. His father couldn't speak. Stella was old. Mortality was everywhere he looked. When he got home, he lifted Stella onto the bed, where she lay with her chin on her paws. The Red Sox were playing in Oakland, the game only in the fifth inning, though it was past midnight on the East Coast. He listened to the game on the radio and to the rain drumming against the top of his window air conditioner and tried not to think about where Tamsen was or what she was doing.

He got online the following morning.

PaulGus: It's raining here today. Is it raining there?
HarrGus: NO
PaulGus: Are you lonely?
HarrGus: NO

PaulGus: Don't you wish you could talk to your wife?

HarrGus: YES

PaulGus: Karen said she felt lonely even when I was home. I knew exactly what she meant. By the end it felt like when you're on an airplane, sitting next to a person you'd like to talk to but you can't figure out how to break the ice. You shouldn't have to break the ice with your own spouse.

HarrGus: NO

PaulGus: The strange thing is, my main memories as a kid are of being alone. I remember being sent to my room. Sitting in my room alone, waiting to get out of trouble. Climbing trees and hiding in them for as long as I could to get away from everybody. I don't know why I wanted to get away from everybody. Don't you think that's odd?

HarrGus: YES

PaulGus: What I don't remember were times when the whole family was together. I mean, I remember the family being together but I'm always on the outside looking in. Sometimes I wonder if it had something to do with the accident. When I was okay but everybody else was hurt.

HarrGus: YES

PaulGus: I used to listen to all your classical records and I remember putting Barber's Adagio on the hi-fi and fantasizing that I was walking somewhere alone. Like I was trying to convince myself I wanted to be alone. I was bluffing.

HarrGus: YES

PaulGus: Mom's worried about me, isn't she?

HarrGus: YES

PaulGus: Are you?

HarrGus: YES

PaulGus: To tell the truth, I'm scared I'm not going to make it. Scared I'm going to always be lonely. I'm tired of giving myself little pep talks. Are you scared?

HarrGus: NO

PaulGus: Because of your faith?

HarrGus: YES

PaulGus: Have you ever been scared?

HarrGus: YES

PaulGus: I mean really scared?

HarrGus: YES

PaulGus: When? Sorry. You can't answer that. Do you want to talk about it?

HarrGus: NO

PaulGus: Are you sure?

PaulGus: Are you still there?

PaulGus: Forget I said anything. Sorry.

PaulGus: Sometimes I don't know when to leave well enough alone. I'll talk to you soon.

13

Pretzel Logic

The postcard from Paris was a print of van Gogh's painting *The Night Café*. On the back, she'd written, "Hey, Paul — how are you? Hope all is well. The food is fabulous here. I think I've gained five pounds. Love, T."

She hadn't mentioned the missed rendezvous — had she forgotten or, more to the point, had she forgiven him?

And were monkeys currently flying out of her butt?

At the bar, the word was that Bender's heart attack was entirely stress related. Paul found this worrisome. Running every day helped with stress, but he also needed to relax, to quiet himself inside. Tamsen had once suggested that he try yoga. He went to the Laundromat and looked on the bulletin board for a flyer for a yoga class, something not too crunchy-huggy. He found one offered by a woman named Amelia, who patiently explained to him on the phone, when he told her he'd always been interested in the martial arts, that yoga wasn't one of them.

Amelia was slender and serene and wore her hair in a fat black braid, and she smiled slyly when he cracked wise in class. It was all he could do to bite his lip and keep quiet one night when she'd led them from a *sarvangasana* or "candle" pose ("lie on your back and stick your legs as high in the air as they'll go, hands on hips") into a *halasana* or "plow" pose ("bring your legs down behind you until your toes touch the floor, your knees touch your forehead, and your rear end is sticking up in the air"), which had caused the gentle young man on the mat next to Paul to fart loudly. Everyone else in the room was too *centered in the moment* to say anything or even snicker.

"Do we have to pay extra for the aromatherapy?" Paul wanted to ask.

He liked the mindful breathing part. The poses hurt like hell, but that seemed to be the idea, learning how to get bent out of shape without getting bent out of shape. Amelia gave him a very cursory introduction to transcendental meditation theory, and he found that if he practiced it on his own at home, even without true instruction, it helped him feel calm, and sometimes the daydreams he experienced were wicked good.

His experience in yoga class was soured when a woman named Marty joined the group. He recognized her as one of his ex-wife's co-workers. She recognized him with a smile and said she'd just been talking to Karen that morning — they were going to sign up together for Amelia's prenatal yoga class.

"It's more effective than Lamaze," Marty said perkily, "and you don't have to drag your husband along to do it."

Until this point, Paul had been unaware that his ex-wife was pregnant.

His friends at the Bay State were sympathetic when he told them, and bought him beers to help drown his sorrows or at least give them a good soaking. It was clearly unfair of Karen to have children without him. Of course, she was a free agent and had hooked up with a nice guy named Kurt (or Kirk?), and she had the right to behave however she pleased and didn't need Paul's consent or permission to so much as blow her nose.

That didn't make it fair.

It probably meant she'd be getting married. That sucked too.

When he got home, he opened the top drawer of his dresser and, in it, the cigar-box-size jewelry case he'd inherited from his grandfather Paul, along with some of the old man's accessories, nothing fancy, a pair of cuff links featuring hunting dogs and flying ducks, a tie clasp in the shape of a Shriner's scimitar. In the back of the jewelry box, Paul found a small ziplock bag containing a folded cocktail napkin upon which he and Karen had written, "Rosemary, Sam (Samuel/Samantha), Henry, Caledonia," and, with a question mark after it, "Booker?" He considered mailing her the list they'd collaborated on, with a brief note saying, "These names you can't use."

Instead, he took the napkin into the bathroom, where he lifted the lid on the toilet and, using the matches he kept nearby, lit the napkin on fire, twisting it as it burned to make sure the flames consumed it before he dropped it into the bowl. He flushed twice.

"Chili for dinner?" Stella inquired from the doorway.

"Would you like to go for a walk?"

"I thought you'd never ask."

He carried her down the front steps. It was a fine summer evening, with a breeze rustling the leaves overhead to let the moonlight sift through. He had to slow down to let Stella catch up. He tried to remember the things he'd learned in yoga class and took a deep breath, in, hold it, out . . .

"Did something happen?" Stella asked.

"I found out Karen is pregnant. And remarrying. Probably."

"She's having a litter?"

"So to speak."

"And you're not one of the fathers?"

"Nope."

"I thought she didn't want kids."

"Apparently she's changed her mind."

He turned left at the corner, heading for the cemetery. He didn't expect Stella to understand, and for her part, she seemed to know better than to probe, though she stayed close to him as they walked, something she'd always done when she knew he was upset about something. He wasn't sure how she knew, but she did.

Back at the house, he lifted the dog, climbed the front steps, and set her down. He told her to lie down, poured himself a scotch, and then rejoined her, sitting on the porch swing. The scotch tasted good. He sipped, even though alcohol had the unwanted side effect of letting the past leak back into the present. Some people said spirits damaged the memory, but he found the opposite to be true — they kept memories alive.

He rocked. It was the same porch swing where he and Karen had discussed when she should stop taking the pill. They'd agreed on New Year's Eve arbitrarily. They made love a few times a week after that, but as the year came to a close and the nights grew longer, they made love less and less frequently as he more often failed to sustain his erections, and he asked himself if he was afraid of the moment when she would go off the pill and the stakes would go up. Afraid of what, though? Then she'd said they needed more money first, so Paul put in extra hours at his computer at his office to get more money, until Karen said he was never there for her. He argued that he couldn't be in two places at once, to which she'd replied that he couldn't even be in one place at once.

Was it Karen who'd stopped believing first, and he'd caught it from her? To have a kid, she had to believe in one of three things: herself, him, or the future. To believe in herself was on her To Do list, but when she looked inside herself for strength, she saw ferocity instead, at the end anyway, like a thunderstorm darkening the midday sky. Then one night the fights stopped, and that was worse than the conflict — that meant she'd quit. To believe in him wasn't much easier. His heart was good, she said, not a mean bone in his body, but at the same time, there was something wrong, missing. She couldn't be more specific. Something made him run away from her, she said, some hidden thing that made it hard for him to trust people. She'd felt kept at a distance, unimportant, unseen, and that wasn't going to change, and she was tired of it.

The future was easier for her to believe in, except that it was a fantasy. She wanted to be a stay-at-home mom in a big house with four kids, she'd said. He tried to make her dream come true, but every time he managed to tuck a thousand dollars away toward a down payment on a house, she wanted to buy a new couch, or take a vacation, or replace a perfectly good appliance, and the money got pissed away. Her pay, working in an art gallery, did nothing to further the cause. The farther they got from their goal, the more they argued, despaired, drifted, until he envied those mythical couples who had nothing but each other and screwed three times a day using their unpaid bills for a mattress. Each time he failed, he tried to shrug it off, but each time he shrugged, another piece of his body fell to the ground, his fingers, hands, arms, legs, internal organs, until he had nothing left to shrug with — and then finally she had to walk away, telling him, "I can't fix this."

His friends told him life goes on, but what they failed to mention was that life goes on indeed, on and on and on and on and on. There was no magic anywhere to be found. The days dragged. He walked around his little town with a giant billboard sprouting from his skull that read DIVORCED. "When does the billboard fall off?" he asked friends experienced in such matters. "It doesn't," they told him. "They just build a road around you."

He went inside to refresh his drink, feeling a bit unsteady on his feet, while the dreaming dog twitched her tail and wuffled in her sleep. In the kitchen, dust bunnies lay undisturbed in the corners. It was the same apartment where he and Karen had tried to make something bigger and better, something more than the sum of their parts. Maybe it was time to move. He saw the walls she'd painted, thinking it would brighten things up and possibly save the marriage, the first of her last-ditch efforts. He closed his eyes and heard the ghost sounds, laughter, music, fragments of dinner party conversations, flitting about the house like moths, eating holes in the fabric of time, sounds of summer barbecues, autumn rakes scraping the sidewalk, a Christmas goose crackling in the oven, because everybody else cooked turkeys, so he and Karen did what they could to start their own tradition. He heard the noise of her screaming at him until the piano rang in harmonic sympathy, and he heard her sobbing softly from across the room, the kind of sorrow you can't comfort because you're the cause of it.

What would the Zen masters do at a time like this? Did their hearts break like everybody else's? Did they drive past their ex's new house at two in the morning to see if the light was on in the bedroom window? He drew a deep, slow breath and focused on the beating of his own heart until a freight train split the night silence, blasting toward Brattleboro, making the house shake. He wondered who was driving the train and whether they were headed toward home or away from home. Did the engineer know where love goes when it dies, or how it was possible that hummingbirds can cross the ocean while words can fail to fly half a pillow's distance? And on those cold winter nights when snow obscured the tracks, did he ever lose faith? That the rails would still be there, that the bridges would hold, that there really was a Vermont, that there really was a train, and that the clickety-clack he heard wasn't just the sound of his own heart moving away from him in the night, growing fainter and fainter, beat by beat.

Paul had weathered the storm and made it to spring, and then Tamsen found him, with her smile and her wet, bright eyes! The phone rang and magic reentered the world, like the day Houdini was born, nurses in fishnet stockings, doctors in top hats and tails, asking for silence as they levitated Mother Houdini, passed a brass hoop around her as she pushed and groaned, the calliope playing "Entrance of the Gladiators," until suddenly and with great flourish the doctors pulled from between her legs a bouncing seven-pound white rabbit, and the hospital gasped, and then a baby was heard to cry from inside a padlocked cabinet in the next room. So Houdini was born, and so Tamsen was delivered to Paul, entering off to the side while he wasn't looking. Her arrival astonished him. It had no explanation. It came after much pain and labor and crying and gnashing of teeth, unexpected and astonishing. Presto — ta-da!

And now she was in Paris with Stephen.

He was too drunk to know whether to laugh or cry, but he thought he might feel better if he did something impulsive. He took his drink and the phone out on the porch and sat back down on the swing, nearly missing it as it bounced off his legs.

"Who are you calling?" Stella asked him. He dialed 411 and got the number for his ex-wife. Stella's ears pricked up when she heard Karen's name.

"Paul," Stella said, "I have to say, I really think this is a bad idea. This is way too late to be calling anybody."

"Aw, come on," Paul slurred, "I just want to congratulate her. I'm sure she's been trying to reach me to tell me the news in person."

"Put the phone down," Stella said. "Seriously."

He put the phone down, then picked it up again and dialed Tamsen's number. He wanted to leave her a message to tell her how sorry he was for having stood her up. He wanted . . .

Bad idea. He hung up after listening to her outgoing message, the sound of her voice soothing to him. He lay down on the porch swing, his knees bent. He was so tired.

When he awoke, it was morning. He sat up, the world swimming for a moment until he remembered he was still lying on the porch swing. His head hurt. Stella was next to him on the floor and opened her eyes and yawned. He looked down and saw that in her sleep she'd had an accident, a turd about the size of a minidoughnut, pressed into the porch floor. He collected his thoughts, got some Kleenexes and picked up the turd and flushed it down the toilet, and then washed the spot with a wet paper towel.

"My bad," she said.

"Not at all — it's my fault," Paul said. "I'm a lousy pet owner. I should have walked you."

"You did walk me," Stella said.

"Oh," Paul said, remembering little of the previous night. He opened the door, and Stella followed him to the kitchen, where he checked and filled her food dish and water bowl, then filled a bowl of his own with cereal and milk.

"Anyway, it wasn't your fault," he told her. "You couldn't help it."

"Help what?"

"The accident."

"What accident?"

"The turd," he would have said but didn't. She'd forgotten already, her memory failing, but he let it go. Her dignity was more important than making sure his apology had registered.

14

The Laughing Club

He slept poorly during the time that Tamsen and Stephen were in Paris, "taking it to the next level." Rather than toss and turn pointlessly, stewing in his own insecurities, he tried to get work done, logging on and using the Internet. Sleep and sleep deprivation seemed appropriate research topics. He learned how the homeostatic system regulates sleep by responding to the body's adenosine levels, while in the circadian system, light stimulates photoreceptive ganglia in the back of the retina to send a message to the suprachiasmatic nucleus in the hypothalamus to tell the pineal gland on the epithalmus to excrete melatonin. Who knew? He typed:

> Rats deprived of REM sleep for a few days start attacking their handlers and one another. They become hypermetabolic and burn huge amounts of calories standing still. Their hair falls out. The first to die, die of sepsis after five days, and the majority die at about the three-week mark, while the hardiest last as long as a month. Dolphins and whales get very little REM sleep, one cerebral hemisphere dozing off while the other half stays awake. Even fruit flies need sleep. Of all the creatures tested, the duck-billed platypus gets more REM sleep than any other animal.

"What does a platypus dream about?" he wondered.

"Probably about being anything other than a platypus," Stella said.

It became relevant when his sister told him Carl wasn't sleeping much, maybe four or five hours a night by his own estimation, and he was probably understating the case. Paul told Bits people who are sleep deprived never know how much they're suffering, forgetting things, making mistakes, never recognize their failures of commission and omission, their attention lapses, because their judgment is the first thing to go, once sleep loss turns their brains to mush, and they can no longer self-assess.

"I talked to Erica," Bits said. "She says Carl's been under a lot of stress since Dad's stroke. She's hoping he'll take something for it."

"He won't," Paul said.

"I know," Bits said. "Though he started drinking warm milk before bedtime. They say that actually works."

He suddenly felt sorry for his brother. He wasn't sure that he ever had before. Until now, Paul had never wanted to admit how much he relied on his brother and needed him to be strong. For a moment, he regretted destroying the list of Carl's PINs. If he had them, he could keep a surreptitious but benevolent eye on Carl's well-being.

He was checking his e-mail a few days after his conversation with Bits when Tamsen instant-messaged him. He'd intentionally tried not to keep exact track of the days. In his fantasies, Tamsen would have flown home early, taken a limo to his door from the airport, and told him breathlessly that all was forgiven and what a mistake she'd made, going to Paris with the wrong man.

TamsenP: hey paul. busy?

PaulGus: Just got in. I was wondering when I'd hear from you.
  Welcome back. How are you?

TamsenP: tired. i would have called you last night but i didn't

get home until two in the morning. they lost my luggage.
they called this morning and said they found it and they'd
ship it to my door.

PaulGus: Bummer.

TamsenP: i tried to e-mail you from paris at an internet cafe
but the guy there couldn't figure out how to get to aol. did
you get my postcard?

PaulGus: Got it. Thanks. So you had a good time?

TamsenP: it was beautiful. i'll tell you all about it when i see
you. if you want me to.

PaulGus: Okay.

TamsenP: would you like to get offline and talk on the phone?

PaulGus: I'd *like* to see you in person. But this is okay, for
now.

TamsenP: how's your car? i was worried.

PaulGus: All fixed. The battery cable was loose. I'm sorry I
missed you.

TamsenP: I was worried that you were stranded somewhere.

PaulGus: Nothing serious.

TamsenP: i'm relieved.

PaulGus: Did you talk? You and Stephen.

TamsenP: yup.

PaulGus: And?

TamsenP: inconclusive.

PaulGus: What does that mean?

He was glad to put the lie about the car behind him. There
were long pauses between their transmissions. He suspected
Tamsen was walking the line as she tried to answer his questions
honestly without betraying Stephen or hurting Paul's feelings.

TamsenP: just that. i think it's still too soon to tell. i don't
think he knows what he wants. he's not even sure he wants

to stay in the east. his brother has a radiology practice in los angeles and he's invited stephen to join it. stephen's ex has been thinking of taking the kids there permanently, so there's a chance they all might move. or stay. or he'd go and she wouldn't, or vice versa.

PaulGus: Would you go if he did?

TamsenP: i don't know what to say. it's a possibility.

PaulGus: It is?

TamsenP: just a possibility. i don't feel like i could leave my mother. i know she'd be all right but i think our weekly dinners mean a lot to her. other reasons.

PaulGus: It's funny how the people you love make your life so complicated, but if you didn't have someone to love, your life would be unlivable.

TamsenP: funny "ha-ha" or funny "peculiar?"

PaulGus: There's a song called "Funny Peculiar," Thelonious Monk.

TamsenP: i know. we were listening to it in class before i left.

PaulGus: How's Sheila? Pick up any good Edith Piaf CDs?

TamsenP: nope. sheila's fine. i assume. i'm going to see her tonight. wickenden cafe. the same place we went after you spoke to my book club.

PaulGus: I'm glad you're home. Safe.

TamsenP: i missed you. i probably shouldn't be saying this but i thought about you every day. just so you know. i almost called you a couple of times. i'm having a hard time.

PaulGus: I'm glad to hear you say that. I missed you too. A lot. Can I ask you a question?

TamsenP: anything.

PaulGus: I know this is just going to make me sound insecure, and I'm sorry, but I really need to ask. Do you still love me?

TamsenP: of course i do.

PaulGus: Why? Humor me.

TamsenP: i can't do this right now.

PaulGus: Never mind, then. It's just been a rough couple of weeks, self-confidence-wise.

He waited for her to respond. For a moment he wondered if she'd logged off. Perhaps she had to take a phone call. Then:

TamsenP: i love you because you're extraordinary. i love you for your sense of humor and your spirit and you have this weird mix of sadness and optimism and self-absorption and selflessness and silly and serious and i don't know why. there's a million things and no real reason. i love the way you see things. the way you get me. i love how fair you try to be. i love how soft your eyes are. i love how you're loyal to your friends. i love the way you are with your dog. i love the way you walk. i love how you're interested in other people, which has always been a sign to me of a fine person. i don't know, paul. i don't spend much time analyzing it. i just go with the feeling. i love how you can make me laugh whenever you want to.

PaulGus: Does Stephen make you laugh?

TamsenP: paul, i'm not going to get into comparisons.

PaulGus: I love your laugh. I live for it. Sometimes I feel like the reason I was put on this earth was to make you laugh. Does that sound too grandiose?

TamsenP: that sounds nice. no one makes me laugh the way you do. no one. even the sophomoric stuff. we're our own little two-person laughing club. no matter how bad anything gets, you always keep your sense of humor.

PaulGus: Whistling through the graveyard, as they say.

TamsenP: it says something about you. it recommends you.

PaulGus: You should come here and live with me. You'd be a kept woman.

TamsenP: and you'd be my sugar daddy?

PaulGus: I'd buy you mink stoles and we'd have T-bones and martinis every night and ride around in my convertible.

TamsenP: now you're talking. i'd have to redecorate your swinging bachelor pad though. apropos of nothing, my feet are killing me.

PaulGus: Why?

TamsenP: i don't know. they're always killing me. i wish you were here. you could hide under my desk and rub my feet

PaulGus: I could do more than that.

TamsenP: change of subject — how is your father feeling?

PaulGus: Hard to say. About the same, I suppose. My mother said his grip is getting stronger but it's still just the right hand. No spoken words yet. He doesn't always recognize people, but she thinks he understands more and more every day. Sometimes he gets confused.

TamsenP: have you been working with him?

PaulGus: Trying. Sometimes I get confused too.

TamsenP: in what way?

PaulGus: I seldom know what to say. The "conversations" are fairly one-sided.

TamsenP: but you knew that.

PaulGus: True.

TamsenP: what do you "talk" about?

PaulGus: Sometimes I try to find out what he's feeling. Not easy to do when your vocabulary is limited to two words. On the other hand, we never had much luck even with the entire dictionary at our disposal.

TamsenP: i'm sure it's helping.

PaulGus: My sister says Carl isn't sleeping. None of my
business, I guess.

TamsenP: give him a call, why don't you?

PaulGus: Maybe. I missed you.

TamsenP: can you come see me next weekend? i thought
maybe we could go to the ihop. you can choose the syrup.

PaulGus: I'd love that.

15

Faith

I have a confession to make," he told her. They were in her living room. They'd gone to the movies. She was happy to see him, and he was happy to see her. He had to spoil it. He could see no alternative. His conscience wouldn't let him do otherwise. He'd spent the time driving down from Massachusetts thinking of what words to use. They'd launched their affair on the premise that they could tell each other anything. Anything less than that, and cascade to failure could be reliably predicted. Full disclosure was indicated, with atonement to follow, if all went well. "You're going to hate me."

"I'm not going to hate you," she said.

"Yes, you are," he said.

He wanted her to say, "No, I won't, I promise," but she didn't.

"The day I went to Fenway with Murph," he said, "I didn't actually have car trouble. I lied."

There was a pause.

"You lied?" The look on her face was more one of confusion or disbelief than one of anger. "Why?"

"I didn't plan on it," he said. "I was going to tell you the truth if you answered the phone, but when I got your machine, I . . . froze."

"That doesn't make any sense," she said. "Froze about what?"

"I was afraid you were going to break up with me," he said. "That that was why you were coming. To clear the way so that you could have a good time in Paris. And the only way I could stop that from happening was not to be there. It was too complicated to leave on your machine."

"So you lied?" she said. "That comes easier to you?"

"Not usually," he said. "If it came easy, it wouldn't have bothered me so much. I couldn't live with it. That's why I had to tell you."

She looked at him like he'd put his underwear on outside his pants.

"I used poor judgment."

"You get that feeling, do you?" she said.

"Tell me what you think."

"I'm trying to think of what to say," she said. "It leaves me a little speechless."

The idea of losing her good opinion was too much to bear.

"You didn't have car trouble?"

"Nope."

"So where were you?"

"At the rest area," he said.

"So you just lied about the —"

"Battery. It wasn't on purpose," he told her. "I mean, not consciously. It just came out."

"That's supposed to make me feel better?" she said.

"I told you you'd hate me," he said.

This was where she was supposed to say, "I don't hate you." She looked at him for a long time.

"Were you . . . ," she began.

"Was I what?" Paul asked.

She paused again, changing her mind about whatever it was she was going to say.

"I'm glad you told me the truth," she said at last. "This just

really raises serious questions about . . . trust. It's so basic. Donald lied to me. It's fundamentally undermining when . . . I know
we're not supposed to judge each other, but I'm just not sure I
want to be . . ."

"Be what?" This was a blank he did not want to fill in.

"I won't get drawn into this again," she said. "It's not my job.
It's your responsibility, not mine."

"It is my responsibility. I'm agreeing with you. The idea of
you spending two weeks in Paris was driving me crazy. I'm not
making excuses. I just wanted to make it clear to you. I feel
terrible."

"Just say you're sorry," Stella had strongly recommended.
"Don't say, 'I'm sorry, *but* . . .'"

"Do you want me to leave?" he asked.

She looked at him in silence for a very long time. Before she
could answer, the telephone rang. It was her friend Caitlin. Paul
felt saved by the bell or, more accurately, the chirp. Tamsen went
into the kitchen to take the call and after a few minutes returned
to Paul, putting her hand over the mouthpiece.

"Do you mind?" she said. "I haven't had a chance to call her
and she has to put Ruby to bed soon. I might be a few minutes."

"Talk all you want," Paul said. Caitlin liked him, he knew, and
would hopefully advocate on his behalf. It seemed like a good
time for Tamsen to vent with one of her friends. "I'm not going
anywhere."

Tamsen went into her bedroom to talk. Paul waited. He
watched the fish in her aquarium. He waited some more, sitting
on the couch. He grabbed a soda from her fridge and sat back on
the couch, and after a few minutes, just to make himself useful,
he started to clean her fish tank, which she'd apparently not gotten around to yet.

Finally Tamsen came out of the bedroom, nearly an hour
after she'd gone in. He'd heard laughter through the closed door.

That was a good sign. Tamsen sat on the couch next to Paul, who faced her.

"How's Caitlin?" he asked meekly.

"She's good," Tamsen said. "She liked the wineglasses I brought her from Paris."

"What else did you talk about?"

"Oh, a lot of things," Tamsen said. "She always helps me get things in perspective." He felt ashamed, exiled. In limbo. Not in hell but close enough to feel the heat through the soles of his shoes.

"Can I just say again how sorry I am?" Paul said.

"Sure," Tamsen said. "I know you are."

"I need you to forgive me," he said.

"I know," she said. He waited. Karen used to drive him crazy, refusing him forgiveness when he asked for it, saying instead, "There's nothing to forgive," which was tantamount to saying, "The pain you feel isn't real," making it worse instead of just making it go away with a simple word.

"Can you?" he asked.

"I just don't want to be put in this position."

"What do you mean?" he asked.

"I'm not sure I can explain it," she said. "I just don't like the way this engages me. I get drawn in, trying to fix somebody else's problem, and I know I shouldn't but I feel guilty if I don't try. And when things don't work out, I feel even worse."

"I don't understand."

"You cleaned my fish tank?"

"Was that okay?"

"Thank you," she said. "I've been meaning to get to it."

"I'm still confused," he said, returning to the subject under discussion.

She took his hand, holding it in both of hers. The gesture meant more to him than he could say.

"I'm not saying, 'It's not you, it's me' — this is definitely you," she said. "But this is also familiar."

"What is?"

"I take on too much, and then I get overwhelmed. It makes me want to hide or run away. It's why I didn't want to stay with my mother in the hospital when my father died," Tamsen said. "She told me she didn't need me to be there, but I knew she was just saying that."

"Where were you?" Paul asked.

"Down the hall," Tamsen said. "Watching CNN. Not paying attention, just letting the news sort of wash over me. Hoping it would happen and he'd die while I wasn't in the room. And praying. I'd been praying ever since he was diagnosed, asking God to save my father. Then when we knew it was hopeless, I prayed for God to take him in his sleep. But I meant my sleep."

"You went down the hall to watch television," Paul said. "There's nothing wrong with that."

"I was hiding," she said. "And God didn't answer any of my prayers, so I decided then and there to stop praying, because it wasn't helping anything — I was just fooling myself into feeling better, and I didn't want to do that anymore. I'm not sure why I'm telling you this. I'm sorry."

"I'm the one who should be sorry," he said.

She looked at him.

"You certainly are," she said. "I'm not saying you can't count on me. I don't walk away from somebody just because they screw up. Which you did. It hurts to be lied to. It just does. But I know you. And just so you know, I am steadfast, and I am forgiving. Caitlin said everybody should get one chance to fuck up. Deep down, I do believe in you. I know how I feel about you. My love isn't going anywhere. If you want to know, I wasn't coming up to break up with you. I was coming up because I didn't feel like I'd explained things properly and I wanted to be clear."

"Oh," he said.

"Just don't . . ." She dropped the thought. He didn't pick it up for her.

"It's not going to happen again."

She looked at him. He suspected that was the same promise her ex-husband had made to her. It was weak. What else could he say?

"I'm reluctant to say too much because I know how down on yourself you get," Tamsen told him. She paused and seemed to him to be choosing her words carefully. "Look, I've made mistakes just like everybody else. I'm no one to sit in judgment. And I'm not your mother either. I just think you need to look at some of the things you do and consider what sort of changes you might want to make. Okay?"

"Okay," he said.

"We can talk about it some more if you want," she said.

"I'm good," he said. "Unless you want to."

"I'm tired," she said. "My internal clock is five hours different."

"I got you something," he told her. He went to his bag and retrieved the Red Sox hat he'd purchased for her at Fenway Park, a genuine MLB model and not one of those one-size-fits-all adjustable hats they sold at supermarkets. She tried it on. It fit.

"How did you know what size?" she asked.

"I measured."

"Measured what?" she said. "I don't have any other hats."

"I measured your head," he said.

"With what?" she asked.

"With a shoe lace," he told her. "While you were sleeping."

"That's a little weird," she said. "Thoughtful but weird. I got you something too. Wait here."

As he watched her aquarium, a blue cichlid about the size of a mint Milano cookie took a nip from the tail of a smaller fish. The tail on the smaller fish had a saw-toothed edge from multiple bites. Paul saw the cruel logic of it, each nip inexorably reducing the victim fish's ability to propel itself, making it slower and slower until it was finally easy to catch.

When Tamsen rejoined him, she sat next to him on the couch, leaned against him, and handed him a present, about the size of a Kleenex box. In it, wrapped in white tissue paper, he found a small brass replica of the Eiffel Tower with a thermometer attached to it.

"You collect thermometer kitsch, right?"

He'd told her how his father had brought him an Empire State Building souvenir thermometer after a trip to New York, and a Washington Monument souvenir thermometer after a trip to Washington, D.C. He was surprised that she remembered.

"I love it," he told her. "It's really thoughtful."

"It would look nice next to my Paul Bunyan snow globe," she said, smiling. Perhaps she hadn't meant to, or maybe he was just reading things into her statement that weren't there, grasping at straws, but unless he was mistaken, she'd just evoked an image of the two of them living together someday.

"I'm so jet-lagged I can't see straight," she said. "Do you mind?"

She lay down on the couch, her head in his lap. He took the acrylic throw from the back of the couch and covered her with it against the cool night air. He stroked her hair.

"Oh — have I said I forgive you?" she asked, her eyes closed.

"Not in those exact words," he said.

She gave him a moment to think about it, then whispered, "I forgive you."

16

The Gathering Storm

He retained Tamsen's good opinion through the summer. He'd lost almost fifteen pounds since he'd started running and cutting back on Klondike bars and doughnuts. Sometimes she joined him on his runs. In his competition with Stephen, he neither gained nor lost ground, as best he could tell, though he tried not to measure.

At the end of August, the students returned, Smithies and their moms, and occasionally dads walking three steps behind, trolling the store aisles and forming lines at the cash registers downtown, buying printer cartridges and plastic laundry baskets and message boards for their dorm room doors. You could tell the freshmen by the dubious glaze in their eyes. He was getting ready to head down to the Bay State one night to check out a blues band when Stella was suddenly in the doorway.

"Don't go. Something is going to happen," she said.

She was panting. It was a warm late-summer evening, maybe seventy-five or eighty degrees, but not so warm that she'd be overheated. A breeze had kicked up, making the air quite pleasant. Saliva dripped from her tongue.

"Just calm down and tell me what's going to happen."

"I don't know. Something bad."

"Something bad?"

"Paul, please . . ."

"What? What do you want me to do?"

"Don't go. Stay here. Make it stop."

"Make what stop? What do you want me to stop?"

"The thing that's going to happen."

"Well, if you won't tell me what you think is going to happen, how can I make it stop?"

Stella was beside herself with fear.

Then he heard it, distant but distinct, a low rumble that could have been a train slowly snaking through town but wasn't. He looked out the window at the sky. He saw a distant flash of lightning. Stella paced and panted, unable to listen.

"It's just thunder," Paul said. "You've been through thunderstorms before."

"This one is different," she insisted.

"How is this one different?"

"I don't know. I just know it is. I have a feeling."

"You have a feeling. Now you're psychic?"

"You don't have to be psychic to know when something bad is going to happen. These things cause fires. I can't run like I used to . . ."

Another rumble sounded, still distant but stronger than the first, which meant the storm was indeed getting closer. That she'd heard it before he did was no surprise.

"Do you want me to close the windows? Let me — "

"I don't care if you close the windows," she interrupted. "What good is closing the windows going to do?"

The sky was lit with a flash of lightning. He heard the first few drops of rain splattering down on the roof. The air smelled of ozone, a stainless steel fresh-cut hay smell. She'd probably smelled the storm coming long before she'd heard the thunder.

"You want to go for a ride in the car or something?"

"Oh God, no!"

This time the thunder was loud and explosive, maybe a seven or an eight on a scale of one to ten. He tried putting his hands over her ears, tried putting his arms around her to calm her down, as the clouds broke and the rains came down all at once. Wind shook the lilac tree outside the kitchen window.

"Stella, it's okay, you're indoors. Nothing is going to happen."

"Make it stop."

"Shhh, shhh . . . Come on."

He led her under the kitchen table and told her to lie down. She often took shelter under the kitchen table during storms, but tonight it wasn't enough. He turned all the lights off, grabbed the bedspread from his bed, and threw it over the kitchen table, arranging it so that the hem touched the floor, and then he got under the table with her. When the lightning flashed, the bedspread blocked the light, save a thin line where the bedspread met the floor. He put his arm around her and stroked her face. She was able to sit, but too nervous to lie down.

"Paul, I don't like this. This is dangerous. This is a bad one."

"Shhh, shhh, shhh, there's no danger, Stell — you're in a big, strong house and you're very safe here. You're very safe."

"This house is made of wood. Wood can catch fire."

"That's your blood memory, Stell," Paul said, stroking her. "Thousands of years ago, back when you guys were still evolving and living outdoors with the wolves — "

Another crackle of thunder.

"Jesus. Shit! I'm sorry, I'm sorry — oh my God . . ."

"Do you remember the story about men and dogs?"

"No."

"You don't remember?"

"No."

"About how we got to be friends?"

"No."

She seemed terribly confused, as if she didn't know where she was.

"Tell me the story again," she asked.

"I'd be happy to," he said. He put his face next to hers. "Thousands and thousands of years ago, back when you were living outdoors with the wolves, sometimes forest fires started from lightning strikes, and those of you in the pack who were too old to run away from the fire got left behind, and now you feel like that's what's going to happen, so that's what you're afraid of, but Stella, that was thirty thousand years ago. That's over two hundred thousand years ago in dog years."

"Tell me the story," she insisted. "Tell me about thirty thousand years ago."

"Thirty thousand years ago is when dogs and people first got to be friends. Today, scientists digging around in the ruins of old Neolithic villages sometimes find the remains of dog bones and human bones lying side by side."

"Were the dogs chewing on the human bones?"

"No," he said. "The dog bones were usually found near where the garbage dumps were, which means that some dogs stayed wolves but others decided to become scavengers and live off what the humans left for them, and then some of you who'd become scavengers got to be very clever and figured out how to make humans your friends."

"How did we do that?"

"By looking us in the eye and not being afraid," Paul said. "Only the very bravest and the very smartest among you had the courage to come up and eat out of human beings' hands, because up to then we'd been the enemy. We'd both been wild animals, humans and dogs, but somewhere along the line, at about the same time in history, we decided there was a better way to live together, and that's when dogs moved indoors instead of hanging around the dumps. And dogs liked it indoors because it was warm and dry and easier to get food, and so out of gratitude, dogs learned how to do jobs for humans."

"Like guard sheep?"

"Like guard sheep, and pull carts . . ."

"And rescue people?"

"And rescue people by using their keen sense of smell. Dogs even guarded children from other beasts in the wilderness. Dogs were very helpful and very happy to earn the table scraps the humans would give them, and the humans were very grateful to have dogs as friends. Humans and dogs had learned to love one another, in a way that no other two species have ever learned to love one another. Out of all the other animals on the planet, there's never been another example of two species that decided to love one another."

"Not cats either."

"No, not cats," Paul said. "People love cats and cats certainly enjoy people, but cats don't lay down their lives and die for people the way dogs do. Cats don't swim out into lakes and pull drowning children ashore, or run into burning buildings, or leap into the darkness when they hear a threatening noise. And if a person dies in a cabin in the woods, and there's a cat in the cabin with him, the cat will eat the human's dead body rather than starve to death, but a dog would starve to death too, rather than betray the friendship. Some people say that makes cats smarter, but I say that makes dogs better."

"So if you died, I couldn't eat you?"

"You wouldn't want to."

"I wouldn't?"

"No."

"Could I roll in you?"

"Sure, that would be all right." The lightning and thunder had stopped. It was still raining.

"So people let dogs live in their houses because they loved them, not just because they needed their sheep guarded."

"That's right," Paul said. "And it used to be that lightning would hit houses and make them catch fire, but that doesn't happen anymore because of lightning rods."

"What's a lightning rod?"

"It's a thing that directs the electricity away from the house."

"What's electricity?"

"That's what lightning is made out of. It's too much to explain right now, but the point is, you're going to be all right in the house because you're safe and dry and I think the storm is over. Do you feel better?"

He listened and heard only the sound of rain drops dripping from the trees.

"A little." She was calmer. She looked at him. "Are you still going out?"

"No," he said. "Feel like lying in bed and watching television?"

"Sure," she said. "The bed is the softest place in the house."

He lifted the bedspread and let her out from their improvised shelter beneath the table. When he looked down, he saw that Stella had had an accident — the storm had literally scared the crap out of her, a solid turd on the linoleum beneath the table. He picked it up using a wad of toilet paper, wiped the floor clean, and flushed it all down the toilet. He saw no need to tell her. He cleaned her up, put the bed spread back on his bed, and lifted her up onto the mattress, where she lay down with her back to him, one leg up, asking for a belly scratch. He complied, turning on the television to *The Tonight Show.*

"Whatever happened to that white-haired guy?" Stella asked.

"Johnny Carson?"

"Yeah."

"He retired a few years ago."

"I miss him. I knew him my whole life."

"Me too."

"He was really kind to animals. These new guys just make fun of them. What's he doing these days?"

"Playing tennis, I guess," Paul said.

"That's good exercise," Stella said. "I love you, Paul."

"I know. I love you more."

"Yeah, probably. Just kidding."

17

Water Bears

Once Stella had fallen asleep, her legs twitching, Paul went to the refrigerator and got a beer. He opened a book he'd been reading about protozoans and spent a few minutes with it but lost energy. It was still raining. On CNN, the pundits were calling for the president's impeachment because he'd lied about getting a blow job in the White House cloakroom. He turned the TV off and logged on to his computer, where he discovered that his father was online.

> **PaulGus:** Are you feeling better than you did yesterday?
> **HarrGus:** YES
> **PaulGus:** Did you have a good dinner? You have to eat, you know.
> **HarrGus:** YES
> **PaulGus:** Are you still having trouble remembering things?
> **HarrGus:** YES
> **PaulGus:** You never complain. I don't mean now. I mean before.
> **HarrGus:** NO
> **PaulGus:** You just soldier on.
> **HarrGus:** YES

Maybe it was his annoyance with the CNN pundits, the hypocrisy of the holier-than-thou Republicans with past and future Lewinskys of their own, channeling their obvious arousal over White House revelations into spluttering outrage. People were emotionally complex. The ones who weren't, or pretended they weren't, were the freaks. For whatever reason, he thought he might push his father a bit, nudge him toward an examination of the inner life.

> **PaulGus:** Good in theory. In practice, that doesn't help children learn how to deal with their problems. Children aren't soldiers. If you spend your life keeping your problems to yourself, your children have no coping mechanisms in place other than to "take it like a man" when the shit hits the fan for them. Pardon the expression.
>
> **PaulGus:** Just a thought I had. No need to respond.
>
> **HarrGus:** NO
>
> **PaulGus:** I met a guy once who bragged that he never cried. To me that's like saying he never laughed. An emotional IQ approaching zero. Anybody who buys the idea that God created us would have to admit he gave us each a complete set of emotions to help us get by, right?
>
> **HarrGus:** YES
>
> **PaulGus:** Doesn't it dishonor God not to use the tools he's given us? I just mean being open to our own hearts and trusting them. Good idea, don't you think?
>
> **HarrGus:** YES
>
> **PaulGus:** Like in the old Westerns where the cowboy gets shot full of arrows and passes out and his horse finds the way home. Give the heart its head.
>
> **HarrGus:** YES
>
> **PaulGus:** Mine would probably walk off a cliff in the dark.
>
> **HarrGus:** YES
>
> **PaulGus:** You needn't agree so quickly. Have you ever loved a woman other than your wife?

HarrGus: NO

PaulGus: Here's another one—who do you think knows more about love, a person who's had a series of complex and involved relationships with a number of different people, or someone who's had a single long-term, deep, satisfying relationship with only one person?

PaulGus: I can't answer that either. I used to think I knew all the answers. Then I thought I knew maybe a few of the answers. Now I'm not even sure I understand the questions. Nobody knows anything.

HarrGus: YES

PaulGus: Did you love your parents?

HarrGus: YES

PaulGus: Just fishing—do you love your son Paul?

HarrGus: NO

It was as if he could hear his father's voice, even though the word *no* had been nothing more than a series of pixels arranged on a screen.

He turned off the computer and went to sit on the porch swing. He heard a peeping sound. A bird of some sort had built a nest in the broken downspout beneath the eave. He listened to the rain, the traffic, the night, then went back to the computer and got online again, happy to find that Tamsen was available for instant messaging.

TamsenP: you're up late.

PaulGus: Working. So are you.

TamsenP: working. is it raining there?

PaulGus: Yup. It was pretty loud thunder a while ago. Stella freaked out a little bit.

TamsenP: it poured here. how's your book coming along?

PaulGus: Researching. I have a book right here that says

there's a little microscopic animal called a water bear that
can survive for 85 years without water in temperatures
ranging from 100 degrees below zero to 200 degrees
above. They can even live in the vacuum of outer space,
bombarded by cosmic radiation.

TamsenP: why do they call it a water bear if they live without
water?

PaulGus: Because they can completely dehydrate themselves
and come back to life years later when it rains, I guess. Like
sea monkeys.

TamsenP: sorry not to be more responsive. i'm not in the
best mood. they laid off 500 people today. i tried to phone
you.

PaulGus: I'm so sorry. You weren't laid off, were you?

TamsenP: not me, but i think it's a sign of things to come.
we've been blowing through untold millions of v.c. dollars
and now they're trying to sell the whole thing to jeff bezos.

PaulGus: Who?

TamsenP: amazon.com. buy stock in it if you have any excess
funds. it's going to be huge.

PaulGus: I always thought that had something to do with
lesbians. Amazons, etc.

TamsenP: it has nothing to do with lesbians.

PaulGus: Are you going to have to start looking for work?

TamsenP: can you keep a secret? i don't have to start looking.
i got a call from the competition, hoping to lure me away.
bottlerocket.com

PaulGus: What do they do?

TamsenP: they don't do anything either, but they don't do a
whole lot more things than we don't do. it's just really hard.
people picked up and moved their families to be here.

PaulGus: I'm really sorry for you. And for your friends.

TamsenP: how are you?

PaulGus: Had kind of a hard night myself.

TamsenP: what happened?

PaulGus: My father told me he doesn't love me. Other than that, everything's peachy.

TamsenP: what do you mean? i don't understand.

He copied and pasted the entire conversation to Tamsen, who said she needed time to read it. He read about water bears. Positing an omniscient and benevolent demiurge ruling over a meaningful universe, why give the most dramatic survival mechanisms to so low an organism? Wasn't it supposed to be man whom God favored above all others? Why make man the weakest, the most vulnerable? Water bears could survive at one hundred degrees below zero for nearly a century. Paul wanted to crawl off and die at a single word.

TamsenP: interesting.

PaulGus: It felt like it was going pretty good. We were talking about love.

TamsenP: you're sure he wasn't goofing with you?

PaulGus: Not his style of humor.

TamsenP: you know you're a fine person, don't you? you don't have to hear it from him to know that. you're lovable. lots of people love you. just because your father can't deal with emotions is no reason to get down on yourself. you're totally cool.

PaulGus: In theory.

TamsenP: paulie, paulie, paulie—this has to be a misunderstanding. it's not his fault. he had a stroke. you can't take anything he has to say . . . i was going to say seriously, but maybe i mean literally. you need to take it with a thousand grains of salt. and put all this stuff out of your mind and wait for the day when he's more rational. he's not himself.

PaulGus: He's not irrational. There's nothing wrong with his mind, other than that he can't get it to tell his body what to do anymore. He's the same guy.

TamsenP: you don't know that. people who've had strokes might have all kinds of issues. he can't talk. he can't ask clarifying questions. he can't tell you what he's thinking. he can only click yes or no. if he could talk, i'm sure he'd explain what he meant.

PaulGus: There's nothing ambiguous about being asked, "Do you love your son Paul?" I don't see how he could misconstrue that.

TamsenP: he's not himself. just forget about it. he played baseball with you and threw footballs and put you through college. you had a few disagreements, big deal. par for the course. you really think he could say he didn't love you?

PaulGus: You're absolutely right.

TamsenP: it must have hurt a great deal to read that.

PaulGus: I used to think that if my dad went golfing, for instance, and they needed somebody to make a foursome, and there was a guy, just like me, hanging around the putting green, some liberal-humanist, agnostic, pro-abortion, anti-death penalty Democrat who likes to go out to bars and listen to music and drink beer — if my dad met a guy just like me, he wouldn't like him. He'd say to himself, "This person is not my cup of tea."

TamsenP: you're wrong. they love you. they know you. they've seen you grow up. they changed your diapers. they looked at your poop. let it be. they know the real you, and they accept that, and they love that. go easy on yourself.

PaulGus: I'll try.

TamsenP: i have another conference in worcester in two days. maybe i'll drive to northampton when i'm done. would that be all right?

PaulGus: That would be good.

TamsenP: i'll call you when i know more. can you hang in there?

18

Hanging In There

When Tamsen arrived, two days later, Paul told her about a terrible dream he'd had, one not particularly difficult to interpret. He'd been with his parents at the Mall of America. They'd become separated and couldn't find one another, which filled him with anxiety, even though he was a full-grown adult and not a child. Eventually he found his mother, who informed him, "Your father isn't with us anymore. His heart is stuck."

"Can you get your father online?" Tamsen asked.

She'd arrived just before six. Paul was cooking her a relatively fancy dinner by his standards, veal scaloppine in a mustard cream sauce with wild mushroom risotto, matched with a spectacular Chianti, or so the wine salesman at the liquor store had claimed. He wanted to do something special for Tamsen, to pay her back for all the things she'd done for him. She said her cooking instructor would have been pleased. Stella was under the kitchen table on scrap patrol.

"Probably," Paul answered her. "I don't think he's going anywhere. Why?"

"Your dream made me think of something."

Paul called his mother and got her to turn the computer on and set it up for his father to use. When they were ready, Paul asked Tamsen what she wanted him to say.

"I usually start by asking him how he's feeling," Paul said.

"Do that, then," she said.

PaulGus: How are you feeling today? Better?

HarrGus: NO

PaulGus: We'll just take it easy today, then. Okay?

HarrGus: YES

PaulGus: It's a beautiful day here today. Is it a beautiful day there?

HarrGus: NO

PaulGus: Well, we're very much enjoying the sunny weather. Have you watched any golf on television lately?

HarrGus: YES

PaulGus: I think this kid Tiger Woods is amazing. Don't you?

HarrGus: YES

"This isn't exactly going anywhere," Paul told Tamsen.

"Tell him you think Tiger Woods's father must be very proud of him," Tamsen suggested.

"Why don't you type?" Paul said, rising from the chair and offering her the keyboard. "He won't know the difference."

"Paul, please," she said.

"If you have something in mind, just go for it," Paul said, gesturing toward the open chair. "I give you permission. It's better than you telling me what to type. If it takes too long, he loses focus."

Tamsen took a seat at the keyboard.

PaulGus: his father must be very proud of him.

HarrGus: YES

PaulGus: last time i asked you if you loved your son paul. do you remember that?

HarrGus: YES

PaulGus: are you proud of your son paul?

HarrGus: NO

"Gee," Paul said, "this is making me feel *much* better."

"Just wait a minute," she told him.

"What does this have to do with my dream?"

"I'm not sure," she said. "It just made me think that maybe you got it backward."

"How did I get it backward?"

"You didn't lose him," she said. "He lost you. He's the one who had the stroke."

PaulGus: do you love your son paul?

HarrGus: NO

PaulGus: let me ask you this, then. do you have a son named paul?

HarrGus: NO

PaulGus: if you did have a son named paul, you would love him, wouldn't you?

HarrGus: YES

PaulGus: but as far as you know, you don't have a son named paul?

HarrGus: NO

PaulGus: i'm a little confused as to why you say that. are you still feeling confused about some things?

HarrGus: YES

PaulGus: do you know what day it is? or what year it is?

HarrGus: NO

PaulGus: do you know the names of all the people who come see you?

HarrGus: NO

PaulGus: sometimes you forget?

HarrGus: YES

PaulGus: do you have a son named carl?

HarrGus: YES

PaulGus: and a daughter named elizabeth?

HarrGus: YES

PaulGus: and you know that because they come to visit you and tell you who they are?

HarrGus: YES

PaulGus: but nobody named paul comes to visit you?

HarrGus: NO

PaulGus: does the name paul gustavson ring a bell for you?

HarrGus: YES

PaulGus: is that person related to you?

HarrGus: YES

PaulGus: is that person your father?

HarrGus: YES

PaulGus: and do you understand that this is paul you're talking to over the computer?

HarrGus: YES

PaulGus: so is it your understanding that you're talking to your father? that all these times, you've been talking to your father?

HarrGus: YES

"Now *this* is getting interesting," Paul said.

His grasp of family history wasn't as complete as it could have been. He remembered his grandfather and namesake as a quiet, stern, undemonstrative man, an architect who designed railroad stations and yard depots for the Northern Pacific Railway. He gave everybody five dollars for their birthdays, always a crisp, unwrinkled, unfolded bill, tucked into special cards with a window cut in the front to frame Abraham Lincoln's face. He'd seen four of his boys leave to fight in World War II and welcomed three home, having lost Inger, his second oldest, in the invasion of Normandy. Harrold had served in the Pacific. Neither Paul's father nor his uncles ever spoke of what happened during the war. Paul's grandfather died when Paul was nineteen.

"So Harrold has thought all this time that he was talking to his father," Paul said.

"Apparently," Tamsen said.

"I'm going to have to go back and reread our previous conversations," Paul said. "Switch seats with me."

Paul typed.

> **PaulGus:** I guess there's been some confusion then. You think I'm your father?
>
> **HarrGus:** YES
>
> **PaulGus:** I apologize, Harrold. And I wanted to tell you how sorry I am that you've had a stroke. There must be all kinds of things that you wish you could say to me. Things you never got a chance to say when I was alive.
>
> **HarrGus:** YES

"What are you doing?" Tamsen asked.

"Pretending to be my grandfather," Paul said. "If that's who he thinks this is."

"That's lying," Tamsen said.

"I know," Paul said, "but when is he going to get another chance to talk to his father?"

> **PaulGus:** I'm very proud of you for the way you're handling this. I'm proud of you for the way you've lived your life. You're a good man and a good father. I imagine there were times when you felt like I could have been a better father.
>
> **HarrGus:** YES
>
> **PaulGus:** I never said this often enough, but I want you to know I always loved you, even though I couldn't always express it.
>
> **HarrGus:** YES
>
> **PaulGus:** We both loved you, your mother and I. And we were always proud of you, even when I might have been harsh

or stern with you when I was trying to teach you things or correct you when you made mistakes. We were always very proud of you. Did you know that?

HarrGus: NO

PaulGus: Well, we were. We love you. I love you.

HarrGus: YES

PaulGus: I have to go now.

HarrGus: NO

PaulGus: I have to go. I can't stay. But Harrold, the next time someone talks to you on the computer, it won't be me—it will be your youngest son, Paul. You have three children, Carl, Elizabeth, and Paul. Paul will be the person contacting you next. Do you understand?

HarrGus: YES

PaulGus: Do you remember your youngest son, Paul, now?

HarrGus: YES

PaulGus: Do you love your youngest son, Paul?

HarrGus: YES YES YES YES YES

PaulGus: Okay. I gotta go.

19

Casablanca

They talked about it at dinner. It was still a bit overwhelming. Paul worried that he might have said something wrong in his previous e-mails, but Tamsen told him not to second-guess himself. It broke his heart to think of how confused and lost his father must be feeling. He couldn't think of a way to rectify the situation, other than to let time blur the outlines and smear the images. He thanked Tamsen for figuring it out on his behalf. She deflected his gratitude, adopting an aw-shucks-it-was-nothing, anybody-would-have-done-the-same-thing pose. Yet, though Paul felt closer to her, he sensed that she wasn't reciprocating. She seemed, he thought, odd, somehow, or distant, as if now that she'd helped him straighten things out with his dad, she had something else on her mind.

Stella thought the veal tasted like chicken. Tamsen appreciated the fancy dinner but ate quickly, rather than savor it. When she told him, sipping her after-dinner coffee, that she really had to be getting back, Paul begged her to stay, explaining that he'd rented a movie and hoped she'd watch it on the couch with him and spend the night. She told him she hadn't brought a change of clothes, which made no sense, because she had a drawerful of clothes she'd left behind during her previous visits.

"What movie did you rent?" she said at last.

"*Casablanca*," he said. "You said you always wanted to see it."

That had to have scored him significant points in the thoughtful/considerate boyfriend department.

"I did say that, didn't I?"

He poured each of them another glass of wine, grabbed a quilt from the bed, and moved next to her on the couch. She lifted Stella up to join them, the dog's head resting in Tamsen's lap.

It wasn't until the movie was nearly over and the Nazis were racing to the airport that Paul realized what he'd done. What was he thinking, showing her history's most tragic love-triangle movie? What an idiot he was! It was like a scene out of a Woody Allen movie. Come to think of it, it was a Woody Allen movie. He could see the film affecting her. He considered pausing the movie and suggesting they go to bed without finishing it, but it was too late to stop it now. What a moron! If art was supposed to hold a mirror to the soul, he'd just presented her with a floor-length 10× magnifying reflector. By the end of the movie, tears were flowing down her cheeks. Afterward, she had her head buried in his chest, sobbing, and he knew why before she spoke. He held her and stroked her hair.

"Is that a great movie or what?" he said at last, trying to give her an out by pretending she was just sad because Bogie and Ingrid Bergman weren't going to be together. She sat up and looked at him, trying to smile.

"Jesus, I can't keep doing this," she said, sniffing. "I can't keep having my feelings pulled in so many directions. It's tearing me apart. Believe me, it's totally my own fault and I have no right to complain to anyone. I take full responsibility. I'm not going to say, 'You do the thinking for both of us.' This is all on me."

"What do you mean?" he said. "Tell me what's going on."

"Same old thing," she said, sniffing again, apologetic and apparently mad at herself. "Something's gotta give, Paul. This is just too hard. I haven't been sleeping. I have bags under my eyes."

"Did something happen?" He found it hard to swallow.

"Nothing specific," Tamsen said. "It's just that Stephen and I had a talk the other night. This is driving him crazy too. It's got to be getting to you too — isn't it? It's not good for anybody. You can't be all that happy about the situation."

"I'm happy when you're here," Paul said. "When you're not, I just sort of go numb and try not to think about it."

She leaned her head toward him and kissed him.

"I'm happy when I'm with you too," she said. "But when I'm with you, I'm making Stephen unhappy, and I hate that. And when I'm with him, I'm making you unhappy, and I hate that too. Whatever I do, it's wrong. It worked for a while, but that's not true anymore. I should have known better."

"Is it wrong for you to be sitting here?" Paul said. "I think it's pretty right." But he wasn't going to try to argue her into choosing him. As much as he wanted to be with her, deep down he had to allow that she needed to feel free to do what she had to do. There were things she wanted. Even a moron could see that Stephen was probably better able to give them to her than Paul was, and if that was true, then the right thing for Paul to do would be to back off and not stand in her way. Maybe the movie was affecting him too. *If that plane leaves the ground and you're not with him, you'll regret it. Maybe not today, maybe not tomorrow, but soon and for the rest of your life.* If she wanted stability, security, a family, then Stephen was her best bet. Paul could see that. Surely she could too. Those were just the facts.

"What does Stephen think?" Paul asked.

"He'd like it if I stopped seeing you," she said. "He's too polite to make it sound like an ultimatum, but he feels like as long as I have feelings for you, we'll never know what we could have between us. I didn't put that very succinctly."

"You don't have to," Paul said. "I get it."

"He doesn't know I'm here, by the way," she said. "He's going to be upset when I tell him. I really wasn't going to spend the night. I promised myself I wasn't going to. And I have to tell him. I'm not going to start sneaking around. That's not an option."

"This can't be easy for you," he was willing to acknowledge.

"I have no one to blame but myself," she said, taking his hands and looking him in the eye. "I wanted to know you. I still do. You're a really valuable part of my life. I can't imagine not having you in it. And all these other parts of your life that are so . . . in transition . . . don't matter, in a way. But they do. I'm sorry I'm so confused. I thought we could do this and be open and honest about it. I've been selfish, and it's unfair. To everyone."

"What do you want me to do?" he asked.

She didn't answer at first. She seemed to be wrestling with her conscience. Finally she put her hand on the back of his neck and pulled him toward her, kissing him gently, lushly, wetly. Her eyes glistened.

"I want you to take me to your bed and make love to me," she said.

If.

Only.

He.

Could.

Failure was virtually guaranteed, a fait accompli.

He nevertheless took her to bed, where Paul in the Bed did everything he could to make Tamsen feel loved, while Paul on the Ceiling looked on. He tried to take his time, breathe deep, relax, slow down, and ignore his dysfunctional doppelgänger. Paul on the Ceiling kept reminding Paul in the Bed that if he couldn't overcome his impotence tonight, he might not get another chance. Paul in the Bed told Paul on the Ceiling that he really didn't need that kind of pressure.

In the end, the best Paul in the Bed could do was to hold Tamsen until her gentle snoring told him she was asleep. He opened his eyes and stared at the spot where Paul on the Ceiling had been, but Paul on the Ceiling was gone. Paul in the Bed felt sick to his stomach. He rose and went into the kitchen for a drink of water.

"How'd it go?" Stella asked him.

"It didn't," he said. "It's not good."

"You're overthinking it again."

"I know," he said. "Why don't you ever have that problem?"

"If I asked myself that question," she said, "I'd be overthinking it."

"I wish I was more like you," he said. "I don't like the way I am."

"Then change," she said.

"I'm trying."

"I know. That's what matters."

He heard a noise from the bedroom, the bed squeaking as Tamsen rolled over in her sleep.

"I don't think she's going to be with me much longer," Paul whispered. "I think she's starting to make a choice. She thinks I'm too much work."

"How do you know the other guy isn't too much work too?" Stella asked.

"Possible," Paul allowed.

"It's up to her, isn't it? Everybody's work somehow. All you can do is be yourself. You're a very caring person. What else could you do?"

"I could step aside and make it easier for her," Paul said.

"Like the guy in the movie?" Stella said. "The one in the white tuxedo."

"Yeah, like him," Paul said. "I'm no good at being noble either."

"I don't understand what you mean."

"That's the line in the movie," Paul said, "before he puts her on the plane with Victor Laszlo."

"Yeah, but why didn't she just say, 'No thanks, I'd rather stay here with you?' Wouldn't that have made more sense?"

"She wanted Bogart to do the thinking for both of them," Paul said. "Besides, the Nazis were coming."

"Are the Nazis coming now?"

"I certainly hope not."

"Do you think Tamsen wants you to do the thinking for both of you?"

"Definitely not."

"I rest my case. You already think enough for one person," Stella said.

"Or more than enough," Paul said. "Do you need to pee?"

"I'm okay," Stella said.

He took her water bowl to the sink, poured out the old water, and refilled it with fresh. The dog struggled to her feet, nearly losing her footing on the linoleum floor before correcting herself, then walked stiffly to the bowl, where she lapped slowly with her tongue.

He went back to bed, sat on the edge of the mattress, and watched Tamsen sleep, lying on her side, wearing one of his white cotton dress shirts for a nightgown, the collar turned up to frame her face. He wondered how much longer . . . then took Stella's advice and stopped himself from thinking too much. He lay down beside Tamsen and buried his face in her chest, feeling the warm rise and fall of her soft skin as she breathed in and out. She awoke just enough to put her arm over him and pull him closer, muttering something under her breath that he couldn't quite make out, something that began, "You don't have to . . . ," before becoming unintelligible.

He wanted to wake her and ask, "I don't have to what?" but he let it go, on the chance that in her dream it wasn't him she was talking to.

20

Time

Then one night, Paul woke up on the couch, unable to sleep. It was two in the morning, and eighty-one degrees, October now but Indian summer, humid, the air not moving, the curtains hanging limp and still at the open window. A moth fluttered briefly against the screen, then disappeared into the night. Of all the things he'd lost to Karen in the division of property, the air conditioner was the only item he'd felt inclined to contest, but by then he was too tired to fight. Their internal thermostats were wildly incompatible — she was invariably too cold when he felt fine, or fine when he felt hot, and they were never comfortable at the same time, though he never complained. Growing up in Minnesota, he'd explained to Tamsen, you learn early to keep your thoughts about the temperature to yourself, on a frozen January playground where everybody is just as cold as you are and where whining about it changes nothing and annoys all.

The dog felt the heat too, her breathing labored — huff, huff, *huff*, huff, huff — in a pattern he could hear repeated from where she lay on her pad in the front room. Paul was uncomfortable enough — imagine living through a night like this wearing a fur coat. If it stayed hot tomorrow, he'd take Stella to the fountain in front of the county courthouse and let her cool off in the holding pool. If it was this hot tomorrow, he'd join her.

He got up and went to sit on the porch.

He sat on the swing in his boxer shorts, rocking slowly to minimize the chain's squeak. All the windows in the student ghetto across the street were dark. Sometimes, on warm nights when people went to bed with the windows open, he could hear the mating cries and coital barks of nubile coeds and college boys who'd yet to experience the joys of erectile dysfunction.

He heard a train whistle and listened as the train passed through town, the tracks half a block from his house. The sounds of trains appealed directly to the heart — the distant rumble of approach, then the thundering crescendo as they passed, and then the attenuated decline, like the memory of love when love is gone. The ta-*tack*-teh-teh rhythm of the train's wheels soothed him.

In the silence that followed, Paul heard Stella wake and struggle to her feet, grunting and huffing to get her hindquarters up and running. She tottered off into the kitchen. The clickety-clack of her toenails on the wood floor was as reassuring as the steel wheels of the train. He heard her return, pause, and then push the screen door open with her nose to find her way out onto the porch, where she stood panting, tongue out.

"What's up?" he asked.

"Hot night," she said.

"Very warm," he agreed. He listened as a car screeched down King Street.

"It's time, Paul," Stella said.

"Time for what?" he said.

"You know what I mean," she said. "It's time."

He considered her words. He'd known, of course, that one day she would tell him.

"What do you mean, 'It's time'?" he said, stalling as the impact of her words settled in. "Why? Why now?"

"Come here," she said, leading him into the front room, where he turned on the light. Her L.L. Bean doggie bed was darkened at the front edge, and a trail of urine led from it toward the kitchen. "I can't control my bladder anymore. It's bad enough that I've lost control of my bowels."

"It's not a big deal," Paul assured her. "I'm used to cleaning up after you. I don't mind."

"This is different," she said. "What if I'm in the car and I lose it? What if I'm on the couch, or at somebody else's house, or at Jake's? I can't be pissing all over everything, now can I?"

He didn't answer right away.

"It's just a little piss," he said. "I don't care — "

"I care," she said quietly. "There's no dignity in it. It's important to me to keep my dignity. You know?"

"I know," he conceded. "You've always been a gracious mutt."

"Thank you," she said. "Which is why this is my decision. So don't blame yourself. But I need you to pick up the phone and call the vet. See if you can get that nice Louise woman. I like her. We should do this tomorrow."

"Tomorrow?" he said. "Stella, I don't want to."

"Paul," she said, "I need you to be strong about this. This is something you have to do for me. I can't do it myself. I would if I could. I'd been hoping to die in my sleep ever since I noticed I'd been leaking, but it's gone too far now."

"But you're still sharp," he argued. "You're mentally all there, you can see and hear . . . I can get a diaper or something for you."

They listened to a police siren howling in the distance.

"I've tried not to complain," she said, "with all that you've had going on, but it's a little worse than you think. It's not just my bladder and my bowels. I can hardly walk. I haven't really smelled anything in weeks, and I can only see a little bit out of one eye. It's getting harder to hear you too. And I get confused. Which is why I'm glad I remembered to tell you these things now while I'm clear. Do you remember what your grandmother said, the last time you saw her in the nursing home?"

"Yeah."

"And what did she say to you?"

"She said she wished she'd died when she felt better."

"That's how I feel, Paul," Stella said. "I told you before. There's a line. And above the line, life is good, and below the line, life is not good. Right now I'm still above the line, but I don't want to wait until I'm below the line. I want to go thinking life is good. I think I'm entitled to that."

He watched the moths gathered about the streetlight. He'd heard once that moths didn't want to fly toward light, that light in fact inhibited the action of their wings, so that whichever wing was in the dark beat faster, pushing the moth inexorably toward the flame. Some of the moths attacking the streetlight were only going to live for twenty-four hours. They too had a line, above which life was good, and below which life was bad. Everything did. For everything there is a season.

"But I love you," he said. "What am I supposed to do with that love, once you're gone?"

"I don't understand what you're saying," Stella said.

"It makes me feel good to love you," he said. "When I pet you or feed you or take you for walks, it makes me feel good. It makes me proud of myself. Like I'm doing something valuable, and that makes me a good person."

"I like it too."

"I know you do. So when you're gone, I won't be able to do that."

"So get another dog."

"It's not that simple," Paul said. "You're special to me. I can't just get another dog."

"It's easy to love," Stella said.

"Easy for you to say. You love everybody."

"You can still love me after I'm gone," she said.

"But it's not you. It wouldn't be you. It'd be the idea of you. The memory of you."

"What's the difference?"

"It's a huge difference. There's a saying: 'Hell is the inability to love.' That doesn't mean not knowing what love is. It means knowing exactly what it is, being fully aware, but somehow being prevented from expressing it."

"Paul," she said, "I've had a great life. I've traveled all over the country with you and I've seen more states than any dog I've ever met. We've been camping and fishing, we've been in all kinds of restaurants and bars where they don't ordinarily allow dogs . . ."

"Because, you're so well behaved."

"Well, thank you. I've done all kinds of amazing things, thanks to you. I don't want to leave you, but it's time. That's all. It's time. I've been richly blessed. More than I ever deserved."

"Ditto."

"I want you to have my stuff. I've made a list. You can have my bed and my bones and my tennis balls and my stuffed animals and my dish. Though I don't know what you'd do with any of it if you're not going to get another dog."

She hadn't had any stuffed animals since she was a puppy, but he didn't have the heart to tell her.

"I'm tired now," she said, eyeballing the wet doggy bed. "I guess I'll just sleep on the floor. I'm sorry about the bed."

He wanted to call someone, but it was two in the morning. He lay on the couch and at some point dozed off, but before he did, though he was not a believer, he found himself uttering a short prayer.

"If you could just take her in the night, I wouldn't mind . . ."

But she was with him in the morning, awake and alert and looking at him with pleading brown eyes. There was nothing to be done, no stroke-of-genius plan he'd hoped would come to him in a dream to change what had to happen. It was simply time. He called the vet and was told they could come in at two o'clock that afternoon. He called Tamsen twice but got her answering machine both times and didn't leave a message because it wasn't the sort of thing you could leave a message about. Finally he called Karen, asking her if she could take time off from work to help him — Stella had been her dog too for a while. They arranged to meet at their former community garden plot at one o'clock.

He spent the morning reading the paper at Jake's. Stella lay in the doorway, where she'd lain for the past fourteen years, watching the street through the glass doors and occasionally checking over her shoulder to make sure Paul was still sipping coffee. As soon as he put his cap on to leave, she started struggling to her feet. Paul lifted her hindquarters, careful not to put any pressure on her bladder, but she tinkled a bit in the doorway anyway. Just as well, Paul thought, in case the next dog to come along wondered whose doorway it was.

He parked in the lot at Serio's Market, an old-fashioned mom-and-pop grocery store with fruits and vegetables displayed in their shipping crates and wooden floors that squeaked. He picked up a half pound of shaved roast beef in the deli section, some meatballs, and a quarter pound of sliced muenster cheese, even though cheese gave Stella diarrhea. That wasn't going to matter. He stopped at the liquor store next door and purchased a bottle of wine.

"Remember that Smith College party where they knocked the cheese tray over?" Paul said, parking the car on the grass at the Northampton Community Garden and lifting Stella down gently from the passenger's side.

"That was good cheese," she said.

She headed straight for their plot, a patch of prairie when they'd first signed up for it. The community garden was located next to the long-defunct state hospital, a collection of decrepit brick buildings with ivy on the outside and asbestos on the inside. Paul had manned the rototiller that first year, pulverizing the sod and turning it over and over until it was workable. The first year, they'd planted mostly vegetables, but over the years Karen had planted more than half their garden with annuals and perennials and rose bushes and cutting flowers. Paul hadn't visited the garden since their divorce.

"Beautiful day," Stella said, raising her nose to the wind. When a bee started up from a patch of Johnny-jump-ups, she made a halfhearted attempt to snap at it. Eating bees was her favorite thing in the world, and Paul wished he could catch one for her. Downtown, in the fall, when the bees buzzing around the sidewalk trash cans grew slow and lethargic in the cool weather, Stella would lie down on the sidewalk and eat bees for hours until her lips swelled up, but she didn't seem to mind.

At the garden, she examined the various sections before taking her usual place in the shade of the willow tree. Paul remembered when Karen had shoved a handful of pussy willow cuttings into the ground. "That'll never grow," he'd predicted. The bush was over ten feet tall now, full and thriving. Karen was good at making things grow. He saw her car pull in behind his.

"Look who's here," Paul said. "Surprise."

"Oh, Paul," Stella said, her tail thumping at the sight of her former mistress. "I thought she was dead."

"I know, I know," he said. "She's fine. Don't try to get up."

"She looks great," Stella said. "I'm not sold on the short haircut."

"It looks fine," he said. "I think she just wanted to change things up a bit."

"She looks like she's gained some weight," Stella said.

"She's pregnant," Paul told Stella. "Due any minute, by the looks of her."

"Hi, you two," Karen said as cheerfully as she could. "Hello, Stella." She looked at the dog and then, reluctantly, at Paul. He'd remembered how the corners of her eyes glistened with tears when she was sad. She put her hand on her belly.

"I was going to tell you," she said. "But I figured in a town this small, you already knew."

"I did," Paul said. "Congratulations."

Karen turned back to Stella, kneeling.

"It's good to see you again. You're still the most beautiful dog in the world, do you know that?" Karen looked at Paul. "How's she doing? What'd the vet say?"

"He says there's nothing you can really do with a dog this old," Paul said. "She's not strong enough to survive surgery. The appointment's at two." He was feeling strong about the decision, but that could change at any moment. "I brought lunch — help yourself." He used the corkscrew on his Swiss Army knife to open the wine and filled three paper cups. Karen sat opposite him, with the dog in the middle. He handed her a paper cup full of wine, then remembered and dumped the wine on a tomato plant.

"I forgot," he said. "You can't have wine. I apologize."

He'd bought a bottle of water. He rinsed and refilled Karen's cup with the water and then handed the cup to her.

"Dig in."

"Actually," she said, "I'm not eating meat these days either." Sure, he thought. Defy sixty million years of evolution as an omnivore. "Kevin is a vegetarian."

"Is he?" Paul said. Kevin, not Kirk nor Kurt. He was never good with names. "That's okay with the pediatrician? I mean, for you. Not for Kevin."

"Obstetrician," she corrected him. "I just have to make sure I get enough protein. You still do dairy, don't you?" she asked Stella, pushing the cheese closer to her, first peeling off a slice and dropping it into Stella's open mouth.

Stella lapped at the wine.

"Excellent bouquet, eh, Stell?" he said. "A delicate balance of wood and fruit, with a smoky finish, perfect with cat turds and stepped-on cheese pizza."

He raised his cup to his ex.

"To Stella," he said, "who . . ."

Suddenly he choked up and couldn't speak. It had been happening like that all morning, whenever he thought about it. It didn't matter if he thought about the past, the present, or the future, because each bore a particular kind of sadness. The past seemed the safest place to dwell, but it was like swimming in a river flowing unstoppably into the now and the next, neither of which held much joy or promise.

"To Stella," Karen said, touching her paper cup to his. He knew she wanted to say something about his drinking, but he knew that today she wouldn't. "Our flower girl."

"This really sucks, Karen," he said. "I can hardly stand it."

"She's old, Paul," Karen said. "It's the right thing to do. You've been the best owner a dog could want — she's been with you twenty-four hours a day, practically. I think that's all any dog would really want, and you gave that to her."

It was true. She'd sailed off the coast of Maine. Attended swank parties in Soho lofts. She'd met Kareem Abdul-Jabbar and Julius Irving at a UMass fund-raiser. She'd had her picture in the paper, twice. She'd been to forty-six states and seven national parks and crossed the country a dozen times with him. She'd dug her nails into the Athabasca Glacier and wandered through fields of wildflowers in Montana. She'd chased seagulls into the surf on the Oregon coast and waded the tidal flats of Provincetown. She'd hiked the Appalachian Trail and chased away a black bear that was raiding the food cache. She'd done a lot. It was time.

They ate and made small talk, updating each other on their families. Karen was sad to hear about Harrold's stroke; she was glad to learn he was getting better and asked Paul to convey her best wishes. The fact that she was pregnant was none of his business. She wore a gold band on her left hand — also none of his business. Sharing even the most mundane things with Karen was awkward now, as if saying merely "What time is it?" or "Pass the salt" was a bad move that could undo the long, laborious psychodramatic process of pissing and bitching and blaming that had allowed them both to move on. They really had said everything they had to say to each other. Chitchatting seemed absurd, and yet he needed her there to do this thing. She'd shared her life with Stella too. He needed to be with someone else who'd known her.

Paul looked at his watch and said, "We should probably go."

In the past, Stella would commence trembling as soon as she recognized the Northampton Veterinary Clinic parking lot, and it had often been necessary to give her shots or examine her outdoors, on the steps, where her anxiety levels were manageable. Today she was calm. Paul kept saying to himself, "It's a common thing, it happens all the time, millions of people do it every day." He looked at the dog to see if there was anything he could read from her expression, any kind of fear or apprehension, but he saw only resolve.

Karen, following him in her own car, parked next to him and waited outside with Stella while Paul went to the reception desk to report in. In the linoleum-floored receiving room, a cat the size of a small bear was wedged into an empty beer case between its owner's feet. The front desk was usually staffed by high school girls who loved animals so much that they were willing to work after school for free.

The receptionist said she'd go get Dr. Larson. Paul said Stella would prefer that Louise, Dr. Larson's assistant, be the one to perform the procedure. Anna said Louise would meet them at the side door.

In the parking lot, Karen scratched Stella behind the ear.

"Can we have a moment?" he asked Karen. "I think she should pee before we go in."

He led Stella around to the backyard, where she squatted for the last time.

"Lunch was delicious, Paul," Stella said, once they were alone. "Thank you very much for that special treat."

He was having a hard time talking.

"Don't cry, Paul," Stella said. "I don't know what to say to you. I know it's hard, but it's only one day. We've had so many good days that it more than balances out."

"God-fucking-damn it, though," he said.

"I know," she said softly. "You know it's the right thing to do, though."

"I know," he said. "Karen was telling me what a great life you've had, and I know that. I guess I can't help thinking how mine is taking a rather dramatic turn for the worse. I'm really sorry—I didn't want to make this any harder for you. You have had a great life, I know that."

"Well," the dog said, "you made it great."

"Thanks."

"There's no chance that you and Karen might get back together, is there?"

"No," Paul said. "There's no chance. Not even if lightning hit us both. Twice."

"Well, then," Stella said. "I always liked her."

"So did I. She's a good woman."

He looked around, hoping that something would be different about the day, but the birds sang and the bees buzzed and the clouds in the sky rolled silently on, just as they always did.

"You will be loved, Paul. Remember that I told you that."

"I will," he said. "You know me. I remember everything."

He looked at her.

"We shouldn't keep people waiting," she said. "I'm sure Louise has better things to do than to wait around for me all day."

Later he remembered the heat, and how the warm sun burned down on them in the backyard of the veterinary clinic, and how somewhere faraway somebody was using a chain saw. How he picked her up and carried her into the room, setting her down on the stainless steel table. How Louise removed Stella's collar. How the room was more like a kitchen than a doctor's office, clammy and cold from the air-conditioning, with sinks and stainless steel basins, and the floor was wet from having recently been washed. How Louise said, "What this is, is simply a very powerful sedative." How she worked silently, moving quickly, as if afraid she'd lose her nerve, first shaving a bare spot on Stella's right front shin with an electric shaver. Paul would remember saying, "It's okay, Stella — it's going to be okay. Don't be afraid," more for his own benefit than for Stella's, and how Karen was saying the same things. "We love you, Stell. We both love you very much." He'd never had to watch love die, all in an instant, right before his very eyes. It had always died somewhere else, in some other town, some other place. He'd remember how they both held her, soothing her, his hands and Karen's hands touching the dog but touching each other as well, and that it was the last time he physically touched his ex-wife, the last time that the circle was complete, the way it had once been, the three of them all in one place at one time. Later he'd remember how Stella looked up at him one last time, and then Louise stuck the needle in. How surprisingly fast the drug acted, stopping the heart instantly, like turning off a light switch, and how the old dog's head went down and she didn't move anymore.

The doctor's assistant said that they could take all the time they wanted to say good-bye and that Stella's ashes would be ready to be picked up in the morning. It was another minute before he could take his hands from her. He wanted to hold on to her. Finally Karen took his hands in hers and gave them a squeeze. She hugged him. He closed his eyes. He hoped some-one would take Stella away while he had his eyes closed, but her body was still there when he opened them, though she no longer occupied it.

It was more than he could bear.

Karen hugged him in the parking lot again. Her tears had made her mascara run.

"Thanks for coming," Paul managed to say.

"Of course," she said. "Call me if you need to talk. I loved her too."

He got into his car and drove until dark, heading north into Vermont, where the leaves were perhaps a third turned. He picked up dinner at a McDonald's drive-through but couldn't finish his cheeseburger.

Part 3

Fall/Winter

Natural selection takes millions of years to effect change, because nature resists rather than encourages change. Most species tend to stick with what they know and go with what works for them, focusing on one prey species or adapting to one habitat until that singularity is modified by circumstances, at which point the majority die off, with those who remain surviving more out of dumb luck than by actually figuring out how to adapt. It's rare when a species learns anything quickly. One exception may be the elk in Yellowstone National Park, who'd lost their fear of wolves over the years that wolves were gone from the park but quickly rediscovered it after wolves were reintroduced in 1986. At first the elks stood and watched as the wolves approached and killed them. Within one generation, mother elks were again teaching their young to fear wolves. Humans seek change despite ourselves and only because we are the lone species with a sense of our own impermanence.

—Paul Gustavson, *Nature for Morons*

21

The Insignificance of Being Earnest

He called Tamsen the next day to tell her what had happened. She didn't hesitate, telling him she was driving up and would stop on the way to pick up something for dinner. He tried to warn her on the phone that he wasn't going to be very good company, and when she arrived, he was mad at her for not listening. He felt sick to his stomach and wasn't hungry. He wanted her to go home and come back some other time because he knew that even though she was only trying to make things better, they would be worse before she left. None of this would be her fault. It would be his. Why wouldn't she listen? He didn't want to be good company. He wanted to be a bastard. He had nothing to give her.

At first, when he said he didn't want to talk about it, she simply cleaned his house, without explaining why, although she didn't have to. She vacuumed, mopped the floors. She vacuumed under the couch cushions and under the couches, the windowsills, the radiators, gathering up all the dog hair that had collected over the years. She put Stella's dog bed and toys in a garbage bag and asked Paul what he wanted her to do with them. He suggested she put them in the trash can. Soon the house smelled of ammonia, Simple Green, and Murphy's oil soap, as if she were performing an exorcism with cleaning products. He stayed in his bedroom. He didn't want to talk. He could hear her in the kitchen going through his refrigerator and throwing out all the

old Tupperware containers that had started to buckle and balloon from the biological corruptions in progress within. She left
him alone. She ordered Chinese takeout and told him his was in
the microwave when he said he wasn't hungry. Every nice thing
she said or did for him only made him want to withdraw further into a dark, private, pissy place where he was free to loathe
himself, convinced that he didn't deserve and hadn't earned her
kindnesses or for that matter anybody else's. He would have
been the first to admit he was not pulling his oar, as his father
might have said, and he knew what his Viking ancestors did with
guys who didn't pull their oars.

Lying in his bed with the shade pulled down, he realized
how unfair it was of him to interfere with her happiness. She deserved better, someone who could do as much for her as she did
for him, someone who could make love to her when she wanted
to make love and be with her for the rest of her life — he had a
pretty good idea of what she wanted. He was only being realistic.
It wasn't fair to make her wait. She should be with Stephen, who
by all accounts was a great guy, just the sort of person who would
make her feel safe. To go on pretending otherwise was point-
less and would only make it hurt more later. They were clearly
fooling themselves. It hurt too much to lose the ones you loved,
and he was going to lose Tamsen one day, he was certain, so the
sooner the better.

He hid in bed, listening to the radio with his headphones on.
When he heard her open his bedroom door to say good night,
he kept his eyes closed, which was just as well because he didn't
think he could look her in the eye anymore. The local NPR station was offering Bach's violin concertos this evening, familiar
but welcome, so he closed his eyes again and listened, each piece
forming a full emotional narrative, clear as any written word,
telling of innocence and experience, love discovered and love
destroyed, struggle and failure and triumph, loss and recovery.

Nothing else that he'd ever heard made as much sense, each piece picking him up and leaving him somewhere better than where he'd been before.

He dozed off. When he woke up, the digital clock said it was 3:46 in the morning. He went to the kitchen, where Tamsen had done the dishes, scrubbed the sink, and lined his booze bottles up on the counter. He poured himself a glass of bourbon, then changed his mind, dumped it in the sink, and filled his glass with cold cranberry juice from the refrigerator. He went to the front room and pulled aside the window curtain to see if Tamsen's car was in the driveway. It was. He turned and saw that she'd fallen asleep on the couch under a quilt she'd taken from the guest room. Even in the dark, he could tell the place was spotless. He sat on the coffee table in front of the couch and watched her. After a few minutes, she opened her eyes.

He couldn't hold it back any longer. He started to sob, even though he was afraid that if he started he'd never stop. He told her he was sorry he'd been acting like such a dickhead. He said he appreciated everything she'd done. She shushed him and held him. He lay on the couch next to her. He said again he was sorry for behaving badly and she told him he didn't have to apologize to her. He was crying about Stella, but he was crying about everything else too, everything he imagined Tamsen was thinking about their relationship and where it was headed.

"Should we go to bed?" she said at last when he'd stopped. "I'm sorry, Paul, but I have to be on the road no later than five thirty. I'd already rescheduled some meetings for tomorrow morning and I just can't miss them."

"Can we just sleep here?" he asked.

He didn't notice when she left, but when he awoke, there was a note on the coffee table, no words, just a drawing of a heart, and the letter *T*.

He spent the day in a haze. He went to Jake's and tried to read the paper but couldn't concentrate. He went to his office and tried to work but ended up playing solitaire for three hours. He ran errands, picked up a few things he needed to pick up, including a small metal box from the vet's, containing Stella's ashes. Time crawled. He felt encased in amber, unable to move forward. He reheated leftovers from the food Tamsen had bought him for dinner and watched ESPN for a while to distract himself, but soon he had to get out of the house. His house felt haunted.

He headed for the Bay State. He needed a crowd to lose himself in and the distractions of multiple voices.

Doyle and O-Rings were at the pinball machine. McCoy, Bender, and Yvonne were seated at the bar. D. J. and Mickey were at the pay phone. Paul took a seat next to Yvonne, who lit a cigarette, took a drag, and blew the smoke toward the ceiling, holding the cigarette above her head as if that could keep her hair from smelling.

"What's wrong?" she asked. "You look like shit."

"Where's Stella?" McCoy said.

"That's pretty much what's wrong," Paul said.

"Aw, jeez," McCoy said.

Then everybody knew. McCoy gestured to Silent Neil to set Paul up with a beer and to bring a couple of shots over. As people bought him drinks in sympathy, he learned another argument for suffering in silence: every time he told anybody his dog had just died, they insisted on telling him about the time *their* dog had died. It really wasn't making him feel better.

He stumbled home, completely plastered. He'd been drunk before, but tonight he might have set a personal best, or worst, depending on point of view. "You need to look at some of the things you do," Tamsen had said, "and consider what sort of changes you might want to make." He was, at present, and in the recent past, and for the foreseeable future, more concerned with all the changes he didn't want to make, and with hanging on to what he had, which, apparently, was not one of his options.

No sooner had he walked in the door than the phone rang. He expected to hear Tamsen's voice but was surprised, instead, to hear his brother's.

"Hey," Paul said. "You still up?"

"I've been trying to reach you," Carl said. "Your answering machine is broken or something."

"I turned it off," Paul said. "I should warn you — I've had a bit too lot to drink."

That didn't come out right.

"I can tell," Carl said. "Bits told me you had to put Stella down."

"She did?"

"I just wanted to tell you how sorry we are," Carl said. "We know how much you loved Stella."

"How did Bits know?" Paul asked. "I haven't told anyone."

"Apparently Karen called her," Carl said. "She didn't want you to be alone."

"Oh," Paul said, surprised to think that his ex-wife and his sister were in touch with each other. "Thanks."

"It's just the worst," Carl said. "It's hard enough when someone you love dies, but when you're the one who has to make the decision, it's a thousand times worse."

"You said it," Paul said.

"You should go to bed," Carl said. "Get some sleep."

"So should you," Paul said. "It isn't healthy to sleep four hours a night."

"Let's both get some sleep, then," Carl said. "I just wanted to call you."

"Thanks," Paul said. "I appreciate it."

"Let me know if there's anything I can do," Carl said.

He was tired and needed to lie down but knew that if he did, it would be a while before he got up again, and he had one last ritual to perform.

He found one of his landlady's gardening trowels in the garage and put it in his back pocket, tucked the metal box containing Stella's ashes under his arm, and walked to the cemetery.

There was a large oak tree in the center, beneath which Paul and Stella had sat on crisp fall afternoons and warm summer evenings to talk or just think, particularly on those occasions when Paul and Karen were going at it and he needed a place to go to cool off. They liked the way the oak leaves turned purple each fall, in contrast to the showier orange and yellow maples in the cemetery.

There, Paul dug a small hole, using the gardening trowel, cutting the sod on three sides and folding it back. From his pocket, he took the brass tag he'd removed from Stella's collar, bearing her name, his phone number, and the message, "If you find me unleashed, please do not call — I'm okay. I'm just waiting for my master." On more than one occasion, he'd exited Jake's or the Bay State only to find Stella missing and, when he got home, a message on his answering machine from some well-intentioned rescuer saying, "I found your dog and took her home because I thought she was lost . . ."

He opened the tin box, set the brass tag atop the ashes, and then buried the box in the shade of the oak tree, dispersing the excess dirt and carefully replacing the sod atop the grave, lest the groundskeepers discover the surreptitious interment. He'd tried to explain the concept of irony to Stella once, saying that burying a dog in a boneyard would be a good example. She'd replied, "Oooh, I like that very much." This was something she might have wanted.

He laid his hand atop the grave for a moment, patting down

the dirt, and considered saying a few words, but what was there left to say?

"I'll see you later," was the best he could come up with. He recalled a hand-painted plaque he'd seen in a pet store once that read, THE FIRST THING YOU SEE WHEN YOU GET TO HEAVEN ARE ALL YOUR OLD PETS, RUNNING TO GREET YOU. It was, of course, only wishful fantasy, magical thinking, and he was above all that.

He rose and turned for home.

22

The Truth about the North Pole

P aul's resolve hardened as the weather turned chilly. He withdrew, holed up with a bottle of vodka to slow his thoughts. He wasn't sure when he would be ready to resume his responsibilities in the universe. There was also, apparently, some kind of unwritten rule, in that world beyond his own four walls, that said he was forbidden to feel sorry for himself, so he wanted to stay where he made the rules.

He was working late one night, researching polar bears online for the book, when Tamsen instant-messaged him. He'd told her after her last visit that he needed to be alone for a while. When she invited him down the following weekend, he said he had to work. She said she understood, but dark thoughts came to him that night and stayed with him. Hopelessness. A wish to become invisible, absent, deleted. A desire to quit, accept defeat, drink the Kool-Aid. He began to pull away, screen her calls. He was emotionally fatigued. The relationship, which had started out with such fire and optimism, so much laughter and engagement, was dying, if it wasn't dead already, starting with his inability to consummate the relationship and flowing in all directions from there. Despite the many times Tamsen had told him it didn't matter, he knew it did. He couldn't untell his story, nor could he lay it at her feet for her to finish. He couldn't keep apologizing all the time or allow her to feel sorry for him, and he couldn't keep feeling sorry for himself in her company. The situation was pathologically pathetic, and he couldn't talk to her about it without pushing the relationship farther in the wrong direction.

He was, in short, wasting her time.

He stared at his computer screen, trying to think of what to do, aware that he was in no shape to make any major decisions. Yet, even in the fog of grief and depression (the hours he was spending at the Bay State weren't helping, but where else could he go and be both alone and not alone at the same time?), he knew he was being indefensibly selfish. He'd apparently been far less ready to enter into a new romance than he'd thought, trying unsuccessfully to fool himself. How to become ready, he hadn't a clue. He really wanted her to break up with him and be with Stephen. He had a sense that she'd been working up to it, before Stella's passing, but who could break up with a man right after his dog died? A temporary delay. The clock was ticking. He could hear it. She should leave him and move on as soon as possible.

On the other hand, he loved her.

He took a deep breath, held it, exhaled.

TamsenP: you're still up.

PaulGus: Working.

TamsenP: on?

PaulGus: Did you know that they once tracked a polar bear wearing a radio collar who walked 4,612 miles straight across the North Pole from the Beaufort Sea off Alaska to Greenland all by himself? They think he was looking for a mate.

TamsenP: did he find one?

PaulGus: One would hope so. What's new?

TamsenP: i'm totally nervous. sheila called and told me she'd accidentally booked two gigs on the same night and she needs a substitute for one of them.

PaulGus: When?

TamsenP: december 5. i think she has to sing at a christmas party. with just a piano player. that means i'd get to sing with her band. she thinks one or two rehearsals is all i need. i know the songs, so we just have to set up the intros and out-tros and decide what keys work for my voice.

PaulGus: You'll be great.

TamsenP: i feel like we haven't talked in way too long. what's been going on? how are you holding up?

PaulGus: I'm okay. One day at a time.

TamsenP: i've been thinking about you a lot.

PaulGus: All good thoughts, I hope.

TamsenP: all good. how is your father?

PaulGus: Hard to tell. About the same.

TamsenP: did you tell him about stella?

TamsenP: still there?

TamsenP: you've been avoiding me. what's wrong?

PaulGus: I'm sorry.

TamsenP: just be honest with me.

PaulGus: I'll try.

TamsenP: i'm going to hang up and call you.

PaulGus: I'd really rather not.

TamsenP: we need to talk in person, paul. not like this.

PaulGus: I prefer this. This is safer.

TamsenP: i'll call you tomorrow then.

PaulGus: Are you breaking up with me?

TamsenP: if you don't want to talk in person tonight, then i'll call you tomorrow.

PaulGus: Are you breaking up with me? Please answer the question.

TamsenP: i'm not going to let you keep your distance like this. we have to *talk*. in person. voice-to-voice if not face-to-face.

PaulGus: I have to go.

He got off-line, turned off his answering machine, poured himself a drink, went out onto the porch, and then listened to the phone ring and ring. It stopped after sixteen rings. A minute later, it rang again, this time for thirty-four rings. When he thought it was safe, he went back inside. He realized his head-in-the-sand approach wasn't going to work for very long. He realized his head-in-the-sand approach wasn't actually working now. He knew what was coming. He'd known it since Stella died. He'd been horrible to Tamsen ever since, and now the cows were coming home to roost, as his mother might have said.

He logged back on, briefly, to see if Tamsen had sent him an e-mail. Immediately she interrupted him with an instant message.

TamsenP: are you okay?
PaulGus: I'm fine.
TamsenP: have you been drinking?
PaulGus: A little.
TamsenP: a little?
PaulGus: More than a little.
TamsenP: can we talk on the phone?
PaulGus: No.
TamsenP: why won't you let me call you?
PaulGus: This way we can't say things we don't mean. Or blurt things out accidentally. I want to be able to read this later. I'm not feeling particularly sharp right now.
TamsenP: this is not the way to do this.
PaulGus: Do what? Are you breaking up with me?
PaulGus: Hello? Still there?
TamsenP: i'm sorry. yes. i don't think we should see each other. i think you've probably been thinking the same things i've been thinking. i think it's evident that something is wrong between us. and i think i should have said

something a long time ago but i let it go on too long and i
shouldn't have done that.

PaulGus: I was thinking earlier that I'm not ready for a
relationship. The problem is, I can't learn how to be in a
relationship again without being in a relationship again. But
that's not your job.

TamsenP: emotionally and spiritually, there's so much that
you already are and so much you could become. you're very
giving. i could see that every day in the way you treated
stella. you're extremely loving when you let your guard
down. but it's like when you're with me, instead of opening
up, you go back inside yourself. you opened up at first and
that's what i responded to, but then . . . i don't know what
happened, but i felt like you turned into the sort of little kid
who runs up to his room when he's upset, hoping mom
or dad will come get him. when i love someone, i want the
other person to hold their position and not run away. you
can't make people chase you. maybe you're just too afraid
of being hurt. i'm afraid of that too, particularly when i think
of how my marriage failed. i so don't want to fail again, or
hurt that much, or hurt someone else. everybody is afraid,
but you can't just give someone glimpses of yourself to see
if they like it and then hide. you have to stick your neck out
a little and give your whole self, 100 percent. you have to
bet everything, even when it would be safer to hold back.
you can't keep parts of yourself secret, thinking, "if i get
rejected, it won't hurt so much because they don't know
the real me." it's also as much my fault for thinking we
could limit ourselves. that was stupid of me. my thought at
first was that we were just going to be friends, and then i
thought, "okay, maybe we can be friends who can kiss each
other and mess around a little bit," but it just kept getting
more and more involved. i should have known i couldn't

keep talking and talking to you and feeling like we were getting closer and closer without wanting to go further and further. that's what attraction is. it doesn't happen in the eyes. it happens in the heart. but it was unfair and weak of me not to say something when i felt myself pulled in the other direction. i haven't lost faith in you, even though i'm sure that's what you think. i've seen you do some stupid things, like when you lied to me. that was hard to get over. and i've noticed how somehow we always end up talking about you and your problems when you're not the only one who's got 'em, but i can also see through all that because if you weren't also a great guy, believe me, i would have walked away a long time ago. i believe in you more than i've ever believed in anybody. but i also think this relationship is getting in the way of your becoming the person you could be, and that makes it wrong to continue.

PaulGus: You wrote that out before you got online, didn't you?

TamsenP: i was writing out my thoughts earlier, yes.

PaulGus: I can't exactly argue you into staying with me, can I?

TamsenP: i'm so sorry. i shouldn't have strung you along.

PaulGus: I don't see it that way. Can I ask you a question?

TamsenP: what?

PaulGus: Has something changed in your relationship with Stephen?

TamsenP: that's a separate issue.

PaulGus: Not really. I see it as losing to the competition.

TamsenP: that's not the way it is.

PaulGus: But you can see how I might feel like it is.

TamsenP: i can see that, yes.

PaulGus: So just answer the question and tell me the truth. The thing I've always liked best about us is that we've always told each other the truth. I'd hate to see that change, even under the present circumstances.

TamsenP: yes, things have changed.

PaulGus: How so?

TamsenP: they continue to evolve.

PaulGus: Don't be coy, please.

TamsenP: stephen asked me to marry him. paul, i would never have told you that this way if you'd given me a choice.

PaulGus: What did you say to him?

TamsenP: i said yes.

PaulGus: Congratulations. When's the wedding?

TamsenP: january 8.

PaulGus: That's Elvis's birthday.

TamsenP: i don't want you to joke right now.

PaulGus: I'm not joking. That really is Elvis's birthday.

TamsenP: that's not what I mean.

PaulGus: My hands are shaking. Hang on.

TamsenP: hello?

PaulGus: Are you moving to California?

TamsenP: that's the plan.

PaulGus: When?

TamsenP: not sure. next summer maybe. maybe sooner.

PaulGus: His ex and his kids too?

TamsenP: yup. they're going after the holidays. we've all met each other, so it looks like we'll be one of those complicated extended families.

PaulGus: Maybe I'll move to Greenland. It's only 4,612 miles by foot.

TamsenP: you'll find someone.

PaulGus: Just don't say that, okay? Just don't.

TamsenP: all right. you didn't do anything wrong, you know. and i know you're going to focus on the sex but that's not it either. let me repeat that: THAT'S NOT IT EITHER. that had nothing to do with it.

PaulGus: If you say so.

TamsenP: paul.

PaulGus: I love you.

TamsenP: i know. i love you too.

PaulGus: No phone calls.

TamsenP: i think not. it just makes it harder.

PaulGus: So we'll never see each other again?

TamsenP: i don't know. i have to go now.

PaulGus: Don't.

TamsenP: it's late.

PaulGus: I love you.

TamsenP: i know.

PaulGus: Okay.

TamsenP: you will be all right. i know that.

PaulGus: If you say so.

TamsenP: i have to go. logging off.

PaulGus: Tam?

PaulGus: Tam?

PaulGus: Are you there?

23

When

The leaves turned yellow and orange and red, then dropped from the trees. The wind blew the leaves up and down the streets of Northampton, past the Smith girls wrapping themselves in more layers of clothing each day, past the black-clad crow babies furtively slipping one another controlled substances in shadowed doorways, past the sidewalk glad-handers and street-corner preachers, past the shopkeepers eyeballing and thumbnailing their storefront windows in advance of Christmas, past the cars with their bumper stickers, past the houses and the factories, and out into the autumn landscape. The November rains fell as if they would never stop, and the roads turned slick and sharkskin shiny. The days grew short, and the nights long, as the stars slowly wheeled into their winter positions. Paul worked, ate, slept, went to movies, went to bars, and stuck to his routine, even though he now knew, for the first time in his life, that it was exactly that, sticking to his routine, that had gotten him precisely nowhere, or less than nowhere, really, because he felt as if he had fallen into a deep hole from which he would never escape.

He didn't know where to turn, until one night.

PaulGus: Hey, Dad. This is your son Paul. Remember me?
HarrGus: YES
PaulGus: Did Mom tell you I'm coming home for Thanksgiving?

HarrGus: YES

PaulGus: How are you feeling today? Better?

HarrGus: YES

PaulGus: I'm not so good myself. There was a woman I was seeing, Tamsen, but she lived in Rhode Island and the long distance thing wasn't working, so we broke up. There was actually more to it than that.

HarrGus: YES

PaulGus: I really feel like quite a failure. She was the first person I'd seen since the divorce. The only person. She was really special. I let it slip through my fingers.

HarrGus: YES

PaulGus: I feel like I need to change things. Get a job. Move, maybe.

HarrGus: NO

PaulGus: What do I do, Dad? I feel like I'll never be happy. I don't know what to do. I can't function like a normal person. I can't fix it alone, and unless I fix it, I can't get someone else to help me. Isn't it ironic?

HarrGus: YES

PaulGus: Tamsen tried but I could tell how frustrated she was getting. It's supposed to be fun. Not work. I could tell her how I felt but I couldn't show her. It was only a matter of time. I don't think I've ever been this down. It's really quite hopeless.

PaulGus: I know what you'd say if you could talk. I'm trying to be honest with myself, but I feel like I can't see things clearly. I'm really lost.

PaulGus: Dad?

PaulGus: You still there?

HarrGus: Q

PaulGus: Q?

PaulGus: Are you there? Somehow instead of Yes or No I

received the letter *Q*. I think there may be something wrong
with the

HarrGus: U
HarrGus: I
HarrGus: T
PaulGus: Quit?
HarrGus: D
HarrGus: R
HarrGus: I
HarrGus: N
HarrGus: K
HarrGus: I
HarrGus: N
HarrGus: G

He read his father's message.

He read it again.

He read it a third time, then gathered up all the liquor he had
in the house and poured it down the toilet. He pissed after it
and flushed the toilet, watching the water swirl in the bowl. He
flushed a second time and went to bed, knowing, all in one moment, that he would never drink again, because there was no further reason to, and every reason not to. He made a mental list of
the things he wanted — good health and a long life, a productive
life, prolonged creativity, a relationship, a family — and then he
asked if drinking was going to help him reach those goals, and
the answer in every case was no, it wouldn't. Using his computer's calculator, he estimated that if he'd averaged 5 drinks a day
for twenty years (and that was a conservative estimate), he'd had
36,500 drinks in his lifetime.

He knew his limit.

Time to say when.

This was change number one.

24

Escape from Berlin

He resumed running, recovering the motivation to exercise that he'd lost after putting Stella down. That was change number two, even though the weather was getting cold and he didn't really have the proper gear or clothing. He ran three miles, five times a week. At the Smith track one day, he timed himself again in the hundred-yard dash. He clocked in at 29.7 seconds, still hideous, but better than his previous time.

He resumed his yoga class. He tried to feel calm and to pay attention to his breathing, as his yoga instructor taught him, but he felt as if he wasn't having much luck, striking the balance between feeling mindful and feeling awkwardly self-conscious. What he did feel was patient, and maybe that was the point.

Some changes were less welcome than others. One day, after running a four-mile loop out in the Meadows area of town, where the floodplain beyond the airport was planted with corn, now harvested to stubble, he was cooling down on Parsons, next to the cemetery, walking hands on hips, when he saw a small, scruffy-looking terrier, charcoal gray, swaybacked and potbellied, with a snout full of wiry white chin whiskers and a cheerful expression on his face, his three-inch tail a-wagging as he sniffed at the contents of a tipped-over garbage can. Stella had introduced them once, and he knew the dog's name.

"Tobey?" Paul said.

The dog turned and looked at him, tail down and not wagging.

"It's Paul. Stella's friend. We met last summer when I was changing the oil in my car."

The dog turned to a forty-five-degree angle in a classic "I may or may not run but I'm no threat to you" signal but maintained eye contact.

"What's up?" Paul said. "You probably heard I had to put Stella down."

When Paul took a step forward, the dog moved a cautious step away.

"Cat got your tongue?" Paul said. "Oh, come on — that was funny."

The terrier ignored him and resumed searching the garbage, but when Paul took another step in his direction, the small dog ran down the street, glancing over his shoulder at Paul once. For a second, Paul wondered if he'd had the wrong dog, some other mutt that just looked like Tobey, but it was the same dog, he knew.

He attempted to communicate with several other dogs that morning, including a Westie on Market Street so fiercely protective of his home that his front feet hadn't touched the ground in years, the dog for all practical purposes two-legged as he strained at the end of his chain, barking and barking without saying a word that Paul understood.

That, apparently, was change number three.

He flew home the Wednesday before Thanksgiving. Bits and Eugene and the boys met him at the airport and hung out with him as he waited for his luggage to slide down the baggage claim. Bits told Paul he'd be staying at her house and said the kids were excited to have their favorite uncle visiting. As they drove, he stared at the still-familiar landscape. The tree limbs were black and leafless, the city solemn beneath a heavy sky.

At his parents' house, he saw that Carl had hired a crew to construct a wheelchair ramp. It looked sturdy and sadly permanent. Paul's mother hugged him and told him Harrold was doing much better. The old man was in his bed in the downstairs sunroom, propped up and watching a college football game on television. Working with his occupational therapist, Beverly said, Harrold had significantly improved the mobility in his right hand and arm. Paul had hoped to see his father's face light up, but Harrold's face was incapable of lighting up in the traditional sense. Yet Paul thought he saw something in his old man's eyes. Maybe he was imagining it.

He went to his father's bedside and took his dad's right hand in his, bending over and kissing the old man on the forehead.

"Hi, Pops," Paul said. "It's good to see you. You look great."

His father looked at him, then squeezed his hand three times.

"I know what that means," Paul said. Then he leaned down and whispered into his father's ear, "I did what you told me."

His mother made him a sandwich, and they chatted while he ate, Beverly filling him in on everything the doctors were saying, while Harrold watched television, using the remote control to switch back and forth between a college football game and a rerun of the old *Perry Mason* show. Beverly was happy to say Harrold's speech and language therapist thought that within three to six months' time, Harrold would be able to convey simple thoughts orally, though right now he was more comfortable using the computer keyboard.

"She thinks part of what's been going on is that his mood has improved," Beverly said.

"The new medications are working, I guess," Paul said.

"Oh, no — they took him off his antidepressants," Beverly said. "They thought they were holding him back in other ways. You know, I've tried to educate myself on all of this, but some things they just can't explain."

They chatted and kept Harrold company until Bits said it was time to go — she had a lot of baking to do for tomorrow. She made sure each of her kids kissed Grandpa good-bye, and then Paul kissed his father one last time on the forehead, saying he would see him tomorrow for turkey and pecan pie.

They drove to his sister's house for dinner, ordering pizza and picking it up on the way. He threw his suitcase in the guest room, and then they all sat together in the den, watching football. When his sister offered him a beer, he declined. He'd felt a bit shaky initially, and his hands had trembled slightly the first few days, but now that he'd gone two weeks without a drink, he monitored himself for any strange or aberrant sensations or emotions and had nothing to report. He'd expected to have some sort of unbearable craving for a drink, but he didn't feel any thirstier than usual, and indeed he felt measurably better, more clearheaded. He slept better, and his skull didn't hurt when he woke up in the morning. The main difference was that time seemed to have slowed to a crawl. He knew he could never have another drink, not even a sip, but it didn't seem as if it was going to be all that difficult. He couldn't drink bleach or antifreeze either. Poison was poison. Unless somebody pried his mouth open and poured alcohol down his throat, it couldn't hurt him anymore.

After the kids were down, his brother-in-law Eugene yawned several times and said he needed to go to bed, leaving Paul alone with his sister. Bits had made two pumpkin pies, two pecan pies, and four loaves of banana bread. Paul couldn't imagine a house smelling any better than hers did. His sister was wearing a bathrobe over her flannel pj's and Polarfleece socks with leather bottoms.

"Can I ask you a personal question?" she said, flopping next to him on the couch and pulling her feet up under her. Paul put down the crossword puzzle he'd been working on.

"Sure," he told her.

"Are you all right? You seem sort of quiet."

"I'm good," he said. "Maybe I just used to be louder."

"What happened to Tamsen? I thought maybe we were going to meet her."

"That didn't work out," Paul said.

"Oh, no," Bits said sympathetically. "Why?"

"Lot of reasons," Paul said. "Stupidity. Ignorance. Cowardice. Speaking only for myself. I'm probably leaving something out." He knew he was leaving out drinking, self-pity, impotence, deception, and the fact that she'd overcome her fear of commitment by choosing someone else, but he wasn't sure his sister needed that much information.

"I'm sorry for you, baby brother," his sister said. "Are you okay?"

"I'll be all right," he said, hoping that it was true.

"That's a shame," she said. "She sounded like she wouldn't put up with your bullshit."

"She wouldn't," Paul said. "That's why she left. It was sort of funny, but right before she told me she didn't think we should see each other, I was thinking how we shouldn't see each other either, but when she said it, I thought, 'Hey, you can't break up with me — I was going to break up with you.' It was just like junior high school. Except worse."

"Have you heard from her?" Bits asked.

"Nope."

"So what happened?" she asked him.

"Her other boyfriend asked her to marry him, for one thing," Paul said. "You gotta admit, I'm not the best marriage material."

"I don't know what you're talking about," Bits said. "Why do you say that?"

"Put yourself in her shoes," Paul said. "What do I have to offer? I don't have a house. I don't have a job. I'm not exactly a portrait of financial stability." There was much he was leaving out. "I'm just being realistic."

"Excuse me," she said, "but if you were being realistic, you'd have to include all the positives. All you're focusing on are the negatives."

"What positives would those be, exactly?" Paul asked. "Because I think I'm kind of a failure."

"That's just stupid," Bits said. "No offense. I just don't know why you see yourself that way. You're the one who left home and went off and had a dream that you followed. That's a lot different from the paths that I took or Carl took. Carl said you've always followed your own instincts."

"Carl said that?" Paul said.

"Can I ask you something else?" his sister asked. "You don't have to answer if you don't want. Did you quit drinking?"

"I did," he said.

"You okay?"

"So far, it's been pretty easy," he said. He pictured jumping over a wall, sort of like escaping from East Berlin in the sixties. He'd made a decision, and now he was on the proper side of that wall. Jumping back over the wall to the wrong side was simply not allowed, even if he couldn't remember exactly all the reasons he'd jumped the wall in the first place. It didn't matter, as long as he stayed on this side of the wall. "I'm actually sort of surprised at how easy it was. Maybe I just got lucky."

"So would you say you're an alcoholic?"

"I would say that, yes," he said.

"Was that a factor in the breakup with Tamsen?"

"Indirectly."

"With Karen?"

"Absolutely." He nearly laughed to consider how many times he'd told himself drinking had nothing to do with the failure of his first marriage. How could he have fooled himself for so long?

"Did Tamsen want you to quit?" Bits asked.

"No," Paul said. "I mean, maybe she did. She never mentioned it. It wasn't like an ultimatum or anything." She had, of course, told him on numerous occasions to look at himself. Was that what she was getting at? "Actually, I quit because Dad suggested I should."

"Really?"

"Really."

"How would he know?"

It was actually a good question. The more he thought about it, the more it puzzled him — how, indeed, did his father know what to say? Perhaps he hadn't been as successful as he'd thought at hiding his problem from his father, but that didn't explain it.

"I should go to bed," his sister said. "I have to go over and help Mom with the turkey tomorrow morning. I'm sorry for you. But I'm also proud of you."

That night, thinking about Thanksgivings past and the question his sister had posed as to how his alcoholism may have affected his marriage, he found some stationery and a pen and wrote a letter, taking care to write as legibly as he could. He couldn't remember the last time he'd written anything by hand, and his penmanship showed it.

Dear Karen,

    Happy Thanksgiving to you and to Kevin and to anybody else who may have recently joined the family. Hope everybody made it home for the holiday. One of the stranger parts of being divorced is losing so many nieces and nephews and brothers-in-law and sisters-in-law — somehow I didn't expect that. Anyway, if it ever comes up, tell them I hope they're all well and thriving. Olivia must have her driver's license by now.

    But that's not why I'm writing. First, I wanted to thank you for helping me put Stella down. I couldn't have done it without you. Thanks for calling my sister too. It kind of surprised me that you would bother, but then you always showed me more compassion than I ever showed you.

That's not really why I'm writing you either.

I'm writing because I had kind of an epiphany tonight. I was talking to my sister and realized you had every right to feel lonely and unimportant during our marriage. I left you alone all the time, and I put everything else first. I'd sit in a bar, thinking, "Gee, I wish Karen was here," and I'd blame you for not joining me, while you sat at home wondering why your husband was never there — how stupid was that? Of me, I mean. I'm not trying to make excuses. I'm just trying to tell you I understand why you felt the way you felt — I used to try to argue with you and tell you you had no right to feel that way. You had every right. I don't know how you could have felt any other way. I was wrong, and blind, and that's no defense, but I am so sorry for causing you so much heartache. I can't make it up to you anymore, I know, so perhaps this is too little too late, but I wanted you to know I know. I'm truly sorry. I wish you every happiness in the world.

Paul

P.S. I'm still right about everything else, but I was wrong about that. Ha-ha.

25

A Pilgrim's Progress

His mother called the following morning to say — though there was no need to call, since it was the same time every year — that the turkey would be ready at four. By two, all were present, early enough for the traditional preturkey walk around Lake Harriet. Carl had run a 10k race that morning and begged off. Paul pushed his father's wheelchair, accompanied by Bits, Eugene, Katie, Elliot, and B. J., who had a new riddle for his uncle Paul: "Dave's mom had three kids — the first one was named Penny, and the second one was named Nickel, so what was the third one named? No, not Dime — Dave!"

Paul didn't mind being fooled by a six-year-old.

The sky was Appaloosa gray, the temperature about forty-five degrees, so they'd all bundled up, Harrold wrapped in a Polar-fleece blanket. The leaves were off the trees, but it had yet to snow. It was easy to push the wheelchair on the smoothly paved footpath. After he'd retired, Harrold had walked around the lake as part of his daily routine. As they walked, other seniors from the lake-walking community passing in the opposite direction greeted him by name. One said, "Welcome back, Harrold." Near the Southeast Beach area, a large flock of ducks had gathered, pausing on their migration southward. An old woman was feeding the ducks corn and gave each of the children a fistful of kernels from her sack to do likewise.

It was impossible, given that this was his traditional lake for Zen contemplation, not to think of Tamsen and wonder where she was spending her Thanksgiving. He remembered small things about her. Eating a picnic lunch in the car in the pouring rain. Finding ten bucks at the mall and blowing it all on video games. Renting *The Music Man* and singing along with every song, including the countermelody to "Lida Rose." Hanging up the phone at three in the morning, too tired to talk anymore. He wondered if she was thinking of him. He wondered if she wondered if he was thinking of her. He wondered if she wondered if he wondered. He wanted to call her but couldn't.

Ever.

When they got back, the house smelled of turkey and stuffing, sweet potatoes and creamed corn. Paul poured himself a tall glass of fresh-pressed apple cider. The tangy-sweet punch as it went down was nearly overwhelming. At four they were called to the table, where they stood to sing grace in three-part harmony, "Praise God, from Whom all blessings flow; / Praise him, all creatures here below," except for Harrold, who sat in his wheelchair with his eyes closed, Bits holding his right hand, Erica his left.

Then the feeding frenzy began. "Don't be afraid of the mashed potatoes," his mother said, directing the flow of dishes around the table. There was turkey, stuffing, mashed potatoes and gravy, creamed corn with bread crumbs on top, sweet potatoes with little marshmallows on top, green beans with canned onion rings on top, dinner rolls and lefse, two kinds of coleslaw, green Jell-O, cranberry relish and jellied cranberry. Paul watched his mother feed his father, touched by the tenderness he saw, but it made him sad too. Who'd be spooning cranberry relish into his mouth when he was down to his last two or three Thanksgivings — who was going to wipe his chin, or hold his hand? Some hairy-backed ape of a minimum-wage nursing home caregiver with a prison record back in the old country, no doubt.

Yikes.

Yet here with his family, and with his nieces and nephews, the idea of simply growing old was not as frightening as it had once been.

After the pumpkin and pecan pies had been polished off, the men adjourned to the den to watch football, a game between the Vikings and the Cowboys. At halftime, the boys wanted to go outside and play football and invited Paul and Carl and Eugene to join them. Carl declined, saying he'd eaten too much to move. Paul played for half an hour, then begged off and went back inside. The women had returned to the dinner table for coffee. In the den, he asked his brother what the score was. Carl didn't answer.

"Do you know who's winning?" Paul said again.

Carl was sound asleep, sitting in their father's recliner, tipped back with the remote control still in his hand. Paul pried the remote from his brother's fingers and turned the sound down, then watched the game from the couch. Carl woke up half an hour later.

"What happened?" he said, still in a fog.

"You zonked out," Paul said. "You've been asleep for at least an hour."

"I have? I'm sorry."

"Sorry for what? It's the tryptophan," Paul said.

They watched the television in silence for another minute.

"I think I need your help," Carl said at last.

"Okay," Paul said. He expected his brother needed to haul garbage bags full of leaves to the dump or something of that order. "Help with what?"

"With everything," Carl said.

Paul looked up from the television.

"What do you mean?" he asked. "What's wrong?"

"Well," Carl said. He swallowed hard, and if Paul wasn't mistaken, he thought he detected moisture welling up in the corners of his brother's eyes before Carl squeegeed away the evidence with his thumb. "I'm not sure, but I think it's me. I don't think I can do this."

"Do what?"

"Do you think maybe you could take over Dad's finances? Just for a little while?"

It took a second for Paul to believe what he'd just heard.

"You're not serious, right?" he said, but Carl didn't appear to be joking. "Didn't you once say an average sea urchin knew more about money than I did?"

"You couldn't do any worse than I'm doing," Carl said.

"What do you mean?" Paul asked. "Are you losing money?"

Carl nodded.

"A lot?"

He nodded again.

"How much?"

Carl tried to shrug. "Six figures," he said. "Approaching six figures, I should probably say."

"How?" Paul knew the stock market had taken a nosedive the previous August, the Dow falling 357 points overnight, for reasons Paul hadn't bothered to pay attention to, something about worsening economic conditions in Russia connected to Boris Yeltsin's political future and recent sobriety. He hadn't worried about it, figuring Carl was on top of it.

"If I knew that . . . ," Carl said. "I've been doing so much research. I thought . . . Everything just goes wrong. They make it too easy."

"Who does?" Paul asked, but Carl didn't respond. It didn't matter. "Does Dad know?"

Carl shook his head.

"You never got him online?"

"I tried about a month ago, but he wasn't ready."

"It's okay, Carlos," Paul said. "Nobody cares. We know you're doing the best you can." He'd read about people trying to micromanage their investments through online trading, how addictive it was and the traps some people fell into. Carl was a micromanager long before the Internet ever came along.

"I can't stay asleep," Carl said. "I go to bed utterly exhausted, and three hours later I'm wide awake. So I figure, as long as I'm up, maybe I'll get some work done. I can't do it. My memory is for shit. I've lost my ATM card three times in the past two months. I fell asleep at work last week. Erica and I . . . it's too much."

Paul could hear his sister and Erica laughing in the kitchen.

"Maybe we should let Arnie Olmstead take over," Paul suggested. "I'm sure he's old school, but he'd do a better job than I would. You're totally right about the sea urchin. I'm not sure I know as much as a below-average sea urchin, let alone an average one."

Carl nodded. He'd probably had the same thought, Paul realized, though his brother would have lost too much face capitulating to his father's former investment counselor directly. He needed somebody to do it for him.

"Do you want me to call him?" Paul asked.

Carl nodded again.

"I'm thinking maybe I should see somebody about all this stress," Carl said. "I know I'm not getting anywhere, trying to handle it alone."

"That's probably a really good idea," Paul said.

They heard the sound of footsteps approaching, the kids thundering down the stairs at a rapid pace, laughing and shrieking.

"I'd really appreciate it if you could keep this just between you and me," Carl said. "I haven't even told Erica."

"You got it," Paul said as the kids arrived, asking if they could watch a movie, Katie hugging a video cassette of *Toy Story* expectantly to her bosom. Paul and Carl agreed to turn control of the television over to the children. Howard climbed into his father's lap, while Elliot and B. J. sat with Paul on the couch. Katie curled up in a beanbag chair on the floor, covering herself with one of Beverly's throws.

"At the very least," Paul told his brother, "you should get something to help you sleep."

"I should," Carl said over the opening credits, staring at the TV. "Man. I should have bought stock in Pixar. These guys do amazing work." He looked at Paul. "We'll discuss it with Arnie. But they do do amazing stuff."

The conversation ended when Howard and Elliot simultaneously shushed them.

The next day, Paul called Arnie Olmstead and asked him if he'd mind resuming his former duties as Harrold's broker. Arnie was amenable. They made small talk for a few minutes, and then Arnie said he'd get the paperwork together.

26

Evthng

He spent his last night home with his parents. His mother was in the sunroom, in the recliner, with her reading glasses on, knitting a sweater for Katie, which she hoped to have finished by Christmas. His father was watching a hockey game, the Montreal Canadiens versus the Detroit Red Wings. Paul pulled a chair in from the living room and sat next to his mother. He felt strangely focused and clear.

"The Red Wings sure have a lot of Russian guys on the team," Paul said. His father clicked on the Yes icon.

"If you want to turn the channel, I'm sure your father wouldn't mind," Paul's mother said. Paul looked at his father, who looked straight ahead at the television. It seemed pretty clear he wanted to watch the game.

"This is good," Paul said. Beverly kept knitting.

"Did you get a chance to talk to Carl?" she asked.

"A little bit," Paul said. He wondered why she'd asked.

"How does he seem to you?"

"Okay, I guess," Paul said. "Too much sweating the small stuff. As ever."

He watched her hands dance, the needles clicking together in a rhythm that reminded him of trains.

"Carl tries to do so much," Beverly said. "Erica said he hasn't been sleeping."

"I know," Paul said, hoping to avoid giving away anything Carl might have wanted him to keep quiet. "We talked about that."

"Oldest children have such a strong sense of responsibility," Beverly said. She looked up from her knitting and smiled. "It's nice that you boys had a chance to talk. I think he really respects your opinions. Do you know what we forgot to do at Thanksgiving? We forgot to draw names for Secret Santa. Do you mind if we draw a name for you the next time we're together? I was thinking—"

"NO," Harrold's computer screen read.

Paul noticed his father was looking at them.

"No what?" Paul said. "I don't mind. Really."

"NO."

"No?"

Harrold was looking at Beverly, who was looking at him. She seemed uncomfortable, focused on her knitting. When Harrold realized Beverly wasn't going to answer the question, he turned to the computer screen and took up the mouse, moving the pointer across the keyboard and clicking until he'd spelled his message.

"TLL EVTHNG," he typed.

Beverly looked at him.

"YES."

"All right, then," she said. "Your father and I were talking last night. It's sort of remarkable, the way he manages to let me know what's on his mind. Anyway, Harrold would like me to tell you a story. Would you like some cocoa? With or without marshmallows?"

"With," Paul said. What did she mean, a story? He looked at his father, who'd closed his eyes. It all seemed very ominous and foreboding. Did Harrold have a second wife and family in Omaha? Had they secretly voted for Clinton?

His mother set down her knitting and went to the kitchen, where she put water on to boil. When she returned with the cocoa, she handed a cup to Paul, set hers on the coffee table, and went to her husband, where she fluffed his pillow and gave him a sip of juice. When Harrold had trouble getting the straw between his lips, she used her hand to insert it in his mouth and then she smoothed his hair back and kissed him on the forehead.

"Now then. As I said, I have a story your father wants me to tell you," she told her son. "It might explain a few things. I don't know. We were hoping it might. As you'll see, it's something we've thought about discussing for some time. Apparently after the things you've been sharing with him in your little chats on-line, he thought you were ready to hear this."

She picked up her knitting again, needles clicking together. Her hands had spots on them, and the grains of her fingernails had become accentuated with time, but they were still quick, nimble fingers.

"We never thought it was useful to dwell on things," she began. "We just didn't want anyone to worry about something that was no longer an issue. There's a time and a place and then you miss the opportunity and eventually it's so much easier to let bygones be bygones. But if your father wants me to tell you, then I'll tell you. I'm sure he'd rather tell you himself. Is this okay, Harrold?"

Harrold blinked.

"Tell me what?" Paul asked. Her reluctance made him worry. What could be so hard to talk about? Had somebody had an affair? Was there something wrapped in plastic under the floorboards in the attic that he might rather not know about? Was Paul adopted, left on their doorstep as an infant by visitors from a distant doomed planet, with a note that said, "Teach him to use his powers for the good of mankind . . ."? In an odd way, he felt as if he'd always known there was something big that nobody was talking about.

"I may get a few things wrong, but I'll try. How much do you remember of the accident?" his mother asked him.

"The car accident? When I was three?" he said.

"Oh, you were too little. You don't remember this. I don't see why—"

Harrold looked at her. His eyes seemed to plead.

"I remember it," Paul said. "I don't remember the accident itself, but I remember staying at Grandma and Grandpa's house, and I remember seeing you guys in the hospital. I remember we were coming home from a party and the road was icy . . ."

His mother was shaking her head.

"The roads weren't icy?" Paul asked.

"I don't know where you got that part of it," she said. "It was September."

On the television, one of the Red Wings' Russians had scored a goal and was pumping his fist in the air.

"Okay," he said. "I just remember we skidded. And hit a bridge. Right?"

His mother nodded.

"Thank God you were in a baby seat. We never had baby seats for Carl or Elizabeth."

"They had their seat belts on, right?"

"Bits had hers on. Your brother didn't, and your father didn't. I had a seat belt on, but it didn't have a shoulder restraint."

"So what happened?" Paul asked. "It was September? In my memory, we were coming home from a Christmas party with Dad's navy buddies, and we hit a patch of ice. That's not right?"

She shook her head again.

"It was Labor Day weekend. A warm summer night." She looked at her husband again. Harrold stared straight ahead. "We were driving back from Madison, Wisconsin, where your father had been to a reunion with the men who'd served with him in the Pacific. It was the first time they'd gotten together since the war. We all stayed at the Howard Johnson. You kids loved the pool. Anyway, we were driving home, and we'd gotten somewhere near Baraboo. Or was it Mauston? I think it was Baraboo, or near the Dells anyway. But your father had had too much to drink. He asked me to drive, but I'd had too much to drink too, and I was exhausted from chasing after three kids all day. Especially you. You were so fast."

Paul looked at his mother, then his father.

"What?"

"We thought about getting a motel room — you know, it had to be the Dells because it was a holiday weekend and all the motel rooms were booked because of all the tourists, so your father thought we should just get home."

"Back up a second," Paul said. "You said you'd had too much to drink?"

"Your father was driving drunk," Beverly said. She let out a big sigh, closing her eyes for a moment, then looked at her knitting.

"What?" Paul repeated. "You don't drink. You never drank."

"No, we don't," she said, looking up. "But we used to."

"What?" he said again. "Let me get this straight. You're saying Dad was driving drunk?"

She nodded. He still couldn't believe it. He remembered how his parents wouldn't even take Communion wine and asked for grape juice instead. How they refused champagne at weddings. How there was never a bottle of anything in the house for guests, and of course how they chewed him out when they smelled beer on his breath after he'd come home from a high school keg party, and did everything they could to keep him from drinking. It all added up now, but he still couldn't picture them drunk.

"And what happened?"

"Well, your brother was singing very loudly and bouncing around in the backseat. He was standing on the backseat, singing 'Ninety-nine Bottles of Beer' at the top of his lungs, and your father was trying to get him to sit down. He turned around to get Carl to be quiet, and he reached his arm back"—she pantomimed the action, her arm hanging in the air — "and when he went back to watching the road, it was too late to turn away from the bridge. God had a hand in saving us that night, because if you'd seen the car . . ."

She looked at Harrold. He had his eyes closed, but he wasn't asleep.

"Carl went through the windshield. Elizabeth was okay except for the cut above her eye. Your father and I were both thrown from the car. Which I don't understand because I thought I had my seat belt on, but I must have unbuckled it. I wish I could tell you more, but I have no memories between just before the accident and when I woke up in the hospital. Anyway, that was what happened."

"And Carl got thrown through the windshield?"

"That's what I was told. He broke his shoulder, and he had some glass pieces taken out of the top of his head, but he was fine. He bounced right back. He used to bring me juice and help the nurse — do you remember that, Harrold? No, he was fine. And like I said, you were fine and so was Elizabeth. It was really a miracle. We've thanked God so many times that nobody . . . it could have been so much worse."

She picked up her skein of yarn to see how much she had left. Paul considered. Carl would have been seven years old and relatively cognizant. He always said he didn't remember anything about the accident. Paul wondered if that was true and, if it was, if Carl had blocked the memory, prevented it from rising to the level of consciousness until it had nowhere to go but to live in the basement of his unconscious, where it gained power over time and came to dominate the way Carl felt and thought about things. Paul had called him a born tight-ass, but now he realized he may not have been born that way.

"At any rate, we never had another drink from that point on," his mother said.

"I can imagine," Paul said.

"I know you always thought we were prudes. We changed a lot of things after that. I know, Paul, that you never cared for church, but for us, God spoke to us and told us he was going to give us a second chance, but if he did, it was on the condition that we become better Christians. He gave us a second chance."

"I had no idea," Paul said.

Harrold was looking at his wife again.

"Pastor Wilson helped us a great deal at first," his mother said. "And we talked to a man at the VA, a psychologist, and then your father attended meetings for years. I had to stay home with you kids."

"AA meetings?"

She nodded.

"When?"

"Every Monday night."

"I thought he was bowling," Paul said. "We thought he was bowling. We bought him a bowling ball."

She smiled. "That bowling ball was one of the best presents you ever gave him."

Paul recalled a time when the whole family went bowling and how his father wasn't very good and barely broke one hundred, and he remembered thinking, "Wow, he sure sucks for somebody who bowls once a week." Now it made sense.

"I'm sorry if it's taking me a while to get this," he said. "I can imagine a bunch of navy buddies sitting around getting loaded and telling war stories, but I always figured Dad would have been the guy sipping iced tea."

His mother had been somber before, but now she was grave.

"I don't think you understand what 'telling war stories' means," Beverly said. "It's not like telling jokes around a camp-fire. By then, two of your father's friends had taken their own lives. That's why they called the reunion. They'd seen some hor-rible things during the war. A psychiatrist suggested it would be a good idea if everybody got together and talked about it. The wives were locked out."

"Do you know what happened?" he asked. "What horrible things?"

She shook her head. She didn't know the answer.

"I thought the right thing to do was not to ask," she said. "Maybe he'll tell you someday, when he's better. Let me get you some more cocoa."

She took his cup and left the room. While she was in the kitchen, Paul looked at his father, whose eyes were cast down.

"Dad?" Paul said. "I had no idea."

His father watched the hockey game.

"Would you mind if I told Carl and Bits what Mom told me?"

"NO."

"No, you won't mind?"

"YES."

"Okay then, I will. I was going to go over to Carl's house to-morrow morning before my flight. You know, if you want to turn the sound back on, I don't care. I know it isn't easy for you to — "

"CN YOU," his father typed.

"Yeah?"

"FRGIV ME?"

"Absolutely."

He saw his father raise the pointer finger on his right hand and hold it up. It looked like a baby bird in a nest. Paul took his father's hand and squeezed, surprised at how hard his father squeezed back. Three squeezes. Three squeezes back. Paul put his arms around his father's neck and hugged him, not for the first time, but for the first time since he was six, when he'd come to understand that men didn't do such things.

27

Brothers

Paul drove out to see his brother the next day. Minnesota in late November was both bleak and expectant, bleak because the trees were bare and the grass was brown, but pregnant with the possibility of winter. Growing up, Paul had watched for the first snowfall, yearned for it. The temperature was in the thirties. He drove around Lake Harriet, then Lake Calhoun. In a month, they'd be frozen over, and a few weeks after that, people would be skating on them.

Over the phone, he'd told his sister everything he'd learned the night before. They'd talked for nearly an hour. She was surprised at first but then saw how much sense it made, a piece of a puzzle she hadn't known was missing.

Paul's brother was in the basement rec room, lacing on a pair of running shoes and dressed in fleece running attire. Despite having taken the scenic route, Paul had arrived half an hour early. Erica had taken Howie to soccer practice and Katie to skating lessons. Carl said he'd hoped to get in a run before Paul got there.

"Go ahead," Paul said. "I can wait."

"You wanna come with?" Carl said. "Bits told me you've been running. I can set you up."

Paul agreed. Carl found him a pair of Yale sweatpants and a matching hooded zip-up sweatshirt in blue and white and an extra pair of socks and shoes, his and Paul's feet being the same size. They stretched in the driveway. Paul wasn't so much into stretching but knew it was something he was supposed to do. The sky was a mat of slate, but there was no wind.

"I hate running into the wind," Paul told Carl. "It feels like the whole universe is against me."

"What makes you so sure it's not?" Carl said, smiling. "Let me know if I'm going too fast. Three and a half okay?"

Paul nodded.

Carl set a good pace, maybe a bit faster than Paul ordinarily went. He felt strong, but then he always felt strong for the first quarter mile. They turned left at the end of the drive and headed up the bike path along Mirror Lake.

"So what was it you had to tell me?" Carl asked. Paul had warned him on the phone that he had some news. "You talked to Arnie?"

"I did," Paul said. "There's some paperwork, but that's about it."

"That's what you had to tell me?"

"There's more," Paul said.

He told Carl the story their mother had told him the night before, leaving nothing out. Carl listened, slowing the pace a bit as he concentrated without comment.

"Pretty interesting," Carl said at last.

"That's an understatement," Paul agreed. "Do you remember anything about the accident?"

Carl didn't answer at first.

"I remember thinking I'd done something wrong," he said.

"Do you remember ever seeing Mom and Dad drunk?" Paul asked.

Carl thought.

"I remember them being goofy. If they were drunk, I didn't know it."

"Did Dad ever talk about the war? He never did with me."

Carl thought again, his pace steady and even.

"I remember him having bad dreams," he said. "Hearing him. And being frightened. He never went bowling?"

"Apparently not," Paul said.

"Mom told you all this?"

"Dad wanted her to," Paul said.

The water on the lake was choppy and broken, the wind picking up now. They ran past a small cove where a dozen mallards had taken transient slippage before heading south, their green heads shining despite the gloom.

"You sleep last night?" Paul asked.

"Nine hours," Carl said. "Triazolam. Point one two five milligrams. It takes about an hour to fully wake up, but it seems to do the trick."

They left the bike path and cut across a footbridge leading to Interlachen Country Club, the famous golf course where Bobby Jones won the United States Open on his way to completing the grand slam in 1930. Despite its being late in the season, a lone foursome of diehards made its way over a hill in the distance, golf carts like beasts slowly grazing.

"I remember," Carl said.

"Remember what?" Paul said.

"Mom and Dad. Drinking. That must have been it. You were crying in your crib and I couldn't wake Dad up."

"Where was Mom?"

"I don't know," Carl said. "He must have been passed out when he was supposed to be babysitting. You were crying and I didn't know what to do. I never thought about it until now." They ran. "Maybe I'll bring it up with my therapist."

"You're seeing one?"

"Friday," Carl said. "A woman Erica knows. She thinks I'm OCD. I'm kind of nervous."

"Don't be," Paul said. "The whole idea is to listen for as long as you can before you realize they're just as big an idiot as anybody else. Then you're cured."

"Speaking from experience?"

"Karen and I saw a marriage counselor," Paul said as they ascended a hill, staying in the rough next to the twelfth fairway. "Talk about a fucking racket. If they were real doctors, they'd be sued for malpractice for losing so many patients. I quit drinking, by the way."

"Bits told me," Carl said. "High time."

"Quite the opposite, actually," Paul said.

They picked up speed at the crest of the hill, moving downhill toward the green, where the pin had been set in the grass just in front of the apron. They turned right at the green for the par-5 ninth hole, heading toward the tee box 518 yards away. Eventually they came back to the shore of Mirror Lake. They saw a man in a wooden canoe, whipping a fly rod back and forth in the air. He looked like a walking Orvis catalog.

"Maybe we should go fly-fishing sometime," Paul said.

"You fly-fish?"

"I tried it a couple times. I didn't catch anything," Paul admitted.

"Me neither," Carl said. "I think it's a crock of shit. I think all those guys who say it's the best way to fish are lying, but they can't admit it because they've already spent so much money. Show me the fish."

"You could be right," Paul said.

"Paul," Carl said, "I never said I didn't think you're smart. You're probably the smartest kid in the family, in a multiple-intelligence way. All I meant, when I compared you to a sea urchin, was that it didn't make sense that you weren't equally smart at everything. Everybody has things they're good at and things they're not. I think I was jealous because you were so much better than me at so many things."

"That's ridiculous," Paul said. "I'm not better than you at anything."

"No," Carl said, "*that's* ridiculous. I couldn't write a book if my life depended on it. And don't argue with me — that is one thing I'm better than you at."

"Are not."

"Am too."

"Are not."

"Am too."

Paul paused.

"Fuck you."

"Touché. You mind if I sprint the last half mile?" Carl said. "I always try to finish with a kick."

"So do I," Paul said.

When Carl picked up the pace, Paul stayed next to him, though conversation was no longer possible. Paul felt good, strong, exhilarated. When Carl increased the pace again, Paul kept up, then surged ahead a few paces as the pavement flew beneath his feet. He felt weightless, the way he'd felt as a kid, streaking across the playground.

He slowed himself when he got too far ahead, realizing that although a kind of final victory was within his grasp, a chance to at last beat Carl in a footrace, it wasn't the time or place to make Carl feel any worse than he already did. When Carl caught up to him, Paul tried to stay close, only to feel his brother slow again. Then it occurred to him: *Carl* was letting *him* win.

Paul slowed. Half a block from Carl's house, both men were walking, out of breath, hands on hips, hearts racing.

Carl turned to face Paul. Paul looked his brother in the eye. Carl waggled his eyebrows.

"Dink," Paul said, sprinting for the house as fast as he could, Carl beside him, both men racing at top speed, laughing in clouds of steam, more full of joy with each other than they'd ever felt before in their lives.

28

Every Mother's Child Is Gonna Spy

The Wickenden Street Café was crowded with young, happy people sipping Grey Goose martinis and manhattans and Long Island iced teas. Paul found a seat toward the back of the bar, in a dark corner where no one would see him, and told the waitress all he wanted was a cup of decaf. She grunted her disapproval.

It had precipitated all the way from Northampton, freezing rain and sleet farther north turning to rain the closer he got to Providence. It had been something of a last-minute decision to come, and against his better judgment, in terms of highway safety, but his mission was critical. The stage in the far corner of the room was lit by colored spots, illuminating a drummer and a bass player, both about twenty-five, and a piano player old enough to be their father, as perhaps he was, for Paul noticed a strong resemblance. The stage was strung with miniature white Christmas lights. At the microphone, Tamsen wore a black dress with a black sequined top, baring her shoulders, and larger earrings than she ordinarily wore, but then she had to sparkle enough for the people at the back of the room to see.

Paul knew he was biased, but he thought she sounded great, with good pitch and phrasings that were unique. Moreover, she seemed utterly confident and unafraid, though he could guess what was going on inside her.

He applauded when she finished. People were for the most part actually listening and not trying to talk over the entertainment. Tamsen looked slightly embarrassed by the applause, but pleased too. She stared at a piece of paper at her feet, then picked it up and showed the audience.

"You guys want to know why I've been squinting at this piece of paper all night?" she asked. "This is how new I am at this — look at this. It looks blank to you, right? It does to me too. I wrote my set list in a red pen. The spots are red too — my set list is invisible."

The crowd laughed. Her stage patter seemed natural and relaxed. He knew all she had to do was be herself onstage and she'd win over any crowd. He felt proud of her. Sheila Clark had taught her well. She seemed happy, which was one of the reasons he'd come, to make sure of that. He saw a man seated at a front table with an extra chair next to him and guessed that he was probably Stephen, a nice-looking guy in a dark turtleneck. Paul would have gone to shake Stephen's hand and congratulate him, but he didn't want Tamsen to know he was there. She sang "Don't Get Around Much Anymore" and "Old Folks" and "This Will Make You Laugh." Finally, after conferring with the bass player, she introduced the last song.

"Thank you so much for coming. You have no idea how much it's meant to me to have you here. We weren't going to do any holiday songs, because I know you've probably been hearing them in every elevator and supermarket, but we'll do this one," she explained. "Written by Hugh Martin and Ralph Blane. As sung originally by Judy Garland in *Meet Me in St. Louis*."

"Have yourself a merry little Christmas," she began. Paul had never listened so closely to the words of the song before. They were really quite sad, if you paid attention to them. It was vain of him, he knew, to imagine that she was singing the song directly to him, but he indulged the notion.

He cut out quickly before the lights came up. Crumpled in his pocket was the note he'd scribbled on a napkin, to give to the waitress, to give to the singer, which read:

Soon you will be known by only one name.

Paul

29

Nature for Morons

When a fare war between airlines, and gasoline prices that were the lowest they'd been since 1949, brought the cost of a roundtrip ticket to Minneapolis below three hundred dollars, Paul bought one with the intention of going home for Christmas and surprising his parents. Only his sister Bits knew of his plan. He needed to shop for presents and headed downtown. It was just after noon and snowing lightly.

Christmas in Northampton meant crowded sidewalks and distant parking spaces, but he couldn't complain. Main Street shopkeepers walked with the extra bounce in their step that only nervous greed could put there and temporarily suspended their petty feuds, with the exception of Stanley Prochaska, the ostracized jeweler and town cheapskate who refused to pitch in to help pay for the strands of small white lights that transformed Main Street into a magical fairyland each year from approximately Thanksgiving to Valentine's Day.

Paul strolled, shopping with nothing particular in mind. He found himself in front of the window of the WindSpirit Gallery, a store featuring western art and Native American crafts. Paul looked at rings, bracelets, pins, picture stone and silver, and earrings made from porcupine quills and feathers, thinking he might find something for his sister, but it was not her style. He could imagine her replying, "What am I — Pocahontas?"

He kept moving. He bought a scarf at Betsy's Threads, and an assortment of Kiehl's lotions and potions for his mother, who liked fine soaps and skin-care products but never bought them for herself, thinking them too extravagant. He found a Gore-Tex running suit for his brother at the Runner's Shop.

UPS had delivered a package from Carl that morning, in which Paul found a Plexiglas cube containing a baseball auto-graphed by Harmon Killebrew, with a note that read, "This is not from Santa — this is just to say thank you for all you've done, for Dad and for the rest of us. Carl."

He bought a whoopee cushion and a fake rubber rat for his nephew Howard, then ran out of steam and went to his office, where he picked up the phone and called his brother. He asked him, just to make chitchat, if he'd finished his shopping, to which Carl replied that he'd been finished since midsummer. Of course.

"I just wanted to thank you for the baseball," Paul said. "Did you know Harmon Killebrew had over eight thousand career at bats and not a single bunt?"

"His arms were bigger than my legs," Carl said.

"Anyway, thanks," Paul said.

"Well, you did a great job with Dad," Carl said. "I don't think I could have done it."

"What do you mean?" Paul said. He was fishing for a compli-ment, he knew.

"Just that your fucked-up marriage paid off," Carl said. "All that stuff you wrote about Karen and your new girlfriend. I think it went straight to a part of Dad's brain that he didn't ordinarily use. I think that really challenged him."

Paul had to pause. Carl had read the instant-message dia-logues? How was that different from Carl reading Paul's mail? Paul had no idea that the dialogues had been saved. He reminded himself that he'd read Carl's computer files and printed out a copy of his PINs, and was hardly in any position to condemn Carl for invasion of privacy. He had no secrets from his brother. Not anymore, apparently. Carl wasn't going to turn into somebody other than Carl, not overnight anyway. Be careful what you fish for.

"Glad I could help," he said.

After hanging up the phone, Paul picked up the binoculars he kept by the window and looked across the street, where a couple of off-duty cops were ringing handbells next to a Salvation Army collection bucket, which seemed like a violation of the separation of church and state, but all for a good cause. He got to work. The good part about being self-employed was setting your own hours. The bad part was you never got a vacation or a day off. Today he felt focused and industrious.

The use of antibacterial antifungal disinfectants, some researchers believe, is actually leading to the spread of bacteria. An antibacterial chemical known as triclosan, used in the majority of commercial disinfectants, has been found in laboratory tests to kill *E. coli* bacteria; however, in about half the cases where triclosan was tested, mutant strains of bacteria able to withstand triclosan grew to replace the previously existing bacterial cultures. In other words, cleaning just makes the world dirtier. In a similar way, the over prescription of common antibiotics like tetracycline and erythromycin has led to mutated strands of viruses capable of resisting all known treatments. We are, in effect, poisoning ourselves with good intentions.

He stopped writing when the phone rang, but he screened his call. The call was from a telemarketer at AT&T, his former carrier, trying to get him to switch back. He was tempted to pick up and tell the guy, "Hey — take it like a man. If I buy a Chevy, I don't get a call from Ford, whining about why I bought a Chevy."

He returned to his work.

Natural selection requires all species to act in their own best interest at all times. True altruism, or the ability to put the interests of others before your own, beyond cooperative efforts to protect personal territory or defend affiliated progeny, has been documented only in the human species.

He picked up the binoculars again. Down the street from the cops shaking their handbells, a street musician was playing folk songs and strumming his Ovation guitar, his face tilted up toward the sky. Perhaps because of the Christmas spirit, passersby were being generous.

Some ethologists question whether even the human species is capable of true altruism. As a social animal, man has learned that cooperative behavior — even things as apparently altruistic as feeding the poor, giving to charity, or tending to the dying — benefits the individual. Such activities function to reinforce the social contract and, in doing so, ensure the survival of offspring. It could be argued that even someone as apparently selfless as Mother Teresa is acting in her own interest, where our unique ability to sense the passage of time and thus our own mortality makes self-interest and altruism the same thing.

His phone rang again. He screened.

"Hi, Paul. It's your mother. I was just calling to check in. Right now I've got a fire going in the woodstove and I have the Christmas lights on. Carl came over and helped me put up the tree. Your sister is having Christmas dinner at her house this year, so that's where we'll be if you want to call. Wish you could be here. Harrold and I had macaroni and cheese because it was all we really felt like. Anyway, I just wanted you to know we were thinking of you and wishing

you were just a little bit closer so we could visit more often. We love
you. Bye-bye."

He was looking forward to surprising them and to eating all
the traditional foods and performing all the traditional rituals.
He wasn't feeling quite as bah-humbug as he had in the past.
Home seemed like a more welcoming place, now that the secrets
were out and the beans were all spilled.

He addressed his computer screen once more.

While man is the only species known to exhibit altruistic behavior, he is not alone in his ability to love. Elephants are believed to know and experience love, have a sense of their own
mortality, and also experience grief, often standing over the
body of a deceased herd mate for days, caressing the body and
mourning the death. The only example of love between species
is that between dog and man, a mutually beneficial relationship
proven to extend the life spans of both species.

Across the street he saw, through his binoculars, a young
father, half his age, walking hand in hand with his daughter,
dressed in a one-piece pink snowsuit. Paul felt envious. What
was it Hamlet said? "The readiness is all." Paul was shocked
to realize he'd just remembered something his college English
teacher had said, but it was bound to happen sooner or later.

He typed:

A squirrel that only needs one thousand acorns to make it
through the winter and has in fact never needed more than one
thousand acorns to make it through the winter will nevertheless not stop collecting acorns at October's end if he reaches
one thousand. He will continue to hoard acorns, most of which
ultimately either rot where they've been cached or are simply
forgotten. Thus the squirrel spends a significant part of his

life worrying unnecessarily, oblivious to the state of plenty all around him.

He spell-checked his work, gave a quick, skipping read-through of what he'd done, and realized, somewhat to his surprise, that he was finished with the book. He needed to send a copy to his agent for his comments, and there would be revisions forthcoming, but for now, he was done. It was good timing, a good feeling to end the year on. He saved a copy of the manuscript to a floppy drive, attached the file to an e-mail, and sent it to Maury.

He logged off and looked at his watch. It was five thirty.

He had time to kill, so he went to where he'd killed so much of it before, shouldering his way past all the shoppers until he reached a familiar doorway. The sign on the door announced that tonight was the Bay State's annual Christmas party, with a full buffet starting at five thirty. He hadn't been back since he'd gotten sober, but now he missed his old friends.

A string of lights had been draped behind the bar. The jukebox had a few seasonal additions, led by Bing Crosby's "White Christmas," with Burl Ives singing "Frosty the Snowman," Elvis doing "Blue Christmas," Gene Autry doing "Rudolph the Red-Nosed Reindeer," the Chipmunks doing "All I Want for Christmas Is My Two Front Teeth," and, perhaps most poignant of all, John Lennon's "Happy Xmas." A group of women at the table by the window were dressed in shiny black cocktail dresses, but Paul's friends looked as they always did. O-Rings and Bender were at the bar. Brickman was at the bar too, seated where the counter met the wall, signaling that tonight he wanted to be left alone. Bender called Paul's name out loud.

"Where the hell have you been?" Bender asked. Silent Neil approached them. "Let me buy you a beer—what are you drinking?"

"Tonic and lime," Paul said. Neil raised an eyebrow.

"That's it?" Bender asked. "Just tonic and lime?"

"That's it," Paul said. "I'm trying to watch my girlish figure. How you feeling?"

"So how you doing, man? Long time no see. Where you been?" O-Rings interrupted.

"Around," Paul said. "This and that."

"Wow, man." O-Rings looked at him for a few moments. "It's good to see you." Paul remembered seeing O-Rings in bars around town and thinking, "Boy, that guy has a problem — every time I go to a bar, he's there." It had eventually dawned on him that seeing O-Rings in a bar meant that he was in a bar too.

"You not drinking?" Bender asked.

"Not right now," Paul said.

"My doctor said I can have one drink a day," Bender said. He held up his glass. "This one is for Tuesday, June thirtieth, 2084."

"How've you guys been?" Paul asked.

"We're okay," Bender said.

"Doyle's not," O-Rings slurred. "Unless you call living in your car okay."

"Doyle's living in his car?"

"His girlfriend kicked him out a week ago," Bender explained. "Let me buy you a drink."

"I'm good," he said, raising his glass.

"What's with the gin and tonic?" O-Rings asked. "You think it's summer or something?"

"It's just tonic," Paul said. He wanted to ask O-Rings how his wife and kid were. He wanted to sing him a song: "Quit your ramblin', quit your gamblin', / Quit your stayin' out late at night / Stay home with your wife and your family / And sit by the fireside bright . . ."

He moseyed down the bar and took the stool next to Brickman.

"Hey, Bricks," Paul said. "You in the mood for company?"

"Fucking lawyers," Brickman said, slurring. "Goddamn fucking lawyers."

"What now?"

"Sonia's lawyer said she wants three thousand dollars a month. Don't ever get divorced."

"I already am divorced."

"You are?" Brickman said. "Women are shit."

Paul stared at Brickman.

"I'm gonna have to disagree with you there, pal," Paul said.

"Then fuck you."

"Jesus, Bricks — take it easy," Paul said.

"Three thousand dollars a month and sole custody," Bricks went on. "I am a good father. I am a *great* father . . ."

Paul moved to the jukebox, where D. J. and Mickey greeted him. He asked them how their boy was. Mickey said, "Don't ask."

"We got him in a program in Stockbridge," D. J. said. "Sort of a tough-love boot camp. I'll be amazed if he isn't worse off when he comes out. They won't let us visit. The guy who founded the school is a megalomaniac."

"Why'd you send him there?" Paul asked.

"He developed a heroin addiction," Mickey said, laughing. "Nice, huh? He's done some stupid shit, but we never expected he'd do that."

Why was she laughing?

"Vaya con Dios," Paul said.

He moved to the buffet and filled a small paper plate with buffalo wings. He looked at his watch. Only twenty minutes had passed. He used to spend entire evenings doing only this. Now time moved excruciatingly slowly. Before, every swallow was an event, marking time. He was enormously bored.

"You hear about McCoy?" O-Rings said, taking a piece of chicken from the chafing dish with his fingers.

"What about him?" Paul asked.

"He moved to Paris. Three weeks ago."

"He did?"

O-Rings nodded.

"I'll be damned," he said.

"Hey, Paul," O-Rings said, "let me buy you a beer to drink a toast to McCoy —"

"I'm not drinking —"

"Hey, Neil — bring Paulie a beer!" D. J. called out.

Paul shook his head to tell Neil not to bother.

He took stock. He saw Bender, Brickman, O-Rings, Mickey, and Yvonne, all of them with glasses raised, all of them drunk at six thirty in the evening. He suddenly realized what should have been obvious. All his friends were alcoholics. All of them were flawed and human and pathetic in their way, all of them determined to keep the party of their lives going, all lost in their own small universe, their personal quest for the next best time, the next happy hour or happy minute or happy moment, and they were good people, and he loved them and wished them well, but they weren't part of his world anymore. More to the point, everything in Paul's new world was changing, and nothing in this world was.

He excused himself and went to the bathroom. He looked up when Silent Neil came in and occupied the urinal next to him. Paul smiled. Neil nodded.

"You on the wagon?" Neil said.

Paul was in shock.

"Beg your pardon?"

"Are you on the wagon?" Neil said.

"Yeah," Paul said, stunned. Neil was actually talking to him. He had a deep, full voice, like James Earl Jones if Darth Vader were from Southie.

"For real? This is a permanent decision?"

"Yeah," Paul said.

"Then don't come back here. They'll just suck you back in with them. I've seen it happen a hundred times."

"They're my friends."

"So see them for lunch. Have breakfast. Just don't come back here. If you want to stay sober, you have to make new friends. There's a meeting tomorrow night at seven at the Unitarian church if you want to go. I'd be glad to sponsor you."

"AA?"

Neil nodded. Suddenly Paul realized Silent Neil was a spy, a mole, working deep behind enemy lines. "Just don't come back here. I mean it."

Neil left.

Paul returned to the bar. From the jukebox, Bing Crosby was singing, "I'm dreaming of a white Christmas / Just like the ones I used to know . . ." When Paul looked out the window, he saw that it was snowing again. Yvonne with her bright red hair was consoling Brickman at the end of the bar. D. J. and Mickey were laughing about something. Bender was hitting on the girls in cocktail dresses. O-Rings was having a spectacular ball on the pinball machine. It felt like the last day at summer camp, and he was standing in the parking lot watching a busload of playmates driving off, except that he was moving and they weren't.

Paul waved to them as he headed for the door.

"I'll see you all later," he said. "Merry Christmas, everybody."

I Thought You Were Dead

P aul turned right on Main Street, stopping at a corner market to pick up dinner. The snow fell lightly, fine flakes that drifted easily in the windless sky. Everything was quiet and clean. In his head, he could still hear Bing Crosby singing, "May your days be merry and bright . . ." A Pioneer Valley Transit Authority bus pushed its way through the snow toward Amherst. Down the street, somebody was ringing a bell.

When he got home, he turned on his television. CNN reported on another billionaire's attempt to circle the planet in a balloon, and the beginning of Ramadan, and a Michigan meat-packing plant's recall of 35 million pounds of contaminated hot dogs (Paul could only recall one), and a freakish cold snap in California that was killing all the oranges. On a local news station, a chick reporter in a fuzzy Santa cap outside a shopping mall told him he had only three shopping days left. The Weather Channel said to expect more snow. It looked as if Bing Crosby's dreams were going to come true.

He was wrapping presents on the kitchen table when he heard a knock on his door. He wasn't expecting anyone. His first thought was that somebody was having car trouble. When he opened the door, his heart jumped in his chest.

It was Tamsen.

"Surprise," she said. He couldn't think of a greater understatement. His heart raced. "Do you mind if I come in? I'm not disturbing you, am I?"

"I was just wrapping presents," he said. He tipped his head to invite her in. If he was going to have a hallucination, this was exactly the one he would have. He took a deep breath to calm himself. She stomped the snow from her boots, then stepped out of them. "You want some cocoa or coffee or something?"

"Cocoa would be great," she said.

She was wearing jeans and her black leather jacket with a black-and-white-checked kaffiyeh around her neck. She took off her coat and scarf, letting her hair fall free, longer than he remembered it. There was snow in her hair. She shook it out. How long had she been standing outside his house? She was wearing an Irish cable-knit sweater beneath the leather jacket, which she threw over a hook on the coatrack. He wanted to take her in his arms and hold her, and kiss her, more than he'd ever wanted anything in his life, but he held off and kept his distance. It was becoming more and more likely that this was not a hallucination.

He heated two mugs of water in the microwave and added two packets of instant cocoa for Tamsen and himself. She took the mug from him, cupped her hands around it, and sipped. He wished he had minimarshmallows. He watched her lips, the shape they took when she blew on her cocoa. In the living room, she sat down on the couch. He'd draped a strand of miniature lights over a small Christmas tree he'd bought at Stop & Shop, a skeletal specimen, more like a large stem of grapes with the grapes all plucked than a respectable conifer, but it had looked as if it needed a good home, and it was cheap. It sat on the table at the end of the couch.

"You have a tree," she remarked.

"Such as it is," he said.

"It's nice," she said, though he knew she was just being kind. "You need ornaments."

He and Karen had started an ornament collection, though where they'd gone, he had no idea. It didn't matter. They were as unusable as his old wedding band.

He waited for Tamsen to say something else. There was no reason to assume her visit was good news. He strove to remain circumspect, though circumspection was hard to come by.

"Just passing through?" he asked.

"I had an errand," she told him. "I have something for you."

She reached into her bag. He thought she might be fishing for some sort of Christmas present and wished he'd gotten something for her, though her visit could hardly have been anticipated. Instead, she handed him a red bandanna, the one she'd given Stella the night she'd met them at the Bay State.

"Where'd you find it?" Paul asked, taking it from her.

"It was under my sofa," Tamsen said. "It must have fallen off her neck when she was sleeping."

He fingered the fabric, then lifted it to his nose and sniffed. The cotton fibers were infused with oils from the ceruminous glands in Stella's ears. He smiled as he recognized the scent, slightly yeasty and all hers.

"I know," Tamsen said. "I was almost going to wash it, but then I thought maybe you'd rather have it unwashed."

"You're right," he said. "She'd appreciate the irony."

"I keep finding hairs," Tamsen said. "But I sort of hope I never find the last one."

"You won't," Paul said. "The other day I dropped a piece of cheese on the floor and I almost called her to come get it. It's hard to get used to the idea that she's not here."

"I know," Tamsen said. "I miss her. I think about her a lot. I can't walk through a doorway without expecting her to be lying outside waiting. Or I'll be sitting in a chair and I want to turn my head because I feel like she's just beyond my peripheral vision. It's a presence. Or an absence."

He nodded to tell her he knew the feeling.

"I appreciate you driving all this way," Paul said. He wondered why she had. "You could have mailed it."

"I could have," she agreed. She turned on the couch to face him, tucking her legs beneath her. "Can you do something for me? I want to tell you something and I just want you to listen. Okay?"

"Okay," he said.

"All right," she said. "I drove up because I've been doing a lot of thinking. About us. I mean, when I think about Stella, I think about you. And even rereading our last online conversation, I'm not all that clear on what happened. Are you?"

"You broke up with me," he said. "I'm pretty clear on that. You had to tell me about Stephen."

"Yes," she said, "but you were also pushing me away. Even before. Before Stella died."

"I was," he acknowledged.

"Why?"

"I'm not sure," he said. "I thought it would be better for you if I removed myself from the equation. I felt like it would be selfish to stand in the way of what was going to make you happy."

"What about what *you* want?" she said. "You're supposed to fight for what *you* want. Why didn't you fight?"

"I did," he said.

"How?"

"I was trying to be nicer."

"Nicer than whom?"

"Nicer than Stephen. That's how Minnesotans fight. We try to outnice our enemies."

He remembered something Stella had said: "Sometimes you

act like you don't think you deserve to be happy. Like the universe is punishing you for something. You haven't done anything bad. You deserve all the happiness you can find. You probably deserve more than you can find."

"You know what I mean," Tamsen said.

"I wanted you to pick me," he said. "I was trying to be pickable. Maybe *lovable* is another word for it. Except that you did love me. You just didn't pick me."

"I couldn't," she told him. "It wasn't safe. I mean, it was the wrong situation to get involved with."

"I know," he said. "For what it's worth, I quit. Drinking."

"I know."

"How?"

"I called your sister. To see how you were doing."

"She didn't tell me you'd called."

"I asked her not to," Tamsen said. For a moment, he felt as if Tamsen and his sister were conspiring behind his back, but then he realized he quite liked the notion. "I was going to call you a hundred times. Just to check in."

"But?"

"That's not how you break up with somebody," she said. "I learned my lesson when I got divorced. You can't simultaneously end something and keep it alive. You can't stay in touch. You have to go cold turkey. It's harsher at first, but in the long run, it's kinder. You get over it quicker. At least that's what Caitlin told me."

"She always was on my side," Paul said. Tamsen smiled. "Can I ask you something?"

"Sure."

"Why didn't you ever say anything about my drinking?"

"Don't think it didn't occur to me," Tamsen said. "Probably the first time we had lunch."

"So why didn't you?"

"Because then you'd be quitting for the wrong reasons. You had to do it for yourself. Not to please me. Or win me. I didn't want to be the prize. I couldn't open my mouth. Does that make sense?"

"Perfect sense." Paul nodded. He got it. You couldn't make other people responsible for your sobriety, any more than you could blame them for your failings. It was nobody's problem to fix but his. It made him wonder why she'd stayed as long as she had.

"Is it hard?" she asked.

"That's what I don't get," Paul told her. "It's not. I know it's supposed to be, but I hardly think about it. Maybe I'm missing something. The hard part was when I used to keep asking myself, 'Yes? No? Should I have another?' Saying no forever takes the pressure off. It seems sort of obvious, like, all right, I'm not going to drink the bleach under the sink, or the antifreeze in my car, and I'm not going to drink alcohol. It can't hurt me unless I let it, and why would I do that?" He shrugged. "Maybe I never really made up my mind about anything before. I know a lot of people have trouble with it."

"I'm really happy for you," she said. "You seem different."

"I do?" he said.

"You seem happier," she said. "Calmer."

He found this curious, in that he felt much the same, and no one else had noticed anything or said anything, but then nobody (this included Karen) had ever really seen him the way Tamsen saw him. He wondered what she saw now, and why she was looking at him the way she did.

"I'm not going to California," she announced.

"You guys are staying here?" Paul asked.

"I'm staying," she said. "Stephen is going."

"Oh," Paul said. "That's going to be a bit of a commute."

She sipped her cocoa, eyeing him over the rim of her mug. He didn't know what the look on her face meant until she squinted quizzically at his apparent density. When it dawned on him, it dawned, as his mother might have said, like a ton of bricks.

"You're not marrying Stephen?"

Tamsen opened her eyes wide and slowly shook her head, her lips tightly pursed and drawn to one side as if to say, "Oops."

"Why not?"

"I have absolutely nothing bad to say about Stephen. But I don't love him," she said. "He's not my soul mate." She paused. "You are. I don't know if you even believe in soul mates, but I was sort of hoping you'd be open to the idea. I had this whole speech figured out and now I've forgotten it. I did the wrong thing, and now I want to take it back. I'm really in love with you. I just am. And I'm not in love with Stephen. And I think that you and I should be together. If you still want me."

He thought of a number of things to say, including clutching his skull with both hands and screaming, "Are you kidding me?" After briefly running down a mental list of options, he decided (though *decided* was not the right word) that a kiss was his best response — rather, that a kiss was inevitable, the impulse unstoppable. They fell together and kissed.

"I'll take that as a yes," Tamsen said, once the kiss concluded.

"Can I just say," Paul told her, holding her close, taking it in, "that if this is your idea of going cold turkey, you're not very good at it."

"No," she said, shaking her head and laughing.

They kissed a second time.

"Just so I understand," he said, pulling back to catch his breath, "you're picking me, right?"

"I'm not picking you," Tamsen said. "That implies I have some sort of choice."

"So in other words, it worked," he said.

"What worked?"

"Being lovable."

"No," she said. "I mean, yes. I suppose it did."

They kissed a third time. This time, she needed to say something, pulling back and tucking her hair behind her ears with her fingers.

"So here's what I propose," she said. "I remembered my speech. We start over. Completely fresh, from scratch. A whole new beginning."

"No more Worcester Compact," Paul said.

"Null and void. Total monogamy and full commitment," she agreed. "And nothing is off the table. I mean, Paul, we can take it slow or fast or whatever you want, but the future is open ended."

"This is really huge, then," he said. He felt like those people who reported near-death experiences, where suddenly a white light beckons at the end of a tunnel, except that in this case it wasn't the hereafter waiting beyond the portal — it was the here and now.

"This is *really* huge," she replied. "Big as it gets."

"So this is like a first date?"

"Sure."

"Do you sleep with people on a first date?"

"Not usually," she said, "but I'm willing to make an exception. Can I just say that it really meant a lot to me to know you came to my gig."

"How'd you know?"

"Stephen recognized you. He'd seen pictures of us," she said. "Why didn't you say anything?"

"I was afraid. I'm a little surprised he told you."

"As I said," Tamsen said, "he's a good guy. If you don't mind, I'd rather not talk about him anymore."

"I don't mind," Paul said.

"Didn't think you would," she said, kissing him again. It was both familiar and strange. He felt them growing closer with each passing moment, drawn back by some sort of emotional bungee cord that absorbed and returned all the energy he'd put into distancing himself from her. He recalled something he'd come across, researching *Nature for Morons*. "Love is a single soul inhabiting two bodies," Aristotle said. Funny how you never heard much about Mrs. Aristotle. Paul had never felt that way before, but he felt that way now. He was lost in Tamsen, and not in a way that he needed to be found.

"There's so much I want to tell you," he said. "I had an interesting conversation with my parents . . ."

She put a finger to his lips and shushed him.

"I know. Your sister filled me in."

"Bed?" he suggested.

"Way ahead of you," she whispered.

AN HOUR LATER, with Tamsen sound asleep and snoring softly beside him, Paul rose from the bed, threw on a robe, and went to the bathroom to pee. He brushed his teeth, then regarded himself in the mirror, stepping back and opening his robe. He turned sideways. His gut was nearly gone. He'd lost almost thirty pounds since he'd started running. He considered adding sit-ups to his exercise regimen, then closed his robe, thinking, "who am I kidding?"

He turned off the light, and only then, seeing his darkened image in the mirror, did he remember his alter ego, Paul on the Ceiling. He was gone, apparently. He would not be missed.

He was about to go back to bed when he noticed a soft

yellowish glow coming from the living room and realized he'd forgotten to turn off the porch light. He tiptoed to the living room and was about to do so when his gaze fell on the red bandanna on the coffee table, still tied in a circle. He picked the bandanna up, ran his thumb across the fabric, then untied the knot and folded it into a square, smoothed the creases, and set it on the bookcase, next to the baseball his brother had sent. He pulled aside the window shade to check on Tamsen's car, not so much because he wanted to see if it was okay but because he needed proof that it was really there. He'd always considered himself a skeptic, putting stock in the saying that if something seemed too good to be true, it probably wasn't true. Key word: *probably*.

But sometimes, possibly, it was true.

He turned the thermostat up two degrees — usually he turned it down at night, but he didn't want Tamsen to be cold in the morning — and went to shut off the porch light. Before doing so, he cinched his bathrobe tighter and opened the front door to see how much snow he would have to shovel in the morning. The cold night air was clarifying. He inhaled through his nose and breathed deeply, closing his eyes and filling his lungs, exhaling in a cloud of steam.

His hand was on the light switch when he looked down to the dusting of snow on the porch deck and saw something that momentarily startled him: a set of footprints or, rather, paw prints belonging to a medium-size dog.

One explanation, the one William of Ockham might have preferred, was that a neighborhood stray had wandered onto the porch to look for food or to investigate an inviting scent, maybe even an Eastern coyote. Coyotes were known to travel the banks of the Connecticut River and wander into town upon occasion, though from where he stood, Paul could not see any tracks leading up or down the steps, where the snow was deeper. A second, more mystical explanation occurred to Paul, one he might have, under ordinary circumstances, rejected as implausible, though tonight, a number of implausible, extraordinary things had happened.

Why not?

"Good night, Stella," he said, then closed the door.

Acknowledgments

I HAD AN ENORMOUS amount of help editing this book down from its original form (or lack thereof) to where it is now. That includes readings, partial or complete, single and repeated, by loved ones and friends and by the writing group I was a part of, as well as by agents and editors. I owe a huge debt of gratitude to all the wise readers who told me what was working and what was not, or what they liked and what they didn't. Thanks to Dean Alberelli and Sarah London, Chuck Martin and Sarah Metcalf, David Hamilton and David Stern, and to my wife, Jennifer Gates, for helping me with the first round of changes. Thanks to Jennifer Gates, Cammie McGovern, Tony Maroullis, Karen Osborn, and particularly Bluie Diehl and Jeannie Birdsall for helping me with the second. It kept getting harder, so extra thanks to my agents at Lane Zachary and to Rachel Sussman, and again to my wife, Jennifer Gates, for their patience as much as for their critical insights, leading me through the closing revisions. The final edit and inspiration came from Chuck Adams at Algonquin, who saw what needed to be done and had faith that I could do it, so thanks to Chuck and to all the other people I've worked with at Algonquin, who are so good at what they do.

The characters in this book are all purely and impurely fictitious, some composited from elements borrowed from people in my life or from the streets of Northampton, though I've generally kept the true good parts of people I know and love and then added fictitious character flaws and/or personality disorders for dramatic purposes. I've also recycled a handful of lines and images cadged from individuals who should be credited: Buddy Rubbish ("recluse driving," page 8), Mark Patinkin ("waffle belly," page 15), John Gorka (butts, page 82), Bill Morrissey ("purse," page 98), and Cliff Eberhardt ("tone of voice," page 113).

Thanks to Jen one more time for her wisdom and her ongoing faith in me, and to Jack for making me strive every day to be a better man. Eternal thanks to my family in Minnesota for all their love and support, and to the town of Northampton and all the cool strange people who populate it. Thanks to the makers of Rolling Rock, Guinness Stout, and Lagavulin scotch whiskey and to Bill Wilson. Closing thanks to Keith Dempster for giving me a puppy named Stella, the best dog in the whole world, and to Alice, who was also the best dog in the whole world, and to Lucy, who is trying really hard to become the best dog in the whole world.

I Thought You Were Dead

The Real Stella: A Note from the Author

*

Questions for Discussion

The Real Stella

A Note from the Author

WHILE, LIKE MOST WRITERS, I use elements from my own life to create a sense of reality in my fiction, most of the characters and events in *I Thought You Were Dead* were created out of whole cloth. There was, however, a real Stella, and she was not so different from the Stella in the book, half yellow Labrador and half German shepherd.

I'd gone to graduate school at the University of Iowa Writers' Workshop and worked at a bar whose owner, also the president of the BMW Motorcycle Owners of America club, lived on a farm he'd converted into a campground for bikers making cross-country journeys. On the campground, he had an outdoor volleyball court with lights. On hot, humid Iowa summer nights, some of us would go there to play volleyball, and often we men would take off our shirts. Stella was one of a loose pack of nameless farm hounds who lived in the weeds beyond the lights, and often as not, one of them would sneak in and steal a sweaty T-shirt, and then they would all rip it to shreds. Stella was always the friendliest pup of the bunch and the first to come forward to say hello. When it was time for me to leave Iowa, I wanted a companion, and so, with the owner's permission, I drove out to the farm, picked her up, threw her into the cab of my pickup truck, and off we went, headed west. I eventually stopped in Portland, Oregon. Stella was so disconsolate, having left her littermates behind, that she pouted all the way to Montana and barely lifted her head from her paws.

I named the dog Stella at the recommendation of a friend who said, "That way, when you call her, you can pretend you're Stanley Kowalski in *A Streetcar Named Desire*." The friend's name was Olivia Wendell Holmes, so I figured she knew a thing or two about names.

One of the reasons I left Iowa was a romantic breakup. Stella helped me recover from the heartache, sleeping on the bed with me, keeping me company, and forcing me to exercise when I walked her every night. I read a book on dog training called *The Koehler Method* and made myself something of an expert on the subject, to the point where I could walk Stella off leash and maintain vocal control over her, which was easy because all she wanted was to get along with everybody. "Never met a man she didn't lick," I used to joke.

I moved from Portland, Oregon, to Providence, Rhode Island, where I roomed with a friend who had two dogs, and I dated a woman named Rosemary who had a miniature poodle named Tumbler. Sometimes I'd walk all four dogs to a nearby high school field to run. I never had to put leashes on any of them. My practice was to walk them around the corner, make them wait until I checked the street for traffic, and if it was safe to cross, I'd say, "Okay — go!" and all four dogs would run at full speed across the street and through a V-shaped opening in the cyclone fence surrounding the field. One night, around dusk, I walked the dogs, made them wait, then gave the command, "Okay — go!" but I failed to notice in the darkness that some time during the day, the city had fixed the hole in the fence. All four dogs ran at full speed, face-first, *smack*, into the fence, then looked at me as if I'd intentionally played a cruel joke on them. They were all fine, but it was a while before they trusted me again. They also may have been mad at me for laughing at them, but it was, frankly, hilarious.

I moved from Providence to Northampton, Massachusetts, where I lived in an apartment on Main Street and then moved to another place that was much like the one I describe in *I Thought You Were Dead*. I wrote books and freelanced for magazines, including *National Wildlife*, which was where I got the idea for a book-within-a-book called *Nature for Morons*. I married, and Stella was our flower girl, and then I got divorced, and my wife moved out, and it was just Stella and me again. I talked to her, and I suppose much of what the dog in the book says is what I imagined my Stella would have said to me if she could. It struck me then as remarkable — and it still does — the way dogs know when a human companion is upset, the way they come to you, out of some sort of pack instinct, and it feels very much like they're trying to help.

Toward the end of her life, Stella became more and more afraid of thunderstorms. One summer day, I'd left Stella at home (she was usually with me 24-7 but not this time), and I was working in my office downtown when, around suppertime, a massive storm rolled in. I rushed home, because I knew Stella would have a hard time of it. I'd come home once during a prior thunderstorm and found her standing in the bathtub, shaking. When I got home this time, I couldn't find her. I looked in the tub, behind the bed, in the closet, all over the apartment, calling her name, wondering where she could possibly be hiding, until I noticed that in her terror, she'd gotten up on the couch and actually pushed through the screen window to get out, jumping down onto the front porch. I drove around town for over an hour looking for her, to no avail. I was, needless to say, concerned. Around 11:30 that night, my phone rang. Stella wore a tag on her collar with my phone number on it as well as a message that said, IF YOU FIND ME OUTSIDE A BAR, LEAVE ME ALONE — MY OWNER IS INSIDE. Thankfully, the caller ignored that message.

"I found your dog," he said. "She's downtown, outside Jake's."

A breakfast haunt of mine.

I drove downtown and parked in front of the restaurant. Stella had her back to me, and she was woofing tentatively and tilting her head from side to side, barking at the darkened eating establishment, a place she recognized. She looked, in fact, exactly like the image that appeared on the dust jacket for the hardcover edition of this novel. I tiptoed up behind her, crouched down, and tapped her on the shoulder, saying, "Hi, Stella." The title of the book, *I Thought You Were Dead*, comes from the greeting she gave me that night.

At the end, I realized that she'd been with me for what were easily the most formative sixteen-plus years of my life, a time when I'd grown, and grown up, in so many ways. She'd been at my side every step of the way, witness to all of it. The day I put her down was one of the hardest days of my life, and as in the book, my ex-wife joined me to help me through it. The day I wrote that scene was no picnic either. A writing teacher in graduate school once advised me, "Never write about something unless you care passionately about it." When I started writing and outlining *I Thought You Were Dead*, I made a list of all the things I cared passionately about, all the things I loved or wanted the most, and all the things I feared the most, and I resolved to try to put them all in my book. Stella was at the top of the list of the things I cared about.

She was there in the first draft, and through countless subsequent drafts, she loomed larger and larger, until by the end of the editing process, she was clearly the second most important character and arguably the most likable. I had no specific plan for her other than to give her a human voice and allow her to say the things I could imagine her saying in "real life," though a large part of the character was also based on my maternal grandmother, who lived two doors down from us and who was also wise and funny and endlessly patient and forgiving.

It's been my experience that memory is fallible, and my memory is not much better than anyone else's and is often worse, but when I bear down to write, I can summon distant memories with an accuracy that surprises me. Writing is, for me, a physical act of memory. In that way, it was not hard to relive the life I'd had with Stella and do her justice, I hope, by committing my memories of her to paper. I intended, from the beginning, to write a book that was more than just "another one of those dog books." I wanted to write about a man whose heart is torn and pulled at in every direction, someone who tries to identify and face down his demons and overcome his bad habits, with some help along the way. Much of that help comes from Stella, who forces Paul to be honest and holds him to account. I think real dogs can do the same thing, force us to be honest, simply because if it's stupid to talk to them, it's even stupider to lie to them. The truth is that although real dogs may not talk, they always listen, and they look you in the eye when they do. They attend.

When I went on tour to promote *I Thought You Were Dead*, I brought a small vial of Stella's ashes with me to return them to the farm in Iowa where I found her. It seemed appropriate. However, when I got to Iowa, I learned that the man who had owned the bar I worked at had retired and sold his farm to a developer, and now, instead of a farm, there was a gigantic shopping mall at the location. I could have taken Stella's ashes and sprinkled them in the potted ferns outside Banana Republic, but that didn't seem right, so I put them back in my pocket. In truth, I like having a small piece of her still with me, just as I am glad to share a part of her with my readers.

Questions for Discussion

1. The author acknowledges that he has brought his own experiences into play in creating this novel. Which parts of the book seem most true to life, and which seem to be literary inventions?

2. How do the conversations Paul has with Stella work as a literary device? Do you think he's *really* talking to his dog? If not, then who is he talking to?

3. How do the ways men talk to one another in this book differ from the ways they talk to women?

4. Why does Tamsen handle her dilemma the way she does? Do you think it makes her likable or unlikable? Why? What are her flaws? Does she take responsibility for them?

5. What is it about Paul that Tamsen finds attractive or compelling? How does Paul fit into, or diverge from, the pattern of men Tamsen has been involved with?

6. Would you want your sister to date Paul, or marry him?

7. How do Carl, Bits, and Paul display attributes characteristic of their birth order?

8. Is Paul more like his father than he realizes? How does the way he relates to his father compare with the father-son relationships you know?

9. Paul's father Harrold is confused by the technology of instant messaging, and yet, his confusion ultimately provides Paul with unexpected insights — how does that work?

10. Do you think it's possible for animals in general, and dogs in particular, to feel love? If they do, how might the love they feel differ from the love humans feel?

11. Do you agree with the argument Stella makes that domestic dogs are more highly evolved than wolves?

12. What is the connection between Stella's death and Paul's quitting drinking? Is the way he quits believable to you? Is his own explanation valid, or do you think he's fooling himself?

13. Some reviewers have said I Thought You Were Dead is a book about male vulnerability — do you agree, and if so, how so? How does the author handle the more emotional scenes in the book?

14. If this book were made into a movie, who should play the main characters? And who would be the voice of Stella?

15. Is the ending satisfying? How else might the book have ended?

PETE NELSON is the author of several books, among them *Left for Dead,* a work of nonfiction. He is not the Pete Nelson who writes about tree houses, but he likes them nonetheless. He lives in Westchester County, New York.